Across the Sands of Time

Across the Sands of Time

Pamela Kavanagh

Robert Hale Limited
Clerkenwell House
Clerkenwell Green
London EC1R 0HT

www.halebooks.com

2 4 6 8 10 9 7 5 3 1

Typeset in 10½/14½ pt Palatino
Printed in Great Britain by the MPG Books Group, Bodmin and King's Lynn

Chapter One

Thea Partington left the house and came out into the shadowed stillness of a perfect June dawn. She was an attractive girl, of average height and willow slim, with bright blue eyes and glossy dark-blonde hair worn in a long plait. On her finger, the diamond and sapphire ring felt new and strange.

Proud and happy to be engaged to Geoff at last, Thea paused to admire the circlet of gold with its cluster of precious stones.

Last night's celebration party had gone so well. Her mother and father had looked better than they had in a long time, ever since the recent agricultural crisis had threatened to shake the very roots of their existence here at Woodhey Farm on the sleepy Cheshire peninsula known as the Wirral.

They were over the worst now, with Chas having made radical changes in farming practice and her brother Richard taking a temporary cut in wages and Mum – hard-working, resourceful, enterprising Mae – pulling out all the stops and turning the big family kitchen into a mini-bakery, where she supplied the local farmers' markets with her splendid home-bakes.

It had proved to be a lucrative money-spinner.

Mae's catering had gone down a treat the previous evening. Geoff's mother, Helen Sanders, had even requested a recipe for the lemon cheesecake – a big breakthrough that had brought the two women closer.

Thinking of Geoff, his crisply curling fairish hair, his kind, light-brown eyes and slow smile, Thea's heart warmed. It had been romantic, the way he had brought her out into the courtyard at the back of the house that Mum had decked with pots of geraniums and a white, scented jasmine on the old sandstone wall, to place his ring on her finger.

'I love you, Thea,' he'd told her, his face serious in the light of a new moon. 'And I'll do my utmost to make you happy.'

'Me, too,' she had murmured. As she had lifted her face for his kiss a cloud had drifted over the moon, throwing the landscape into sudden shadow.

Despite all the fun and feasting and the dancing that had gone on into the small hours, this morning Thea had awoken feeling refreshed. She threw a rueful glance at her sister's window where the curtains were tightly drawn. Bryony would surely emerge, dewy-eyed and flushed with slumber, long after all the clearing up was done and the best china washed and put away. That was her style.

It was Sunday and the faint pealing of church bells mingled with the muted slap of the tide in the distant estuary and the plaintive cries of seabirds. Thea crossed the farmyard and, calling a greeting to her father who was hitching the trailer to the tractor prior to getting in the round bales of hay from the thirty-acre, headed for the field where her ponies grazed.

She had six now, not counting the foals, attractive little Welsh ponies with which she was making a name in the showing ring.

Breeding show ponies was what Thea called her hobby and Geoff said was more a way of life. And he could be right, she thought ruefully, recalling how every morning, come hail, rain or snow, it was ponies first and then a dash to get ready for school and a challenging day with her infant class at the local primary.

Reaching the field which ran alongside barren stretches of salt-marsh, Thea called to the ponies and rattled the bucket of feed she carried. Heads shot up and the mares, three with foals at foot, came charging over to the gate to see what she had brought them.

All except one, that was. Seeing her current show prospect, a pretty dappled grey, come limping up behind the others, Thea froze.

'Dancer? What is it? What's wrong?'

With growing dismay she entered the field. Tipping the contents of the bucket into the metal feeder for the others, she latched the leadrope she carried on to Dancer's headcollar and led the little mare back towards the stables.

In the farmyard, Chas Partington stopped what he was doing and regarded the slow procession with concern.

'Trouble?'

'Could be. It's a foreleg. She must have pulled something, Dad, could you call the vet while I take a look?'

'Sure thing.'

Chas, a thick-set man with wind-reddened cheeks and a head of iron-grey hair, wiped his oily hands on a rag from the pocket of his blue boiler suit and set off instantly for the house.

Not long afterwards the vet's mud-splattered pick-up pulled into the yard. To Thea's surprise, instead of the usual man, a stranger sat at the wheel, and her spirits sank accordingly. She didn't want an inexperienced student messing about with her ponies!

The man – not quite as youthful as she had first thought – let down the window and stuck his head out.

'Good morning,' he called in a voice that was decidedly Irish. 'Would I be right in thinking this is Woodhey Farm?'

Incredibly deep-blue eyes viewed her from a lean, intelligent face. He had thick, wavy black hair and the sort of mouth that could twist readily into a smile and just as easily tighten in displeasure. Gazing across at him, captured by that blue, appraising gaze, Thea felt her heart give a treacherous and totally unexpected leap.

'Yes, this is Woodhey,' she replied, collecting herself hastily. 'Good morning. I'm Thea Partington. I was expecting Freddie Barnes.' Freddie was the equine specialist of the practice.

The new man smiled engagingly.

'Sure now, Freddie was out on another call so they sent me instead. My name's Dominic Shane, and this little lady is Trina.'

He ran his hand over the smooth, domed head of a very beautiful, shiny-coated red setter on the passenger seat beside him.

'Right then, where's the patient?'

To Thea's huge relief the new vet was thorough and obviously knew what he was doing. With increasing reassurance she watched as his sensitive fingers gently probed the troubled knee joint which had now swelled alarmingly. At length, he straightened.

'I think it looks worse than it actually is. You say she's been turned out with the others? Sure, isn't that the best way to keep equines? Anything as close as you can get to their natural environment. My guess is she's either received a clout from one of her mates, or she's pulled a tendon having a scamper around.'

'That's what I thought.' Thea looked glum. 'How long will it take to come right? She's entered for the shows. I expect that's it for this season.'

'Not necessarily,' Dominic said. 'She's in peak condition. With a bit of treatment she could get over it in no time at all. I'm tempted to go for a simple comfrey poultice and rest. I'll give you a muscle relaxant to mix in her feed and we'll take things from there.

'We could fix her up with a magnotherapy boot as well. They used them with good results at a racing place I attended back home in Ireland. Will you be around if I call back tomorrow?'

She looked doubtful.

'I don't generally get home from work until after five, but Dad or my brother will be here. You can safely leave any instructions with either of them.'

He smiled again, and once more her heart gave a powerful leap. It was the most compelling, most disarming smile she had ever encountered and in spite of her worries, Thea smiled back.

'At least Dancer hasn't broken anything,' she said brightly. 'I'd better see if we've got any comfrey. There should be some in the garden.'

'D'you know how to make up the poultice?'

'Oh, yes the pony we had as children was always knocking himself. I grew up wrapping his legs in comfrey leaves!' She paused. 'Are you in a hurry, Mr Shane? Mum's sure to have the kettle on if you'd like a cup of coffee or tea.'

'Coffee would be great, thanks, Thea … and it's Dominic.'

'Right, this way, Dominic. Don't worry about the dog. We don't have one at the moment so your Trina's fine to come inside. If my sister's there she'll probably get spoiled rotten.

'I'm afraid you'll have to take us as you find us this morning,' she added as an afterthought. 'We had a party last night. It was to celebrate my engagement, actually. We haven't cleared up properly yet....'

Dominic spread his hands in an eloquent gesture of acceptance.

'So congratulations are in order?' Well, I wish you every happiness.' He smiled. Stowing his bag away in the car, he followed her indoors with Trina loping at his heels.

Mae Partington added the final piece of Old Willow to the stack of afternoon tea plates and aimed the tea towel with remarkable accuracy to land on the top of the washing machine.

'Phew! What a chore washing up is! Still, I don't like to risk the best china in the dishwasher.'

'It's probably wise, Mum.' Thea returned the silver spoons she had been buffing to their case. 'That's those done. Only the cake stand to polish and then we're finished. Remind me not to put silverware down on my wedding list. It's too much like hard work.'

'But well worth it. You can't beat silver for adding class to a table, especially old silver like this.' Mae pursed her lips in remembered satisfaction. 'Helen Sanders admired it last night.'

'I bet she did! Geoff says his mum's idea of an outing is a day doing the rounds of the antique shops in town. She's actually quite good fun once you get to know her.'

Thea dipped her cleaning cloth in the metal polish and applied it to the ornate Victorian cake stand.

'What a morning! I could have done without Dancer being put out of action.'

'Let's hope the vet's right and it's not serious.'

Mae smiled encouragingly at her eldest daughter. She was a cheerful woman in her early forties and still pretty.

She wore her ash blonde hair in a bob and had the clear blue gaze that she'd passed on to Thea and to Richard, the middle one of her brood.

Bryony, the youngest and her father's darling – though Chas would never have owned up to it – was possessed of the golden-haired vivacity attributed to Mae's own mother in her youth.

'What did you make of the new vet?' Mae asked suddenly.

Startled, Thea looked up.

'He's seems OK, Mum. Why do you ask?'

'I rather took to him myself. All that Irish charm!' She chuckled. 'Good-looking too.'

'Mum, honestly!' Thea sent her mother a glance of laughing reproof. 'Where's Bryony, by the way?'

'Oh, she's still sleeping. You know your sister … she'll come down when she's ready. Seriously though, it's about time the Parkgate practice brought in some new blood. Freddie Barnes must be reaching retirement age and the other two aren't far off it. Donegal, Mr Shane said he was from. Do you remember going there on holiday when you were small? It was the first break we'd had for years. Dad kept ringing home to make sure the cows were all right. As if your granddad couldn't cope!'

'Dad would be no different even now,' Thea commented, exchanging polishing cloth for buffer. 'We mightn't do dairy any longer but there's still the grain crop to worry over, or the chicory harvest or whatever. Nothing will change him.'

'Nor would I want it to,' Mae agreed affectionately. 'I only hope your brother feels the same way. I've a niggling feeling that Richard hankers for pastures new. Not that he's said as much. He spends a lot of time at that jazz club.'

'Well, he's twenty-two, Mum. And he plays in the band, so of course he spends a lot of time there.'

'The lovely singer wouldn't be an added attraction, of course?' Mae suggested shrewdly, and her daughter grinned.

'Tracey Kent? Geoff and I went along to listen to them the other night, Mum. They're really good. They're into traditional jazz and Tracey has a terrific voice.'

'She's a very pretty girl,' Mae agreed. 'That always helps.'

Thea glanced round.

'Is Richard here or is he helping Dad with the bales? I need someone to hold Dancer while I fix the poultice.'

'I'll do it, love. Knowing Richard, he'll be off to Tracey's once they're done on the fields. Will you be seeing Geoff later?'

'Yes. We thought we'd take a run into Chester and look in on some estate agents.'

Mae nodded thoughtfully. 'Mike and Helen Sanders were discussing it last night. Your father mentioned applying for planning permission and building something here at Woodhey for you. Mike Sanders said they could look into converting Roseacre into two separate units. A barn conversion was mentioned, too. Helen seemed to think you might like that. I had the impression they'd prefer it if Geoff continued to live there.' She sighed. 'Mike's not a well man, is he? I thought his colour was bad.'

'He had that mild heart attack last year. The specialist told him to take things easier, but you know farmers, Mike's like Dad, lives for his land – or in Mike's case, his pedigree dairy herd.'

'What a nice man he is. Geoff's so like him. His state of health must be such a worry for Helen. But getting back to the subject of houses. At least you've got some options.'

Thea nodded.

'I'd rather stop in the Parkgate area, if possible. There's school to consider. I know Heswell isn't a million miles away but I'd prefer not to have to travel if I can help it. Then there are the ponies. Geoff's dad says he needs his grass for the cattle, and you know horses, they're such fussy grazers.'

'But nice with it,' Mae chuckled. She caught her breath. 'I've just had a thought … there's The Harbour House. Granted, it would need a lot of work, but it's available and with a bit of flair it could be turned into a lovely home. You could coax Dad into leasing you a few acres of grass, and you'd have a house with land within walking distance of the school.'

Thea stared at her mother, her eyes brightening with interest. The Harbour House, a rather neglected property on the edge of Woodhey land, was situated, as the name suggested, right on the quayside.

At one time the sea had come right in and fishing boats had traded busily where now were vast stretches of saltmarsh, criss-crossed with deep channels that could be treacherous during certain tides. The marsh was haunt to seabirds and the cockle and shrimp fishers, who knew the narrow waterways and the whims of weather and sea as well as they knew their own boats.

Over the years the Harbour House had been a tied residence for the Woodhey farm workers. More recently, with the rearing of live-stock having been replaced by arable, the need to employ a cowman was no longer necessary and the house now stood empty.

Chas had talked of turning it into a holiday home, but that was as far as it had got.

Thea thought hard. The house was available and it met all their requirements. And it had character.

'Mum, you're brilliant!' she said at last. 'Why didn't we think of that?'

'Because you lot are so quick to go surfing the net when you want something, you can't see what's right under your noses! It'll need a lot of attention, mind, new plumbing, electrics and decoration.

Thea made a wry face.

'Oh, well, at least we've got time on our side. It looks as if it might be a good thing we're not planning to get married for another year. I'll pop down there later on and have a look round. It's been ages since I went inside, but I've always liked it. It's so old. It's got atmosphere.'

'That could be a touch of dry rot,' Mae said, ruefully. 'And you're right about it being so old. This farmhouse dates back to the late eighteen-hundreds and the Harbour House goes back even further. Talk it over with Geoff, love. You never know, he may not want to be so far from his work. Think of winter mornings, getting up before the crack of dawn to get to Roseacre in time for milking.'

'That wouldn't bother Geoff. And he likes salt water fishing. He'd be right on the spot there – a great carrot to dangle!'

They laughed.

'If you've finished here we'd better go and see to Dancer, then I must do my shopping list for tomorrow's bake. We had a request for more currant cakes. I must remember to get extra fruit. All go, isn't it?'

Geoff jumped at the prospect of making the house by the old harbour their home. His parents accepted with good grace the young couple's argument for being based at Parkgate and seemed genuinely pleased that the matter of the future marital nest was settled.

Oddly, the only one less than enthusiastic about the idea was Chas. When Mae quizzed him as to the reason why, he spread his big, work-callused hands wordlessly, as if he could think of no logical explanation.

No, he had no specific plans for the house himself, he stressed. And no, sorting out a few acres for Thea wasn't a problem. He'd simply never had any great fondness for the place, stuck as it was on the edge of the saltings, at the mercy of the four winds and bleak as a tinker's curse in winter!

The couple had gone immediately to look the house over. Geoff, a handyman himself, and with some useful contacts in the building trade, saw no reason why they shouldn't go ahead and start drawing up plans.

'It's more spacious than it looks from the outside.'

Geoff paused on the road to look back at the old building with its dipping roofline, small windows and cluster of outbuildings. Inside was a peculiar hotch-potch of old and fairly new, the preponderance of dark beams and flagged floors vying uncomfortably with various less than attractive attempts at modernization.

Outdated lead water pipes snaked along ceilings and disappeared through holes drilled into the thick stone walls. The electrics looked lethal. Seeing the house through Geoff's eyes for the first time, Thea felt a twinge of doubt.

'Bit of a mess, isn't it?' she said, biting her lip nervously.

'So it needs gutting and a complete makeover.' Geoff shrugged. 'We can do it up to suit ourselves. We've loads of time. And it's a good, solid building with great views of the estuary. The lounge could be really something with those exposed beams and the flagstones resurfaced. I wouldn't mind betting we'll find an original inglenook behind that hideous modern fireplace. Nice-sized kitchen. Have you any idea how you'd like it to look?'

'Not yet. I've asked Bryony to pick up some brochures from that new DIY store.'

Bryony worked in a boutique in Birkenhead, and was often called upon to carry out some small errand while she was in town.

'I think we need to keep the kitchen low key and natural. Lots of white, with maybe some walls taken back to the original brick?'

'I agree.' Geoff took her hand in his. 'Chin up, love, we're in no hurry. There's loads of time.'

'Loads of time to fall out over it, don't you mean?' Thea said with a mischievous sideways glance.

He gave her hand a squeeze.

'That'll be the day! When did you and I ever have a cross word? Not counting the time I put a white mouse in your school bag, of course!'

Stray tendrils of hair whipped by the wind that seemed constantly to blow here strayed across her face, blocking her vision. Brushing them away carelessly, Thea went into Geoff's arms.

Life was good. She had a career she enjoyed, she had Geoff, the prospect of a lovely home and, of course, she had her ponies. Even Dancer hadn't turned out the worry she'd anticipated. With Dominic keeping an eye on the injury and regular treatment and care, the little mare was improving fast.

'Dancer by name and dancer by nature,' Dominic had commented lightly on his next visit.

'She's registered as Dawn Dancer,' Thea told him. 'I haven't named any of the foals yet. I can never make up my mind which to keep.'

'You'll have to let something go or you'll be overrun.'

'So Geoff keeps telling me. Doesn't make it any easier, though. What about you? How are you finding your new job?'

'Sure, I like it fine. Everyone's friendly and there's plenty of scope here for equine work. Oh, there's something I wanted to ask you. My boss mentioned you were secretary to the local history group. I wouldn't mind joining.'

'Great! I'll look out an application form. We meet every second Wednesday of the month at the church hall. We take trips to places of interest, digs, the usual things. They're a good crowd. You'll enjoy it.'

I'm sure.' Dominic held her gaze for just a little longer than necessary and, to her chagrin, Thea had found herself blushing.

Richard drew up by the village green at Willaston, where Tracey stood waiting for him. She looked young and carefree in her blue and white striped top and white cargo trousers. Her glorious auburn hair shone and she carried a white canvas shoulder bag which she waved in greeting.

Richard leaned across to open the passenger door for her.

'Hi, sorry I'm late. We had trouble with one of the tractors. Managed to get it sorted, though. Dad needs it tomorrow. Are you OK?'

'I'm fine,' she replied, sliding into the seat, planting a kiss on his lips and latching up the safety belt – all performed in one easy, fluid movement. Her amber eyes smiled across at him, mischievous, provocative.

'Have you said anything to yours folks yet?'

Richard checked for oncoming traffic, then he released the brake, sending the car gliding smoothly away.

'I haven't had the chance yet, love. Well, there was Thea's engagement party. I didn't want to spread a cloud over that. Then what with the silaging and the haylage it's been all go. I might even wait until the corn harvest is over and done with. Dad'll be more relaxed then.'

'But, that's not till September and we're due to go off on tour then. It won't give them time to get used to the idea.'

'It's best this way, trust me.'

'You know I do.' She glanced out. 'Where are we heading?'

'The Thatch at Raby? It's a nice evening. We can take our drinks outside and talk.'

Smiling, Tracey reached out and rested her hand lightly on his arm for a moment in one of the impulsive little gestures he loved so much, then she sat back to enjoy the drive through the gentle Wirral countryside.

Richard drove fast but safely, his sun-browned hands sure on the steering wheel, his clear-cut profile set, his eyes fixed on the road ahead. He was casually dressed in a tan-coloured polo shirt and lightweight trousers a few shades darker.

No one would have placed him as a farmer's son who had been up at first light and done a full day's physical work on the land. His hands, strong, sinewy, the fingers long and tapered, gave him away as the musician he yearned to be. He had started with the guitar as a seven-year-old at school. Now he played classical, blues, jazz, rock – anything. He loved all kinds of music.

Richard grinned suddenly.

'What's so funny?' Tracey asked.

'I was thinking of Dad when he got me my first tenor sax. I think it was for my fourteenth birthday. I couldn't put the thing down. Dad said it sounded like a cow in labour!'

They both laughed, well aware of how far Richard had come since those early days. At school a bunch of them had got together and formed a jazz band. The years had seen some chopping and changing within the group, but Tracey and Richard had remained constant.

Eventually the band had settled down to its present form. The bookings had rolled in; first the youth club, then the local jazz society which had a keen following. They called themselves the Richie Dene Band – Dene being Richard's grandmother's maiden name.

They were now booked for gigs all over the north-west, and what was more, the sessions were satisfyingly lucrative. Despite his depleted wage packet from the farm, Richard was never short of cash.

In the autumn, all five players and Tracey planned to pack in their jobs and head for Ireland, where the jazz scene was big, and a twelve-week tour was scheduled.

The very thought brought a surge of excited anticipation to Richard, swiftly quelled by the prospect of having to tell his parents that he wouldn't be around to work on the farm. He loved his parents deeply and respected their views and values, and knew how hard his news would hit them.

But he had to do it. He wasn't a farmer and had never wanted to be one. The land and the livestock that were life and soul to his father left Richard not exactly cold, but with the clear certainty that this wasn't his path in life. Music sang in his being every moment of the waking day and sweetened his dreams at night.

Hanging on his bedroom walls were his guitars – bass, classical and rhythm, a banjo, mandolin, trumpet, saxophone, French horn … and he played them all. Bookshelves were crammed with sheet music and books about jazz greats. His CD collection was legion; nobody ever had trouble wondering what to get Richard for birthdays or Christmas.

They arrived at the pub and took their drinks outside. Settled, the conversation turned inevitably to the tour.

'Mum's being great about it,' Tracey confided. 'She's running me up some lovely evening outfits. It's great having a mum in the rag trade.'

'Your mum's a star,' Richard agreed.

'Oh, did you notice Thea and Geoff at the club the other night?' Tracey went on.

He nodded.

'I let it slip to Thea about the tour. She's pleased for us, though she understands the trouble it's going to cause.'

'And Bryony?'

Richard almost choked on his orange juice. 'You're joking! My kid sister could no more keep a secret than fly to the moon!'

Bryony and her best mate, Liz, had met up for lunch at the salad bar of a popular café on Grange Road. Beyond the window the stream of Birkenhead traffic ebbed and flowed in rhythm to the traffic lights on the corner.

'I really envy your sister,' Liz said, checking her hair in the window, spiked this week in hues of electric blue. Evidently satisfied with her slightly bizarre appearance, Liz went on, 'She's one of those people everything goes right for. I should be so lucky.'

Bryony grimaced.

'Me too. Trust Thea to have a guy like Geoff Sanders.'

'Oh?' Liz studied her friend through narrowed, light-blue eyes. 'Fancy him yourself, then?'

Bryony coloured guiltily.

'I think he's OK, that's all. Anyway, he's far too old for me. Twenty-six! Thea's twenty-four.'

Liz studied her false nails.

'My landlady knows a woman whose kids are in Thea's class. She says they love her to bits.'

'That's no surprise. Thea's great with kids, sort of firm but fair.'

'I've never fancied having kids myself. What about you?'

Bryony considered, pouring the last of her sparkling water into the glass.

'I guess if you're happily married and settled with someone, then children are the next step.'

She looked up at Liz.

'Yeah, I would, actually. Just like my mum, always tearing round after us, picking us up from swimming or tennis, dropping us off at youth club. She took everything in her stride and still managed to help Dad on the farm.'

Liz looked at her friend as if she had taken leave of her senses.

'Sounds like hard work to me! Anyway, I thought you wanted to come with me, back-packing in Australia.'

'I do!' Bryony grinned, bright and bubbly. 'Get a grip, Liz. I don't mean I'm having kids tomorrow. Got to find a man first.'

Her smile faded as Geoff Sanders's face rose in her mind. Trust Thea to have all the luck. If it was her, she'd have Geoff to the altar double quick, before anything happened to change his mind.

Thea glanced around the church hall – a spacious, convenient, if chilly, venue, where the Parkgate local history group were assembling with much chatter and a some laughter. On the long central table was a large cardboard box of documents, out of which members were taking random piles before splitting into groups. Spotting Dominic enter the room, Thea went to greet him.

'Hi. You made it, then?'

'Just about. I swear evening surgery makes a point of being extra crowded when you particularly want to get away!' He laughed his words off. 'Well, Thea. No other half tonight?'

'Not so far, though there's time yet.' Thea paused. She had been in two minds whether to come herself. A headache had niggled all day, and she had felt generally out sorts.

Maybe she was coming down with the bug that was raging through the school, she thought. But it was a lovely evening and anyway, as a member of the committee she felt obliged to attend.

'Chances are Geoff has been held up,' she went on. 'There's always something needs doing on a farm, as you know.'

Dominic gave a nod.

'That's livestock for you! In fact, I was at the Sanders's place this morning. They had a cow in trouble calving.'

'I bet it was a bull calf – they always cause the most trouble.'

'A heifer, so she was, and Mike Sanders couldn't keep the grin from his face. The mother's been a big prize winner and he thought the calf looked as promising. They really know their cattle at Roseacre. Their Friesians are the best I've ever seen.'

'Yes, they win loads with them. Is it a popular breed in Ireland?' Thea asked, curious.

'So-so.' A shuttered look crossed the good-looking face, so fleeting that Thea thought she may have been mistaken. Then the smile was back.

'So what's on the agenda tonight?'

'Well, one of the members went to a furniture and bric-a-brac auction and came out with that box of tricks you see on the table,' Thea explained. 'It's full of old documents – maps, deeds to local properties, fishing rights … that sort of thing. It'll take weeks to sort through it all. I expect there's a good deal of rubbish amongst it, though there's always the chance you might come across something really interesting.

'Anyway, we thought the best thing was to sort it roughly into categories and then go from there. I'm doing house deeds and shops.' She held up a fat bundle of yellowing papers. 'Think I've landed myself in it. The legal wording takes some swallowing. It's all herewith, hereto and what have you!'

'Want some help?'

'You're on,' Thea said, handing him a pile of papers.

For several minutes they worked in silence, sifting, sorting, placing the documents into separate piles. Dwelling houses, farmsteads, holdings, shop premises. All at once Thea let out a startled little gasp.

'Look at this! It says *The Harbour House*. It must be a set of deeds to the place Geoff and I are going to do up. I thought Dad had them all.'

'It's easy for these things to go astray, particularly when the building's got a bit of age about it. Is it all there?'

She sorted hastily through her pile and found another page. Dominic did the same and came up with the final section.

'Well now, and isn't that a turn up for the books?'

'Isn't it just!' More excited by the minute, Thea ran her eye over the faded copperplate with its stilted wording. 'It's headed *The Harbour House School For Boys*. Goodness! I never knew it was once a school. I don't think Mum and Dad did either.'

Dominic took the documents from her.

'It says for fifteen boys aged from seven years to sixteen. Not very big, was it?'

'No, but that's how it was in those times. Does it give a date? Oh, yes, look, *Twelfth Day of August in the Year of Our Lord Eighteen Hundred and Thirty-Five*. I've got to tell Geoff. When we break for coffee I'll ring him.'

Her headache forgotten, Thea delved further into the box.

A little later, she went outside and took out her mobile phone. Geoff answered instantly.

'Deeds, eh?' He chuckled. 'Wow!'

'Geoff, the house was once a school and none of us knew. Isn't that weird? I'll take them home with me if you like, then you can see them.'

'Sorry I couldn't make the meeting tonight. Dad wasn't feeling too well and by the time I'd done the milking and fed everything the evening was half over.'

'Not to worry. How's Mike now?'

'He's OK. Just been overdoing it. Look, I was going to call at the Harbour House later on.'

'What for?'

'I want to measure up outside.'

'For a garage, you mean?'

'No, a boat.'

Thea grinned. She might have known what Geoff's priorities were.

'Why not meet me there later?' he continued. 'And bring those deeds with you. We'll read through them together.'

'OK. See you later, darling. 'Bye.'

Some time afterwards she was driving carefully along the main street known as The Parade, graced on one side with houses and small shops in a pleasing mix of black and white timber, sandstone and old brick, and on the other by the saltmarsh with its criss-crossing waterways and ancient low harbour wall.

As she travelled, the feeling of being out of sorts returned in full force. Putting a hand briefly to her hot forehead, Thea thought longingly of home. She half wished she hadn't promised to meet Geoff, and then felt a rush of guilt. It would be good to see him and show him her find.

Her route took her right through the village and down a rutted farm track, at the end of which stood her future home. She drove round to the back of the house and pulled up on the weed-matted cobblestones of the yard.

Geoff hadn't arrived yet, Thea saw. Leaving her car, she delved into her bag for the big black iron key to the premises and fitted it into the lock. The solid oak front door, its layers of paint scratched and scored by the years, swung open with a creak.

Making a mental note to bring a can of oil next time, Thea went on and through into the main living area. At the far end of the room was a bow window with a seat and she made for it thankfully, aware of a sickly weariness.

It was very quiet and warm in the window, with the last rays of the evening sun slanting in through the dirty panes of glass. Yawning, Thea recalled she still had things to do before she could turn in. She hoped Geoff wouldn't be too long.

Dust motes jigged and swirled in the golden beam of light before her eyes. Fighting sleep, Thea thought she heard the surging of the tide against the harbour wall beyond, where no tide had come for decades. She frowned, too overcome with tiredness to be bothered to look. Closing her eyes, she gave herself up to slumber.

'In heaven's name, wench! How many times do I have to tell you? Fetch me another flagon up from the cellar, won't you?'

Polly Dakin steeled herself, hating the smell of brandy on her father's breath, determined not to give in.

'Father, it must be nearly the hour for the mail coach to arrive. The driver will need you to help change the horses. Remember last time? You stumbled and almost got trampled on. You mightn't be so lucky again.'

Wallace Dakin's coarse red face turned an ugly purple hue, and his pale grey eyes bulged in anger. Giving in with a regretful little cluck of her tongue, Polly whirled round and smartly left the busy tap-room.

Directly opposite was the door to the cellar. She yanked it open, descending the steep stone steps to the bottom where the kegs of ale and casks of wine and spirits were stored. The former was delivered openly and legitimately by the brewer's cart every Monday.

The latter Polly felt fit to wonder about. There was more here now than yesterday. How had it got here? And when had it come? Shrugging the matter aside for now, she seized a flask of good French brandy and remounted the steps.

She was a pretty girl with a lot of curling chestnut brown hair and bright, intelligent hazel eyes, the legacy of her mother who had been a Platt before her marriage. The Platts were a well-to-do Parkgate family and it was common knowledge that Marion had married beneath her.

Polly loved her attractive mother and even had it in her to feel a spark of fondness for her father. Wallace, when not in his cups, was a handsome, larger than life man with a mane of red-gold hair and bushy beard and eyes that flashed with humour.

She could see how in his youth a girl might have been swept off her feet by him. A charmer, her mother had once said. Polly's brother Edward, the elder by eleven months, had inherited a fair share of the Dakin charm.

As had Polly, although she was not aware of the fact. Swinging the door shut, her lips tightly compressed, she went to place the brandy on the table in front of her father, where he sat on a stool by a sizzling fire of peat and driftwood. Without a word she gathered up her thick woollen shawl from the peg behind the door, threw it across her shoulders and went outside.

Sharp October rain stung her face as she made her way carefully across the straw and dung-strewn tavern yard, heading for the harbour where the ferry from Flint would dock once the tide was fully in. The boats ran infrequently now, due to the canalizing of the river to run on the Welsh side and the subsequent silting up of the harbour at Parkgate.

Father told of how it used to be when the ferry boats put in at regular intervals and Parkgate had been a thriving fishing port, with cod and herring being salted on the quayside and the air ripe with the smell of fish and rowdy with the banter of the fishwives.

Coming to the edge of the quay, Polly stood peering into the distance, the wind blowing her hair and billowing her brown homespun skirts about her small, determined figure. Sometimes, John's boat could be seen out on the estuary when he returned from checking the herring nets.

Thinking of him, his merry brown eyes and ready smile, Polly could have hugged herself. She and John Royle had been meeting in secret for the best part of six months now. What with Father never in the best of humour and her mother in poor health, they had thought it best not to disclose their feelings for the time being.

Polly did not mind. John loved her and she him, and for now that was all that mattered.

There was no sign of John's boat, the *Lady Mary*, but Polly's quick eye caught in the middle distance the outline of a figure on the saltmarsh to her left. Whoever it was had clearly been caught out by the tide and was rushing this way and that in panic, aware of becoming trapped, but not knowing how to escape.

All around was the bluster of the wind and the slap and gurgle of water as the running sea sent ever-increasing eddies along the narrow channels cut into the marsh for access for the fisher-folk. If the person – a woman, by her flying cloak and hair – did not receive help she would be cut off and would surely perish.

Polly cupped her hands to her mouth and hollered.

'Stay where you are! I'm coming!'

Without a thought for her own safety, she skimmed down the slippery weed-slimed steps which would very soon be under water, and made off across the saltmarsh to where the woman stood stranded. Polly was at home on the marsh and followed a well-known path. Sure-footed, bending into the wind, she reached the person, who carried a wicker trug filled to the brim with seaweed.

Polly recognized her as Meg Shone, a reclusive person who dealt in cures and charms and lived in a small cottage behind the village.

'This way! Quickly!' Polly cried and, seizing the woman by the arm, she guided her back across the soggy ground and up the steps to safety.

There, gasping, soaked and wind-tousled, the two women faced one another. Meg Shone was younger than Polly had supposed; a tall, strong-looking person, swarthy skinned, with far-seeing black eyes and a wide, mobile mouth.

'My thanks to you, missy,' she said simply. 'You've saved a foolish body's life. Gathering the seaweed, I was, and lost count of the time. Meg Shone never forgets a favour. If ever you need a friend, and one day, you surely will, remember me.'

Sending Polly a nod, she gathered her bounty to her and sped away, vanishing into the October murk.

Thea came to her senses with a start. The sun had sunk below the horizon; dusk stole across the area where she sat. The papers had slithered from her grasp and lay at her feet on the dusty floor. She stared at them, her mind in turmoil. What had just happened? Who were those people, and how come she had seen them?

A car door slamming made her jump and she looked up with relief. She would have to tell Geoff about this vivid, weird kind of dream … would he think she was crazy? What on earth was happening to her?

Chapter Two

Thea's first thought was one of gladness that Geoff was here, coupled with a feeling of surprise that she had dozed off so readily. She'd never nodded off like that. And as for that weird dream....

She bent to pick up the documents that had fallen to the floor, smoothing them out, her face puzzled and frowning. She had been here in this very room. It had been so real! The innkeeper, the girl, the gypsy woman at the mercy of the oncoming tide. She had even felt the woman's fear.

Geoff's echoing footsteps in the empty hall brought her head up abruptly and a moment later he was in the room with its peeling wallpaper and smell of dust and damp.

'Hi there,' he said, going to where she still sat in the window casement to drop a kiss on the top of her head. 'Are you OK, love? You look a bit wiped out.'

Thea rubbed her throbbing temple absently.

'Just a headache. I've felt a bit off all evening. There's one of those bugs going round at school. I must have picked it up.' She smiled at him, making light of it. 'Better keep your distance. Can't have you catching it too. Who'd do the milking in your place?'

'Oh, you know me. I never seem to catch these things. An outdoor life sees to that. There's nothing like a good old westerly for blowing away the nasties.' He stopped, looking at her more closely. 'There's something else.... What is it, darling?'

'I had this dream. Geoff, it was so real.' Hesitantly, she related what had happened. 'Dreams generally fade when you wake up but this one hasn't. I can remember every detail as if I'd seen it in a movie. It's weird.'

Geoff sat down beside her and took her in his arms.

'You've been overdoing things, that's all, Thea. A good night's sleep and you'll be fine. Are these the deeds?' He picked them up. 'That accounts for the nightmare, then. You were looking through them, dozed off and your overworked imagination did the rest.'

Thea was silent. Common sense told her that Geoff could be right. Deep down, however, she didn't question. Somehow, the past had opened up to her.

'A schoolhouse, eh?' Geoff was glancing with interest through the papers. 'Knocks your dream on the head. A tavern's a far cry from what it says here.'

'Actually, I remember Dad saying the Harbour House had been a coaching inn at one time. The tide would have come in every day then. There was a ferryboat service from across the estuary and transport laid on to carry travellers on to the station. I wonder what happened to bring about the change? It all looked to be thriving to me.'

Geoff was looking at her with something close to exasperation.

'Forget it, Thea. Strange dreams, freaky Fridays. It's like I said, you fell asleep and your mind wouldn't let you rest. And no wonder. School all week, horse shows every weekend. I hardly ever see you.'

A sudden and totally irrational irritation rose up.

'I could say the same for you, Geoff,' she snapped. 'When was the last time we went out without you having to dash back to catch up with something at the farm? What about tonight's history group? I waited and waited for you to show up! So don't talk to me about never having time to spare, Geoff. You're no different!'

'But I told you when you rang on your mobile,' he insisted. 'There was a lot of catching up to do. Heck, Thea. You know as well as anyone that the milking doesn't do itself.'

'Well, the same goes for my schoolwork. The ponies, too, come to that. And you're wrong about the shows. I haven't done one in weeks because my best prospect has been out of action. That wouldn't concern you, of course. Ponies don't count as much as cattle.'

'That's not true!' Geoff drew in a calming breath. 'Look. I'm sorry about the history club tonight. I fully intended being there but Dad was taken poorly. There was a bit of a panic on, to be honest. We were in the middle of the milking. I had to leave off and get him into the house.'

All Thea's anger evaporated. 'Geoff, I'm sorry. You did say when I rang. I thought he was just feeling under the weather. How was he when you left?'

'A bit brighter. Mum called the doctor – well, you can't be too careful. Doctor Malone was off duty so they sent a locum. She was very thorough but it's never the same when someone isn't familiar with the patient.'

Thea nodded.

'Sorry, I was prickly.'

'You weren't.' He kissed her tenderly. 'What happened just now … your dream. It hasn't put you off the house?'

'Of course not. I love the Harbour House.'

'That's all right then. But you really do look exhausted. Why don't you get off home? You hang on to the deeds for now, Thea. I'll see them another time.'

He pulled her to her feet and together they went out into the deepening evening. Dusk had gathered and the murmur of the distant tide was loud on the soft summer air. In the deep channels that criss-crossed the saltmarsh, the water sucked and gurgled.

Still under the spell of her dream, Thea gave a shiver. She remembered the raging wind and rain against the wooden window shutters, the roar of the oncoming tide. The inn had seemed a rough and ready sort of place. A place with a past, maybe a dark one.

Getting into her car, bidding Geoff goodnight, she drove slowly home. The tiff had upset her more than she had realized. They never argued. Her head was now throbbing and she turned with relief into the drive at Woodhey. An early night would put her back on track. She'd check on the ponies and then go to bed.

Home at last, she sipped a comforting mug of hot chocolate and couldn't resist another glance at the bundle of deeds. Her father and sister had both been out when she arrived back; Dad to a darts match at the local and Bryony clubbing with her friends. But Mum had been there and was as intrigued as Thea at the night's find.

'A schoolhouse! Well, I wouldn't have thought it was big enough.'

'Dominic said the same thing. I guess in those days they'd only have needed a few boarders to make it pay. Maybe they made the attics into a dormitory and had the schoolroom and other facilities downstairs.'

'You could be right. What stories that old house could tell if only it could talk,' Mum had commented innocently.

Finishing her drink, Thea put mug and documents down on the bedside table, switched off the lamp and plumped up her pillows. Tired though she was, sleep wasn't immediate. Fragments of her tiff with Geoff ran distressingly through her mind.

Superimposed over Geoff's irate face was that of Dominic's as he sifted through the large box of documents and drew out those all-absorbing papers. He had been so pleased for her, as if he'd found gold. Inevitably, Thea's thoughts went to the house itself.

Her eyes closed; she heard the sea slapping against the harbour wall with an oily sound, the murmur of voices. Turning on to her side, she tried to blot out the memory, but it was too strong for her and she slept, her breath quiet and even, her eyes behind the closed lids describing a series of twitches as the scenes took shape.

John Royle stepped out from the shadows of the boatshed and Polly flew into his arms.

'John! I'm sorry to be late. I was worried in case you'd given me up and gone.'

'Never. I saw the ferry come in this morning and guessed you'd be busy. There looked to be a lot of passengers. Was it a full house?'

'Yes, they all came in clamouring for food. I didn't know if I was on my head or my heels!' Polly paused. 'Mam's not well either.

That's what delayed me. I couldn't very well leave her with all the pots. Still, never mind. I'm here now.'

She gazed up into John's lean, clever face and her heart skipped a beat. How she loved him! Loved the way his dark-brown hair fell endearingly over his brow and the blue eyes that shone when they beheld her, as if she was everything to him. He had never said as much, not yet.

How could he, when all they had were snatched meetings and whispered words to mark their growing attachment for each other? Polly knew that if her father were to find out he'd take his strap to her. His daughter and a common fisher lad?

Useless to tell him that John held ambitions over and above the usual. Da wouldn't listen.

'I'm sorry about your mama,' John said. 'It must be a worry for you. She's such a lady. Not really cut out for the life of a tavern-keeper's wife, is she?'

Polly sighed. It was true that Marion Dakin, with her frail good looks and gentle manners, was more suited to sitting with her embroidery than coping with an inn full of travellers, well-to-do though many of them were.

She wondered if her mother was aware of the others, the ones that came stealthily at night, their boats sliding soundlessly through the waves.

Polly bit her lip.

'John, there's something else. It concerns my father. I've reason to believe he's involved with the moonlighters.'

There, it was said. The fear that had possessed her ever since she had discovered the mysterious haul in the cellar was now shared. Knowing the serious nature of her suspicions, Polly was unprepared for the wry smile that came to John's lips.

'Oh, Polly, my sweet innocent,' he said. 'You'd be surprised how many Parkgate folk have a finger in that particular pie! I see much of what goes on when I'm out on the boat. There's been a marked increase in contraband activity ever since the Custom House and the Watch Tower ceased to operate. People think they are safe.'

'And are they?'

'Not as such, there's always the risk of discovery.' His hands held her shoulders as he turned her towards him. 'Polly, you must have a care. For your own good you'd be wise to turn a blind eye to what goes on. If ever it came to official ears that your father was involved and you were questioned, you could then answer with all honesty that you know nothing.'

'But Da would be in serious trouble. It would kill my mother.'

Touched as she was that John thought enough of her to bestow the warning, Polly wanted further proof that her father was involved.

The pile of unaccounted-for goods she had inadvertently stumbled across preyed on her mind. Polly wanted to establish how they arrived in the cellar and where they were going.

'The tide's on the turn,' John said. 'I shall have to see to the nets. Take care, Polly. Remember what I said.'

His lips came down lingeringly on hers. He tore himself away and went loping off along the quayside to where his fishing boat was moored. Polly was reflective as she made her way back to the tavern.

When she entered the kitchen however, all thoughts of contraband fled. Her mother was bent over a pail of root vegetables she had been peeling, her hand to her brow, her face ashen.

'Mother!' Polly darted to her side. 'What is it? Are you ill?'

'It's nothing, Polly love.' Marion Dakin made a visible effort to pull herself together. 'I came over a little faint, that is all.'

'You must go and rest. Never mind the evening meal. I'll see to it. Here, let me help you upstairs.'

Polly helped her mother to bed and made her comfortable, then hastened back to the kitchen to pick up where Marion had left off. Voices and spontaneous bursts of laughter issued from the tap-room where the overnight boarders were gathered.

Glancing up, Polly then swung the stock pot over the fire. It was going to be a long evening....

Midnight had struck before she had finished. Wearily, Polly put the gruel to steep for the morning and dragged herself off to her room under the eaves. She was drifting into sleep when the sound she most dreaded brought her abruptly back to consciousness – the creak of the trapdoor to the cellar below being opened.

Getting up, Polly flung her shawl around her shoulders and crept down the steep wooden stairs, keeping to the shadow of the wall. Sure enough, in the lobby below, her father and two burly seamen were stowing away a shipment of goods.

There was a murmured exchange of words, a furtive handing over of money, and the men melted silently away into the night. Before Wallace Dakin could ascend the stairs Polly had darted off back to her room.

Her heart was thumping in her throat. So her suspicions had been correct. Her father *was* involved with contraband.

The enormity of it drove all prospect of sleep from her head. Wallace Dakin was not renowned for his discretion, especially when in his cups. One slip, and everything would be lost....

The next morning, Polly, heavy-eyed from lack of sleep, sought out her brother and told him what she had seen.

'Da's making a few pennies on the side?' Edward simply grinned, his tawny eyes dancing. 'That doesn't surprise me. Forget it, Polly. How's your John?'

'He's not "my" John – well, not yet.'

'No more is Susanna mine.' He sighed heavily. 'Why is it that the love of my life has a clergyman of all people for a papa? The rector, Mr Marsdon would never allow marriage between us. Never.'

'Edward, I'm sorry. You are serious in your affections for Susanna?'

'Never more so, and Susanna returns my feelings. For the moment there's nothing can be done. We shall have to be content with secret meetings and subterfuge. Something will turn up for us. For you and John Royle, too.'

'I do hope you're right,' Polly said bleakly.

She went through to the kitchen where her mother – up and about again despite Polly's protests – was standing at the stove frying bacon in an immense black pan. Polly could hardly confide in her mother, not in her present state. That left only one other person she could turn to.

'Mother, I might go and see Aunt Jessica later on. Have you any messages for her?'

'Not especially, but give her my love. Mind you take her some preserves from the pantry; Jessica always did have a liking for them. And change your gown, young lady. You know what a stickler my sister is for correct form.'

Polly gave a little laugh.

'I won't forget.'

That afternoon, she was on her way out, a cape over her pretty afternoon gown of sprigged muslin, for the day was wet, when her father's deep voice stopped her in her tracks.

'Polly, is that you? Come in here, girl. There's something important I want to tell you.'

Polly's insides quailed. Had Da found out about John? Worse, had he spotted her last night and wanted to make sure of her silence?

'Polly!' Wallace's voice roared again.

Polly straightened her back, lifted her chin and went to answer her father's summons. The battered old door of the tap-room swung shut behind her with a bang.

Mae took the final batch of currant buns out of the Aga and put them with the rest to cool, slamming shut the oven door with a sigh. There, that was the market bake done for another day. Chas, glancing through the newspaper as he drank his mid-morning coffee, looked up sharply.

'You look worried, Mae, What is it?'

'Well, since you ask....' His wife brought her own coffee to the table and sat down.

'Chas, do you think there's something worrying Thea? When I took her a cup of tea first thing this morning she started up in the bed as if she'd seen a ghost.'

He shook his head.

'She's got a lot on her mind, builders at the house, things not always going to plan. It's enough to make anyone edgy.'

'Perhaps, but she seems so distracted. It's not like her. I hope she's not regretting her engagement. You know how it is. Doubts start creeping in once the initial excitement wears off.'

He gave her a sidelong look.

'Really? Is that what happened to you?'

'Of course not.' Mae smilingly reached out and touched her husband's work-callused hand. 'Silly thing! I'm not too happy about Bryony, either. Out until all hours, never saying where she's going. I hate to think what time she came in last night.'

'But that's how it is with youngsters, Mae. They're off on a jolly when we're thinking about turning in for the night. I shouldn't worry, Bryony can look after herself.'

'You spoil her,' Mae scolded. 'You always have. Bryony can do no wrong in your eyes.'

She broke off abruptly as the door opened and their younger daughter came in. It was her day off. In her denim mini-skirt and skimpy white top she was clearly dressed to go out.

Her blonde curls were scrunched up with a diamante clasp on the top of her head and on her feet she wore clumpy mules.

Her two daughters, Mae thought with amused affection, couldn't have been more different.

'Off out on the town?' Chas asked her.

'I'm picking Liz up,' Bryony nodded, 'then we're going to Liverpool. Dad, could you lend me some money for petrol? I'll pay you back at the end of the month.'

'I've heard that one before.' Chas grinned indulgently, then dug into his wallet and handed her a couple of notes. 'Mind how you go. Traffic's bad at this time of day.'

'I will.' She dropped her father a kiss on the top of his bushy head of hair. 'Thanks Dad, you're a star.'

On her way out she made to seize a newly-baked bun from the tray.

'Not those!' Mae cried hastily. 'They're for the market. Have an apple if you're hungry. Or better still, have some cereal.'

'No time, Mum. I told Liz I'd be there for eleven and I'm already late.'

'It might help if you didn't stay out half the night. You'd be better able to get up in the mornings then.'

'Oh, Mum. Don't start.'

'What do you expect? I lie awake worrying until I know you're back safely. It's not on, Bryony. Your sister never behaved in this way.'

Mae hadn't meant to make an issue of it but it was too late now.

Bryony glowered as only Bryony could.

'Thea wouldn't. Anyway, she was at university at my age. You don't know what she got up to while she was there, do you? You're always having a go at me.'

'Bryony, that'll do,' her father cut in. 'Your mother's only concerned about you. There's no need to speak to her like that.'

'Mum treats me like I'm still a kid at school,' Bryony retorted. 'Who'd want to be the youngest in this family? Oh, I've had enough, I'm going!'

'What time do you expect—' Mae began, but her daughter had slammed out and she turned to her husband in despair.

'See what I mean?'

Chas raised his hands in a conciliatory gesture and let them fall again.

'It's just a stage. She'll sort herself out.'

'Meanwhile I have the worry of it.'

'All mothers worry over their chicks. Look, try and see this for what it is, Mae, and give the girl some space. Cut yourself some slack, too, love. You're always slaving away till all hours, doing the market bakes on top of everything else.'

He gave a knowing smile.

'I haven't heard Richard's name mentioned yet. Does that mean he's behaving himself?'

'I wish you wouldn't humour me like this, Chas,' Mae said crisply. 'It only makes things worse. I wouldn't be at all surprised if Richard isn't making plans of his own.'

'Plans? What d'you mean?'

'Just a hunch. Haven't you noticed how he avoids talking about the future? Like yesterday when you were thinking about what to put the Long Acre down to. Richard's usually keen to air his knowledge when it comes to crop rotation. I thought he was down-right evasive.'

'Is that all?' Chas shrugged his broad shoulders. 'Happen his mind was elsewhere. On his girlfriend, maybe.' He paused. 'Come to think of it, Tracey let slip something that had me thinking when she was here the other evening. We were jawing on about the new identity cards the government seems to think we need.

'Tracey made the point that a passport should suffice. Then she laughed – you know how she is – and said what a fright Richard looked on his new one. Has he spoken about having a passport photograph taken recently?'

'No, not a word,' Mae said quietly. 'Maybe they're planning a holiday abroad?'

'Could be. Strange he's never mentioned it....' He grinned suddenly. 'Blue skies, golden sand and Tracey. No wonder he doesn't want to talk about farming!'

Mae smiled, hands cupped around her coffee mug.

'Oh, I bumped into Dominic Shane at the supermarket last night. Apparently he's just moved into one of the Dee Cottages. Lovely big garden, he said – well, he's got the dog. Couldn't have been easy for him in digs.'

'The new vet, you mean? I didn't know he was thinking of buying a place in Parkgate. He must have decided to stay, then. I had a feeling he might move on. Just shows how wrong you can be. He's a good vet, I'll say that for him. If I still had my cows he'd be the one I'd use. Quite miss my cows,' he mused.

'I know you do.' Mae's tone softened. 'Maybe one day we'll be in a position to put a dairy herd together again. Something along the lines of the Roseacre stock. Talking of Roseacre, Dominic was saying how Mike Sanders hadn't been very well. Funny Thea never mentioned it. I must give Helen a ring. What a worry for her.'

Chas nodded.

'Good thing they've got Geoff there. They'd never cope on their own.'

'Apparently Dominic got roped in to help the other day. They were short-handed for the milking and he happened to be there. It would be for the vaccinations, I expect. He seemed to have enjoyed himself. I get the impression his people were farmers.'

'Really?' Chas finished his coffee. 'You know more than I do then. Bit of an enigma, that young man. I got to chatting with him a bit when he was calling to see that mare of Thea's. Tried several times to get him into conversation about his home ground, but he wouldn't be drawn. I wonder if he's ever been married.'

'And it all went turn and turn about, you mean? I wouldn't know. People are entitled to their private lives, Chas.'

'I don't deny that. But there's something guarded about him, that's all. Show me the man or woman who doesn't like to enthuse about their homeland when they've moved away. But Dominic Shane? He couldn't get off the subject fast enough!'

'Here, Trina.' Dominic ushered the red setter into the pick-up, shut the door and turned to Geoff with a nod.

'Right then, that's the lot for jabs for now. I've signed the certificate of proof and left it in the house with Mrs Sanders. You'll know about needing to get it copied for the official records, of course?'

Geoff made a wry face.

'Tenfold, you mean? Yes, I know – bloody red tape! Don't know how we'd manage but for Mum. She's got to grips with it all splendidly. Everything's filed on to a computer and she knows exactly where to find it.'

Dominic nodded.

'I expect Thea's pretty well in touch with the ins and outs of farming paperwork, too?'

'I wouldn't be so sure about that. As I understand it, Richard and Mae do the books between them at Woodhey. Thea's busy with her show ponies.'

'She's won a lot with them, hasn't she? You must be very proud of her.'

'Oh, yes. You like the equestrian side of things, don't you? Is that what you specialized in back in … Donegal, was it?'

'Yes,' Dominic answered.

'Thea's never got over to Ireland with her little lot yet. Is the showing scene big over there?'

'Fairly. I didn't have much to do with it myself. I dealt with the big fellows.'

Dominic paused, his blue eyes inward looking. Then he stirred himself.

'Well, that'll be all for now, Geoff. I'd best be getting along. I moved house at the weekend. Lots to do.'

'Now that's something I know I can safely leave in Thea's hands when the time comes – home decorating! Cheers then, Dominic. Thanks for everything.'

'No problem.' Dominic climbed into the car, letting down the window. 'I hope to see your father up and about again next time I come. See you, Geoff.'

He was smiling as he drove off. It was good to be returning to his own place at last. Beamed and flagged and beautifully maintained, it had all the character he looked for in a home.

The Donegal house that Aisling had been doing up for them had been all minimalist and stainless steel. Dominic felt infinitely more at home in Woodhey's big farmhouse kitchen, with its good smells of baking and the farm clutter piled on the vast dresser.

Roseacre was in a similar mould but the rooms were tastefully understated with well chosen antiques, deep, comfortable sofas and muted colours. He tried to picture Thea as mistress of it – which she was sure to be eventually – and found to his surprise that he couldn't.

He slowed for the traffic lights ahead, glancing round while he waited for them to change. The great oaks and beeches that lined the road were in full leaf, dusty now after the spell of dry weather. The fields and hedgerows were neat and well tended.

It was a far cry from the rugged spaces of his homeland but possessed a charm of its own. Dominic was glad of the total change of scene, happy to look ahead.

'Sure, haven't we landed on our paws here, Trina me girl,' he said to the dog in the back seat, reaching to fondle her silky head. The setter had been a gift from Aisling; she always had been one for extravagant gestures.

Aisling – pronounced Ashleen, and woe betide any poor unsuspecting soul who got it wrong! – rose unbidden into his mind. The fey darkness of her, the sultry appeal, utterly irresistible and every bit as lethal as a rattlesnake. Dominic's expression was grim.

When the lights changed, he indicated right and swung round for Parkgate and his new home.

Later, after a sketchy meal and a desultory attempt to unpack a few belongings that still lay in large boxes and bin liners in the narrow hallway, Dominic took Trina for a walk along the estuary.

The sun was setting in spectacular streaks of amber and crimson and shadows were long-drawn across the open expanse of salt-marsh. As he walked, a few lines from a poem by Charles Kingsley ran through his mind.

> *Oh, Mary, go and call the cattle home*
> *Across the sands o' Dee*
> *And call the cattle home,*
> *And call the cattle home*
> *The western wind was wild and dank wi' foam*
> *And all alone went she.*

He'd come across the poem in an anthology he'd picked up in a small second-hand bookshop recommended to him by Thea. The words appealed to his Celtic soul; the open aspect of his surroundings and salt-laden air stirred stark memories and dark thoughts of Donegal.

So you're running out on me.... Great.

Get a grip, Aisling! What d'you expect after what's happened?

A bit of understanding would help. I did it for us, can't you see that? It would have come off, too, if you hadn't interfered, damn you!

And then another voice, harshly male, incredulous rather than accusing.

For God's sake, Dom! Whatever possessed you, man? You must have known the risk you were taking. You certainly know what the consequences would be if I did the required thing and took this matter further. You'd get struck off!

39

It hadn't come to that. Dominic had done the only possible thing and given notice. Relations between himself and Aisling had turned sour and he'd had no choice but to finish it.

The opening with the Parkgate practice had been the first on the list of situations vacant and Dominic had blindly put in his application. Parkgate on the Wirral peninsula seemed as good a place as any to start afresh. At the time he hadn't cared where he went. Nothing could ever live up to the job he had just given up. Nothing ever would. If he had to spend the rest of his working life in general animal practice, then so be it.

As things turned out, someone – as his mother would have said – had been watching over him. The employment he had walked into had turned out ideal. His colleagues were genial, the work varied and interesting, the environment pleasing. Surely if there was anywhere he could settle and put the past behind him, it was here....

Trina had gone loping off chasing seagulls and Dominic whistled her back. A little way ahead on the promontory, the Harbour House sketched a dark outline against the sky. Builders' materials and a skip full of rubble stood on the frontage.

He was debating on whether to turn back when Thea's car appeared on the track and drew up outside the house. Thea got out and waved to him and the dog immediately went bounding off to greet her. Dominic followed at a more sober pace.

'Thea. Good evening.'

'Hi, Dominic. All right, Trina, I've said hello. Now sit. Good dog.'

'I didn't expect to see you at this hour. It'll soon be dark.'

'I know. Geoff rang about some measurements he needed. I thought I had them but could I lay hands on them? It was easier to jump in the car and pop down here with the tape measure. How did the move go?'

'Fine. It didn't take all that long – well, I only brought a few bits and pieces with me from back home. I shall send for the rest once I'm properly settled. It's a nice property. I've struck lucky there.'

'That's great. There's a lot to be said for going for a place that's in good order.'

Thea directed a wry glance towards her future home. The

Harbour House, in the process of being gutted, was at that trying stage where you wonder if it will ever be finished. She shrugged ruefully, smiling at Dominic.

'I expect you'll be touring the salerooms now for furniture.'

'It's a thought. You must call some time. I'll show you round.'

'That would be lovely, Dominic. Would you like a look at the Harbour House? You'll need to stretch your imagination. At the moment it's shambolic.'

She rooted through her pockets.

'Now, where's my door key. Ah, got it. Come on in. You too, Trina. You can both help me measure the kitchen.'

Laughing and talking, they unlocked the front door and vanished into the house. Neither of them had noticed the small, watchful figure who stood in the shadows of the derelict boathouse a short distance away.

'You said *what* to Dad?' Richard asked Tracey with dismay.

It was Jazz Club night. The show was over and everyone had left the premises. As always, Richard and Tracey had stopped to tidy up and sit and discuss the gig over a coffee. Tracey spooned sugar into Richard's mug and shunted it across the table to him.

'It was nothing, Richard. We were talking and I mentioned your passport photo. I don't think your father thought anything of it.'

'Don't you believe it! Dad picks up on everything. He takes on board a lot more than you think.'

She shot him an accusatory look.

'Well, you should have put them in the picture about the tour. This is their farm we're talking about, Richard. They're entitled to know what's happening. Your father might have to take on another guy in your place.'

'I doubt it, not this side of winter, anyway. Everything goes quiet once the corn harvest is over'

'All the same, they should know the situation. Look, why don't I follow you home now in my car and we'll tell them together?'

'Why don't you just let me deal with this? Give it a break, Tracey. We've got Manhursts booked for next week.'

This was the firm of agricultural contractors who dealt with the harvests.

'They're bringing the combines in on Monday. Let's hope this good weather holds. With luck the fields will be cleared by the end of the week. Then I'll tell Dad.'

But Richard's plans were thwarted. The following morning, Saturday, he intended going into town to kit himself up for the tour. Over breakfast, Chas turned to him with the news that he wanted to get on with opening up the fields; a procedure that involved mowing a single track round the outside edge of each field to clear it of weeds and let in the air to the main crop.

Richard gazed at his father in exasperation.

'We can do that tomorrow. It won't take long if we use both tractors.'

'I had a look at the cornfields last night,' Chas replied. 'There's a lot of bracken and other hedgerow stuff this year. Some of it is very high indeed. No, we're better tackling it today. The forecast for the weekend is good. A bit of sun on the crop tomorrow will make all the difference.'

'But I'm going out, Dad. I've things to do.'

'Then I'm sorry but it'll have to wait. It's harvest time, Richard. I don't have to spell it out to you. The farm comes first.'

'Blast the farm!' Richard snapped, the weeks and months of pent-up frustration boiling up inside him. 'I've said I'll do the fields tomorrow and that's it.'

'Oh, is it?' Chas said, dangerously quiet. 'What's so crucial that it can't wait till next weekend, Richard? It wouldn't have anything to do with that new passport, would it?'

Richard's heart sank. So he was right. Tracey should have kept her mouth shut! Mustering calm, he said quite reasonably, 'Yes, it would actually. Dad, you're not going to like this … I'd meant to hold off until after the corn was in before I brought the subject up. But you may as well know now. I'm leaving the farm.'

'What, for good?'

'I'm going professional with the band. I'm sorry to have to spring it on you like this but that's how it is.'

42

There was a shocked silence in which Chas stared at his son as if unable to take in what he was hearing.

'We've made an album, Dad,' Richard went on desperately. 'The guy who's sponsoring us thinks we're good. We've got a tour of Ireland booked.'

'Oh, have you now!' Chas found his voice at last. 'And what about Woodhey? The work doesn't come to a stop with the corn harvest. What about the winter wheat? The ploughing and sowing? Had you thought of that?'

'Dad, I—'

Chas stood up, almost knocking back his chair.

'I might have known there was something up. And where does that leave your mother and me? In the lurch! Well, Richard, I'm telling you this. You've obviously made up your mind, so you might as well go now!

'Go on, before I say something I might regret. Get your things together and clear off out of it! That's what you want, isn't it?'

Chapter Three

'I knew Richard had plans to go off with his band, but I didn't reckon on his leaving under quite such a cloud,' Thea told Geoff ruefully. They were shopping in Chester and had stopped for a coffee.

'He and Dad had a blazing row. You could hear them all over the farm. Neither would give way – they're a match for each other when it comes to stubbornness.'

'It's a pity Richard hadn't come clean before now, though. It would've given your dad a chance to get used to the idea,' Geoff suggested.

'Oh, you know how it is, nothing matters except the farm. There wouldn't have been a moment's peace for any of us.'

'Perhaps not. How has your mother taken it?'

'Mum's miserable. She hates confrontation, but I think she'll eventually see this Richard's way. If farming isn't your thing it can be awful. And Richard's got talent. He'd be a fool not to take it further now he's got the chance. Bryony and I are in agreement for once. She really stood up for Richard. Dad did a lot of blustering but I think he took some of what she said on board. If anyone can talk Dad round it's my sister!'

A smile crossed Geoff's affable face.

'Well, she's a born charmer!'

'Dad's golden girl.' Thea smiled ruefully. 'Bryony always could twist him round her little finger.' She gave a little slight laugh. 'They'll be in Dublin now. The initial plan was to go after the corn harvest but Richard texted me saying there was nothing to keep them now and they were leaving immediately – or as soon as Tracey could make it. She's a fancy dresser. Lots of packing to do.'

'Are she and Richard an item?'

'It looks that way.' Thea poured the last of the coffee. 'They're well matched. I'm glad for them. Can't wait for their album to come out. The Richie Dene Band and Tracey Kent. Imagine!'

'Sad it's been the cause of a rift, all the same. What about the farm? How will Chas manage?'

'We'll have to take on a man in Richard's place. I don't suppose you know of anyone wanting a job?'

'Not offhand, but Dad might come up with something. Meantime I'll send one of our lads along to help with the ploughing. It needs tackling while the weather's good.'

'Oh, would you?' Gratitude shone in Thea's eyes. 'That'll ease a lot of the strain. But lucky Richard … how marvellous to be free to follow your dream.'

Geoff snorted.

'I call it being downright selfish.'

'Well, if it was me I'd have done the same thing.'

'It wouldn't have mattered quite so much though, would it?'

'I don't see why not. Women run farms these days and make a good job of it, too.' Thea was annoyed by his comments. 'Anyway, have you finished your coffee? We might as well go. Just the final decision on the kitchen units. Do you want me to see to it?'

'OK. Let's head back, then. There's something I need to get on with at Roseacre.'

'Yes, I rather thought there might be,' Thea said wryly.

They were quiet on the journey back, separated by their thoughts. Geoff's face wore a preoccupied expression, his mind evidently was on whatever task awaited him at the big dairy farm.

Thea was disappointed that he had shown such little interest in what she considered a brave move on her brother's part. The fact that they seemed to hold quite opposite views on things these days troubled her.

Geoff dropped her off at Woodhey and sped away to pick up the

Heswell road. Watching until the car had disappeared from view, Thea turned and walked slowly up the track to the farm. Lunchtime was close but she wasn't hungry. Instead of going indoors, she jumped into her car and headed for the Harbour House. She might as well get her kitchen choice done with.

A familiar figure walking his dog on the narrow lane ahead caused her to slow down. She drew to a stop beside him, letting down the window.

'Hi, Dominic. How's things?'

'Hello, there, Thea. We're fine, aren't we, Trina?'

The setter laughed up at them joyfully and Thea reached out to stroke her burnished red coat.

'It's my day off,' Dominic went on. 'I've been doing some decorating. Just a dab of paint, nothing fancy.

She nodded.

'We're keeping things simple at our place, too.' Thea paused. 'Have you heard about Richard?'

'That he's gone off with the band and the delectable Tracey? Yes, I did hear something of the sort. It's true, then?'

'Absolutely. I hope you're not going to bang on about shirked responsibilities?'

'Why should I? Richard's a grown man. Thea. It's up to him how he chooses to live his life.'

'My sentiments exactly. Geoff can't get his head round how anyone could up and leave without a backward glance.'

'Quite easily, I should imagine! Music is to a musician what the land and stock are to a farmer. And Richard's got talent. I've heard them play. And Tracey Kent is a natural.'

Try telling Geoff that, Thea thought.

'When the album comes out I'll get you a signed copy.' She grinned. 'It might be worth a fortune one day, like my gran's Beatles programmes!'

He laughed, his darkly handsome face becoming suddenly warmer.

'I'll keep you to that. When do you go back to school?'

'Monday. This coming term is a hectic one – long too.'

'So, do you enjoy teaching, Thea?'

'Well … yes. There's a lot I don't like, such as all the paperwork.' She shrugged. But I suppose there's a downside to every job.'

'True. My pet hate was a certain type of horse owner at Ferlann. Not all, I might add. And the horses made up for it.'

'You were at the Ferlann Ridge Bloodstock Sales?' Thea's interest sharpened at the mention of the famous sale. 'Were you the resident vet there?'

'One of them. A girl I knew worked on the clerical side. She was a jazz buff, too. Sang at the gigs.'

Then the shutters came down. Dominic brought the dog to heel.

'Well, I'd better press on. Tell your father I've got that information he wanted about organic farming. Better still, call in for it on your way back. You haven't seen my place yet.'

'I've been busy. You know how it is.'

'Sure I do. See you later then, Thea.'

Sending a farewell salute, Thea drove away, his words whirling in her head. Why had Dominic abandoned such a highly-thought-of position for a post with a small country practice like Parkgate? And who was the girl? Was there a broken romance here? Something more…?

It struck Thea, a little wistfully, as she turned in at the drive to her future home, how understanding he had been over Richard.

Inside the house, Thea spread out the kitchen brochures on the wide window seat, trying to decide between the latest fashion in limed wood and an attractive golden oak.

But her heart was not in it. She'd think about it later … her thoughts kept straying to Dominic Shane and the mystery behind his reasons for leaving his homeland.

Thea fished in her bag for a bottle of water and sat down in the sunny window embrasure. She'd go to Birkenhead and hand in her order at the kitchen suppliers, she decided, before school started.

How the holidays had flown! Despite her best mare being out of the ring earlier she had made up for it since, coming home with several first rosettes and a trophy to add to those on the dresser shelf.

At the thought of her ponies her heart warmed. Once she and Geoff were married he'd surely take more interest in them. It would be great to do the shows together, she mused, yawning, her eyes growing heavy in the warmth from the golden September sun....

'I won't beat about the bush, Polly,' Wallace Dakin said to his daughter. 'George Rawlinson has asked for your hand in marriage and I've given my agreement. It's a good match. He's not short of a penny or two. Big house, his own ferry company, wise investments. You'd not do better. Don't stand there gawping, girl! Say something.'

Polly stared at her father in shocked disbelief. Marry George Rawlinson?

'But Da, he's old,' she blurted out. 'And he's fat. He's got a son older than I am.'

'Rubbish, George is in his prime, and a fine figure of a man. He's been lonely since his wife passed on, what with the son residing in London and nothing but an empty hearth to return to each night.'

'But I don't love him,' Polly protested chokingly.

Wallace's eyes narrowed.

'What's that got to do with it? He's a good man who'll look after you, so let that be an end to it.'

Recognising the stubborn note in her father's voice, Polly bit back the argument that trembled on her lips. Mama hated raised voices. She must not be upset. Polly picked up her basket and took her leave. A few moments later she was speeding along the road, passing the row of Coastguard Cottages, heading for her Aunt Jessica's in the centre of the village.

As a rule the Parade would have been crowded; strolling couples admiring the view of the estuary, nannies taking the air with their young charges.

Today, with rain sweeping in from Wales, the road was deserted, and Polly was glad to turn off into Mostyn Place where her aunt's house stood, staunch and welcoming, in its big garden.

Fernlea was the Platts' family house, a stone-built residence with wisteria-clad walls, mullioned windows and tall chimneys.

Jessica Platt must have been watching out, for the front door opened and Polly was enveloped in her aunt's patchouli-scented embrace. Dark where her sister was fair and handsome rather than beautiful, with flashing black eyes and a healthy complexion, Jessica had a manner that brooked no arguments.

'Polly! Give Agnes your cape and come and sit by the fire, dear. Some tea I think, Agnes.'

'Yes, ma'am.'

The maid bobbed a curtsy and vanished into the nether regions of the house, whilst Polly was ushered into the comfortable parlour of plush-covered chairs and polished surfaces.

'Now, tell me your news. I vow it is weeks since last we spoke.' Jessica smiled to take the sting out of her words and arranged herself on the sofa with a rustle of silken skirts. 'First your dear mama. How is she?'

'Not very well, Aunt Jessica.'

'Then you must call the doctor. Marion never was robust and she works too hard. I'm surprised your papa doesn't engage some help in the tavern.'

'I'm sure Da isn't intentionally thoughtless. It's just that Mama has always managed. She's sent you a jar of the strawberry preserve you are so fond of.'

'Oh la! Give her my thanks.' She studied her niece closely. 'You look wan, child.'

'Oh, Aunt! It's Da.' Polly hardly knew where to start. She lowered her voice conspiratorially. 'I fear he could be in big trouble. He's involved with *smugglers*.'

Aunt Jessica patted her hand.

'Dear me, is that all? I'm not a whit surprised. A tavern on the harbour couldn't be better placed for a spot of crafty trafficking. Polly, my love, don't look so shaken. You'd be amazed at the number of people – many of them very well respected – with a finger in that particular pie.'

She preened her hair and the collar of her frock.

'How else do you suppose one obtains the material for one's gowns or the wine for the cellar?'

'I ... I hadn't thought,' Polly stammered. 'Aunt Jessica, that's not all. Da says I'm to be married – to Mr Rawlinson the ferry owner!'

'To ... to George?' At this Jessica looked stunned. 'My goodness me!'

The maid entered the room then with the tea-tray, giving Jessica time to restore her scattered wits. Busy with silver teapot and delicate china, she heard Polly out.

'I won't do it! I cannot marry someone old enough to be my father! Besides, I love another, but I dare not make an issue out of it for fear of upsetting Mama.'

'There, child. Mayhap it will come to nothing.'

Jessica handed Polly her tea, plied her with cake and, cleverly changing the subject, launched into an entertaining tirade on a dinner party she had attended the previous night.

Mollified by her aunt's bright company, Polly then returned home to more trouble.

'It's your brother,' Marion wept. 'The rector has found out that Edward's been secretly courting his daughter and is in a fine fury. Your father's forbidden Edward all further contact with the girl. My poor boy! I know he's high-spirited but he means no harm and he truly loves Susanna.'

'And she him,' Polly agreed. 'Hush, Mama. You mustn't distress yourself or you'll be ill again. See what Aunt Jessica has sent you. Some lace trim for a gown and a bottle of cordial she says will help boost your blood. Oh, and there's a new anthology of verse by Mr Browning. Shall I read it you?'

'That would be splendid. Dearest child, what would I do without you?'

Polly opened the book. She had arranged to meet John Royle at high tide. Now she would be late.

When, eventually, she sped to their trysting place in the lea of the boatshed, John was no longer there. He had left a note. Polly read it feverishly.

My dearest Polly, John began in his flowing hand. *It has come to my knowledge that you have been spoken for. I was at the Harbour*

House earlier and happened to overhear your father with a group of friends, celebrating your imminent betrothal to the man who owns the ferry boats.

Polly, I know this will have come as a great shock and my heart goes out to you, but I am sure you will understand the position it puts me in also. Even when my ambition to have my own school for boys is realized, as one day it surely will be, I can never hope to compete with a man such as George Rawlinson. Therefore I deem it best to end our relationship at once.

You will be always in my thoughts. Respectfully yours, John Royle.

The rain had started up again, the stinging drops blending with the tears on Polly's cheeks, blurring the ink on the page so that the words were no longer legible. And still she stood there, her head bowed, until a salt-laden breeze snatched the letter from her grip and carried it away.

Thea woke with a start. The dreams again, and so real! She bit her lip, peering around her, reluctant to accept that these strange dips into the past were somehow tied up with the house. The house that was to be her future home. Could she face living here? Did she want to try?

Some superstitious streak deep within her cried out against it. But the real Thea, the sensible down-to-earth side, rose in challenge. All things had a rational explanation and this was no exception.

Getting up stiffly, rubbing her aching neck, she gathered together the material for the kitchen suppliers and left the house.

She drove slowly along the Parade, fragments of the dream still running through her mind, and turned into the street where Dominic lived. On the side lawn Trina was getting to grips with a large marrowbone.

Dominic opened the door.

'You remembered about the brochures ... well, come in. Coffee's brewing.'

It wasn't until she had entered the newly-decorated beamed and flagged-floored living-room that she was swamped by a feeling of déjà vu. She had seen this place only moments ago, when Polly had poured out her troubles to her aunt! Thea swallowed hard, trying to check the peculiar swimming sensation in her head.

'Hey, are you all right now?' Dominic's soft Irish voice came from what seemed like very far away. 'Here, sit down, put your head low. That's the way. Better?'

'Yes, I think so.'

She sipped the water Dominic handed her, avoiding his concerned gaze.

'I can't think what came over me.'

'It could be the fumes from the paint. I noticed myself how strong they were. Let me open a window.'

Fresh air rushed in, salty, reviving.

'I'm fine now, really. What a lovely room. Bigger than it looks from the outside.'

'Yes, it's a conversion. The big house was made into two smaller ones at the start of the last century. The people I bought this one from made a lot of improvements. Central heating, that sort of thing.'

She hardly took in what he was saying. She did not understand this – any of it. She swallowed again and thought, a little hysterically, what an extraordinary topic this would make for the Historical Society if only she had the nerve to speak of it!

Bryony steered her way through the hordes of afternoon shoppers, heading for Grange Road and a place to eat. Normally she met up with Liz for lunch but today the other assistant at the boutique had gone home poorly and the midday break had been delayed waiting for the boss to come and relieve her.

She was rounding a corner when she literally collided with Geoff.

'Hi, there. Where are you off to in such a hurry?' He laughed.

'The nearest café. I've missed my lunch and I'm famished!'

'Me, too. Come on, the Vine's across the road. I'll treat you.'

He ushered her into coffee-scented and discreetly-lit confines of the wine bar and placed their order.

'This is nice,' Bryony glanced round, relishing having Geoff to herself for once. 'Do you come here with Thea?'

'Sometimes. She's got a weakness for the Danish pastries. Want to try one?'

'Do I!'

Their food came and though Bryony did her best to talk, Geoff seemed distracted.

'Is something wrong?' she said at last.

'Sorry. Got things on my mind, I guess.'

'Well, spill. Tell Aunty Bryony all about it!'

He sent her a smile, quick, apologetic.

'Oh, you know. Dad laid up, and just when we've increased the milking herd. Can't be helped but the double workload....'

'It's worrying for Ma, too. And Thea expects me to drop everything and shop around for fittings for the house. Why it can't all be got from the same place I can't imagine.'

'Is that what you're doing here now?'

'No, I've dropped in to see the accountant. Dad offered to come instead but he's not up to it.'

'I'm truly sorry about your father, Geoff. He's a lovely man.' On impulse Bryony reached across the table and gave his hand a sympathetic squeeze. At that exact moment, unbeknown to the pair at the table, Thea walked by on her way to the kitchen suppliers and happened to glance in.

She stopped short, staring, and then collected herself and hurried on.

'You have Dominic Shane looking after your cows, don't you?' Bryony continued. 'He and Thea are getting a bit chummy. I saw them laughing together down by the Harbour House. They didn't see me, though.... Oh, well, I suppose he walks his dog a lot along the estuary.'

Geoff's face tightened. Realizing she had gone too far, Bryony decided on a swift change of topic.

'Anyway, tell me about the additions to the herd. Have you bought in new stock or are they home-bred cattle you've run on?'

She'd evidently hit the right note. Geoff, coaxed into talking about the subject dearest to him, relaxed visibly and Bryony was astonished at how he made what seemed a dry subject fascinating. Plates cleared, he glanced at his watch.

'My appointment's at three. I'd better make a move.'

'And I should get back to the shop. Thanks, Geoff. It's been great.'

'My pleasure,' Geoff said, smiling.

Outside they parted company. Geoff made his trip to the accountant and returned home in time for milking. He had promised to meet Thea at the Harbour House that evening and was a little late setting off – an all-too-frequent occurrence recently, he acknowledged with a stab of guilt.

On the Parade he passed Dominic Shane, who sent him a smiling salute. With Bryony's words still smarting, Geoff acknowledged it curtly and drove on to the house where Thea was waiting.

'I'd just about given you up,' she greeted, kissing him. 'Five more minutes and then I was leaving. I've a show tomorrow, so I need to groom the ponies. How's your dad?'

'Brighter, I think. The audits were good from the accountant so that's bucked him up a bit.' He glanced into the bare, echoing lounge. 'Looks great now the walls are plastered, doesn't it? I like the roughcasting between the beams.'

'Me too. Makes it look more authentic.'

'Thea, I'm sorry about all this. I fully intended doing more here myself but—'

'I know, you've got enough on your plate right now.'

Impulsively she gave him a little hug to show that there was no ill feeling. The gesture, so typical of her, only served to increase his present feeling of inadequacy.

'I saw Dominic Shane on the way up here.'

'Really? I was at his house earlier. He'd got some brochures for Dad and gave me a guided tour while I was there.'

'Is that right? You and he seem to have got remarkably friendly.'

Thea looked taken aback.

'Dominic's our vet. Of course we're friends. Geoff, what is it? Why are you glowering like that?'

'I just don't like it. After all, we're supposed to be engaged. Oh, I've nothing against him as a vet. We have him ourselves. It's his attitude. Has he been here?'

'I've shown him round, yes. What's wrong with that?'

'Depends on the way you look at it.'

'Like you and my sister, you mean? Oh, don't try and deny it! I saw you together this afternoon at the Vine.'

'You were in town? Why didn't you come in and join us? I bumped into Bryony on the way to the accountant and—'

'Oh please. Spare me the lies. I saw you both. She was holding your hand.'

'Thea, it was nothing.'

'Oh really? It didn't seem that way to me. I considered the Vine our special place. Bit insensitive, Geoff, to take her there.'

'It's not as you think. I came across Bryony in town and bought her lunch and that's all there was to it.'

'But you more or less told me that something at Roseacre couldn't wait. And then I find you eating out with Bryony! What do you expect me to think?'

She took a deep, shuddering breath.

'It's not working between us, is it? I know you've been under a strain lately and I've tried to make allowances for it. But I feel you've lost interest ... in us.'

She looked around the echoing room.

'Who's made most of the decisions over the house?' she went on. 'Me! Who's done all the running around and chasing the builders when they've failed to turn up? Me! We never even have a proper evening out any more.'

Once started she could not stop. She was aware of Geoff's incredulity as she removed his ring from her finger.

'You'd better have this,' she said, her voice wobbling on the brink of tears. 'We can discuss everything else another time.'

Spinning round, she left the house and ran to where she'd

parked her car. Geoff, collecting himself, went after her, but by the time he had negotiated the piles of builders' rubble and stacks of unused materials, she was already firing the engine.

He stood on the cluttered forecourt, running dismayed fingers through his hair, watching the car go bumping off down the rutted track in a cloud of dust. Presently the dust settled, and there was nothing but the whine of the motor growing fainter, and, overhead, the mocking screech of a lone seabird.

The jazz club off O'Connell Street was crowded and noisy. Richard, having checked that the instruments were ready for the second session of the night, elbowed his way to the bar.

'There you are!' Tracey beamed at him over her tall glass of chilled fruit juice. 'Everything OK?'

'Couldn't be better.'

Richard regarded her appraisingly. In her short black dress that glittered when she moved, her dark-red hair upswept, jet earrings bobbing with every vivacious turn of her head, Tracey looked the part of a lead singer.

The Irish were known to be a discerning audience and the roar of applause had been gratifying. Richie Dene and his band, Richard thought with a joyful lift of his heart, were on the road to success!

'Mind if I join you?'

The sultry tone was arresting. Richard turned to see the young woman who had hit the limelight in the visitor's spot smiling at him. Her close-fitting, off-the-shoulder white dress was in sharp contrast to Tracey's black, and she had a rippling mane of chestnut hair and smoke-grey eyes full of mystery.

'I'm Aisling Cleary,' she continued.

'Would that be Ashleen spelt A-I-S-L-I-N-G?' Richard said, aware of the sudden silence of his mates and Tracey's wary attention.

'It would, so! You're a quick learner, Richie Dene!' Again the lazy smile. 'And how're you liking Dublin?'

'Very well – what I've seen of it. And it's Richard, actually,' he countered. 'Richard Partington. Dene's our stage name. Drink?'

'A glass of white wine would be perfect. Thanks, Richie.'

Giving the order to the barman, he then did his best to respond to the questions that were fired at him in a voice that slithered like silk around his senses.

No, they weren't planning to stop long in Dublin, the band was due in Wicklow the following week. No, they weren't London based but were from the north-west.

'A place called Parkgate on the Wirral peninsula. Shouldn't think you'll know it.'

'Would that be Cheshire?' Interest flickered in the amazing Irish eyes. 'Oh, but I do. My ex went over to work there. Dominic Shane?'

'Your joking! Dominic's your ex-what? Boyfriend? ... Husband?'

'Just my ex,' she said with a little shrug of her shoulder. 'He was resident vet at the Ferlann Ridge Sales.'

'Was he now!' Richard's mind boggled. He had always suspected there was more to Dominic Shane than met the eye.

Why had he come to Parkgate if he already had such a good job?

The buzzer went then for the second half of the performance and there was a rush for the best seats at the front of the room.

'See you around.' Aisling's eyes swept the group with a mischievous glance before she slinked off to join her companions.

'Wow!' the saxophonist said softly, and the other three grinned.

'That's one trouble!' Tracey muttered with a sideways glance at Richard.

He smiled broadly.

'You're jealous!'

'No ... I just don't like her type. She's got a good voice, though, I'll give her that.'

'Absolutely,' Richard endorsed. He turned to the others. 'Ready? We'll start with that Duke Ellington number....'

Midnight was striking when Richard at last left the venue.

As always the others had gone on ahead and as he came out of the side door into the damp warmth of the autumnal Dublin night he glanced around for Tracey. They always met up after a gig to discuss the performance and iron out any glitches.

Tracey was not there, but someone else was.

Richard's gaze widened as he took in the white-clad form that left the shadow of the building and smiled up at him.

'Well, hello again, Richie,' Aisling Cleary said silkily.

'Thea darling, what's wrong?' Mae asked breathlessly. 'I thought you were setting off early to the Gredington Show. When I came down and saw the car and trailer still in the yard I wondered what had happened.'

She had crossed directly to the stables and discovered Thea in Dancer's box, her face buried in the pony's mane, weeping bitterly.

'Is it Geoff?' Mae enquired gently.

In response Thea held out her ringless left hand. Sighing, Mae fished in her trouser pocket for a clean tissue and handed it to her daughter.

'It's all gone horribly wrong, Mum,' Thea said on yet another gulping sob. 'It all started when we began the renovations on the house. Maybe it was the dreams.'

'Dreams?' Mae frowned, mystified. 'Are you having nightmares, love?'

'No, it's not like that! I keep getting these strange images of the past. Remember those house deeds I came across at the history group meeting? That's when it started. Geoff shrugged it off as me being over-sensitive.'

'Well, there could be something in that. You're very like Gran Dene. She gets affected by places too. Was Geoff not sympathetic?'

'Oh, Geoff's too distracted these days to be bothered with anything,' she said morosely.

Mae stroked her daughter's hair.

'His father taking ill again can't have helped, love … I don't think it's looking too good for Mike.'

Thea looked up sharply.

'Mum, it's more than that. Yesterday I came across Geoff in town when he'd told me specifically he had to be at the farm. He was with Bryony! They were holding hands.'

Mae was justly shocked. Without another word she put her arm around her daughter's shoulders and led her indoors, easing her gently down into a chair.

'I got up to do the show. But I just couldn't,' Thea said, having spilled out what had happened the previous evening between herself and Geoff. 'The last show of the season, too. What a waste!'

'There'll be other shows,' Mae soothed, offering tea. She'd never seen Thea in such a state. That Bryony! Wait till she got her hands on her. All Chas's fault of course. He'd spoilt her rotten!

By the time Bryony came in from work Mae had worked herself up, rounding on the girl the moment she walked through the door.

'Well, Bryony, what's this about you and Geoff?'

'What?' Her daughter had the grace to blush. 'I don't know what you mean.'

'You were seen at the Vine together. Bryony, what were you thinking off? Thea's so upset, she's broken off the engagement.'

Bryony snorted.

'She's pathetic! Yes, I was at the Vine with Geoff but there was nothing in it. Not that anyone will believe me, nobody here ever takes any notice of what I say. Oh, I'm sick of being treated like the airhead of the family, fluffy little Bryony! Liz and I have been thinking about sharing a flat. Maybe now's the time to go for it!'

Mae looked startled and put a hand on her daughter's arm.

'No, Mum! Don't try to talk me out of it. I'm going as soon as I've packed my things!'

Soon afterwards she stormed out of the house, slamming the door with a force that made Mae wince. Hearing Bryony's car go speeding down the track, Mae flopped down weakly into a chair. How had all this happened? Thea's life in tatters, their only son apparently lost to them … and now Bryony had upped and left.

Chas would be in shortly for his meal. What on earth would she tell him?

Chapter Four

'What do you mean, you don't know how to drive the combine?' Chas snapped at Jem, the new farm hand. 'Didn't they teach you anything at agricultural college?'

'It's a contractors' job,' the lad muttered, aggrieved, as Chas stomped off.

Mae, who was organizing her market bakes in the kitchen, closed the window on the disgruntled voices with a sigh. As if they hadn't enough on their plates without problems with the harvesting. The contractors had turned up as arranged, only to have a machine break down with the job three-quarters done. They'd called out a mechanic to fix the redundant vehicle then moved on to the next job, leaving Chas to finish off himself.

Mae knew her husband to be perfectly capable of the task, and that his ill-temper stemmed not so much from the unfortunate mechanical hitch but from a deeper source.

Chas was taking Bryony's departure from home very hard indeed. Mae had tried to reason with him, pointing out that they hadn't lost their youngest for good and this unprecedented bid for freedom was merely part of the growing up process – phrases he'd used himself many times before. But her words fell on deaf ears.

Her pleasant face troubled, Mae began packing her pies, cakes and bread into containers, hands working automatically, her mind mulling over the traumas of the past weeks.

When Richard had gone off to Ireland with the band, the girls had stood up for their brother. Then, Mae had sided with Chas. Now, with the passing of time, she could see her children's point of view. Woodhey Farm didn't come into it. Richard was his own man and Chas had to realize that sooner or later.

Aware that Thea had kept in touch with Richard, Mae had been eager for snippets of news. The band appeared to be doing well and in his latest text her son had sent his love. Unbeknown to Chas she had responded at once with a text of her own, hating the deception, but knowing the move to be the right one for Richard.

Thinking of her son's tall figure, his good-looking face with the grey-blue eyes that twinkled when he smiled, Mae's heart contracted. How she missed him, missed the music that rippled magically from behind the closed door of his room tucked strategically away at the back of the house, the sound carrying through the house nonetheless.

The old farmhouse had been painfully quiet after he had left.

It was the same with Bryony. Mae never thought she would yearn for the fierce, feral throb of the heavy metal sound Bryony liked, but she did. She missed it achingly and would have given anything to have Thea berating her sister to 'turn that racket down!'

Thea. Slipping the last crusty granary loaf into the container, Mae shook her head wordlessly. Who would have thought that far-thinking, sensible Thea would have given up a promising future with a steady chap like Geoff? It didn't make sense. None of it made any sense.

And now her eldest was seeing a lot of the young Irish vet. Oh, Dominic Shane was likeable enough. He knew his subject and as far as the local farmers and horse folk went, there were no complaints. And yet there was something about the handsome, lean-faced Irishman that niggled. Something ... well, guarded.

Carrying the containers out to her van, Mae sent a worshipful wish that she wouldn't bump into Geoff's mother at the Heswell Farmers' Market. Helen Sanders was a nice enough woman once you got to know her, but she might be taking the broken engagement hard. A chance meeting could prove awkward for them both.

A chilly autumnal wind blew in from the estuary, reminding Mae that winter was approaching. Noting that Chas had taken himself off to the fields without a word – nothing new these days – Mae jumped into her van and set off for the market.

As always on a Friday, Heswell seethed with shoppers looking for tasty treats for the weekend. And, as always, Mae's stall was the first to empty. She was delving into her bag for her flask of coffee and biscuits, when she heard a brisk voice.

'Hello, Mae. How are you?'

Straightening, Mae looked into the expertly made-up face of the very person she had hoped to avoid, and felt her heart sink.

'Oh, hello, Helen.' She managed a smile. 'I'm fine thanks. What about you? And Mike – how is he keeping?'

'I'm very well, thank you. Mike could be better, I think, though he doesn't complain. But there it is. We have to keep going, don't we? Geoff's been marvellous, taking on the brunt of the work. He's out all hours.'

Helps to keep his mind off things. The words dropped unspoken between them, followed by a strained silence, into which intruded the chatter of shoppers and the throb of the traffic that streamed past.

'Was the lad Mike sent any good?' Helen went on. 'He did some supply milking for us earlier in the year, and when he turned up looking for a permanent job, Mike thought he'd be ideal. He's not afraid of hard work.'

'He's absolutely fine,' Mae replied, closing her mind to the grumbling and complaints from her husband that she knew were unjustified. 'I just hope he stays. You know how it is. You get them trained up and then they move on.'

Helen glanced around the stall.

'Well, I see I'm too late for your delicious home bakes, so I'd better have a look round the other stalls. 'Bye Mae. My regards to Chas.'

Conscious of a huge sense of relief, since the encounter had not been too awkward, Mae watched the smart figure in trim trousers and jacket walk off into the throng. There had been no mention of Thea, though that wasn't surprising. Frustration at her daughter for being the cause of restraint between the two families rose within her and was immediately quashed.

You couldn't live your children's lives for them, Mae realized. If Thea had doubts over a future with Geoff, then she had been right to act as she had.

Fortified by hot coffee and a snack, Mae started stacking her empty trays and returning them to the van which was parked behind the row of roadside stalls. She had completed her journeying to and fro and was checking her now-cleared stall for litter, when the woman next to her who traded preserves and honey, approached her.

'Have you heard the news, Mae?'

'What news? You don't look too pleased, Frances. What's up?'

'Well, remember back in the summer how there were complaints about the market blocking the road to traffic? They've started up again. It looks as if we could lose the venue.'

'But that's ridiculous!' Mae retorted. 'The market does well here. You've only got see how quickly the stalls empty to know how popular it is. People would miss us if we closed down.'

'Try telling the complaints committee that,' the other woman said drily. 'One short morning a week, and they want us gone! It's crazy. When I think of all the preparation that goes into coming here, I begin to wonder if it's all worth it.'

'Well, my line definitely is. I could bake double quantities and still sell the lot.'

Mae bit her lip. Money wasn't quite as tight as it had been at Woodhey but they still depended on her earnings. How would she break this to Chas?

'Are you sure it's not all hot air?' she queried hopefully.

'No, it seems definite. We've got till the contract runs out at the end of the year, after which we have either to find a new venue here in Heswell or finish altogether.'

By now the entire row buzzed with the news. People had begun to pack up their wares for the morning but all stopped to discuss the new developments. Mae, needing to get back to get the men's lunch, bid her fellow traders goodbye and, filled with trepidation, set off for home. She wouldn't let on to Chas until she knew something more positive, she decided.

Chas, however, had already heard from a different source. Having put the lunchtime soup to heat, Mae was filling the kettle for a much-needed cup of tea when her husband entered the kitchen with a scowl fit to crack the plates on the dresser.

'Never rains but what it pours, eh?' he muttered. 'What's this about a handful of troublemaking busybodies wanting to close down the farmers' market?'

'You've heard, then,' Mae replied woodenly.

'Aye. The lad mentioned something.' Chas always referred to the new hand this way even though Mae made a point of calling him by name. 'Apparently his girlfriend helps out on one of the stalls. She'd heard last week but hadn't thought it could be true.'

'Oh, it's true, all right! Nothing specific yet but just our luck, eh? When things were starting to look up, too.'

She went and put her arms round him.

'It'll be all right, love. We'll find another venue and everything will go on as before. And there's still the Neston market on Wednesdays, remember. That will never close down.'

'That's as may be, but I'm surprised you never thought to mention it. Imagine hearing something like this from the farm hand.'

Mae's arms dropped limply to her sides.

'Chas, I didn't say anything because I didn't know about it. The first I heard was an hour ago when Frances broke the news. Be fair, Chas. I'm fed up with bearing the brunt of your ill-humour.'

Chas looked faintly ashamed.

'Sorry, love. It's not your fault.'

'Apologies accepted.'

She almost mentioned having seen Helen, but bit it back. She didn't want to give him an excuse to start on about the recent split between Thea and Geoff. Not today.

'Cup of tea, Chas? I kept back a current loaf for after lunch. I'll butter a few slices. Is Jem around? Will I give him a shout? Oh look, the sun's broken through all that cloud at last. Could be a good omen.'

'Chance'd be a fine thing.'

Her husband parked his stocky frame at the kitchen table, accepting the steaming mug she handed him.

Thea drove slowly into the quiet cul-de-sac where Dominic lived and pulled up outside his gate. All looked quiet. Clearly he wasn't home yet from the Saturday surgery.

Gathering up the newly released local Historical Society booklet she was delivering, Thea scrambled out of the car and let herself into the garden, walking round the side of the house to the back, where Dominic had placed a rustic seat by the rose bed.

The day was cool but here it was sheltered and pleasant. Sitting, Thea lifted her face to the thin November sun and let herself relax.

It had been a long week, ending in a Hallowe'en party organized by the school's PTA. Not exactly an event to relish, since the professional requirement to promote good parent-teacher relationships vied understandably with the altogether human need for a change of scene after a day with lively youngsters. This year's was more trying than usual.

Last year Geoff had been at her side, genial, smiling, supportive. If the talk had turned to classroom issues – and what parent didn't seize an opportunity to query their child's progress – he was there to counter it, neatly steering the conversation to more neutral grounds.

This time there had been no such help, and Thea had found herself battling through a barrage of questions more suited to an official parents' night than the social gathering the occasion purported to be. She was left at the end of the evening with a thumping headache and a vague notion of changing her profession.

And since every other member of staff had other halves in tow, she had felt painfully the odd one out.

Breathing in the sweet scent of late flowering tea roses, her mind turned to the scenes that had haunted her dreams these past few weeks. The latest one had been so detailed, so … involving.

It had begun with a visit to the inn by that sparky but likeable individual, Jessica Platt. Fashionably dressed in rustling mulberry silk, fringed shawl and high-crowned bonnet, she carried in her basket some tempting treats for her sick sister....

'Marion, my pet, how are you?' Jessica fluttered a kiss on her sister's pale cheek and subsided on to the chair at her bedside, her basket at her feet and her gaze scrutinizing the frail figure in the bed.

'I came as soon as I received Polly's message. Tell me, has Wallace called the doctor?'

'Doctor Gordon came this very morning. He couldn't have been more kind and considerate but, Jessica, I'm afraid the news wasn't good,' Marion said weakly. 'Oh, it came as no surprise to me. This lump.' She fluttered a hand vaguely in the direction of her chest. 'Poor dear Mama had the same affliction.'

For a brief moment Jessica's iron composure slipped, a complex mix of anger, irritation and compassion battling within her. Foolish and impulsive Marion might be, but this was undeserved. What sort of a life had she had? Barely out of the schoolroom and rushing headlong into a totally unsuitable marriage.

For love, she had said when probed. Love! All it had done was to condemn her to a lifetime of drudgery and unhappiness! Jessica recalled the miscarriages, the two tiny graves in the churchyard, the silent sorrow and suffering. And through it all Marion had smiled courageously and carried on. And now this ...

'You're sure there is no mistake?' Jessica queried in a gentler tone.

'Quite sure. Oh, my dear sister, don't look like that! I've no complaints with my lot. I know you're no respecter of Wallace but he's been a good husband in his way. And my two children have been a great solace to me.' She halted, biting her lip. 'Jessica, there is something that bothers me. Something I must ask you.'

'It's Polly, isn't it? You want her away from here.'

'How clever you always were at reading other's thoughts! Jessica, you'll probably be aware of Wallace's little ... dealings ... in certain goods. And I'm sure Polly will have told you that her father has arranged a match for her.'

'With George Rawlinson. Yes. What of it?'

'I have reason to believe that he also is also involved in the contraband trade. Oh, I'm not as green as you think! I know what goes on. Always has and probably always will as long as the ships are able to get into port. I also know my girl. Jessica, Polly's as honest as the day. She'll not turn a blind eye the way I've done. The smuggling will bother her and wear her down. She'll know no peace of mind.'

Her breath caught in her throat.

'I don't want that for my Polly.'

She paused, clearly upset and growing visibly weaker.

'Don't try to talk any more, dear. Have a little rest,' Jessica said gently. 'I think I can guess what you're asking. You want Polly out of Parkgate, and you'd like me to find her somewhere suitable. A place with a respectable family, perhaps, where she can earn her keep and not be a victim of circumstance.'

It seemed a tall order for a girl in Polly's position, but Jessica was tactful enough not to say so.

Marion nodded.

'You know so many good people, Jessica. You move in the right circles.'

'I shall look into the matter right away,' her sister said briskly. 'There's a Chester family I've heard of who are seeking help in the nursery. Polly should suit admirably. Now don't fret about the ins and outs of it all, my dear. Polly can be spirited out of here in a wink if needs must.'

Jessica reached for her full basket of goods.

'Look, I've brought you some fruit and a new novel. Shall I read you a chapter or two?'

Jessica's thoughts raced. She was pleased to have eased her sister's mind. Deep down, however, to her shame and chagrin, she knew a sneaking gratification that the matrimonial arrangements between her niece and George Rawlinson now looked to be scotched.

She rather liked George. Upstanding, courteous, a gentleman in every sense of the word, he was part of her own circle and, when all was said and done, a good deal closer to her age than Polly's. Up until quite recently Jessica had relished her single state, but of late the thought of the companionship and protection a suitable union could bring was sweet. If she played her cards carefully, George could be hers.

Thea had woken, moaning a little, disturbed by what she was experiencing. She had drifted back to sleep, only to have the dream pursue its relentless course. Plainly some time had now passed. The scene swung to John Royle.

He was regretting his impulse to end all contact with Polly. He loved her so much, missed her so terribly it was like an ache that would not ease. His wish to have her as his wife had refuelled his earlier ambitions. Wanting to be worthy of Polly and provide a sound existence for her, since the life of a fisherman was notoriously spiked with danger and insecurity, he had stepped up his quest to leave the trade and start his own school for boys.

John left the house he had looked over in vain with a view to renting, determined not to be disheartened. This was the fourth unsuitable premises in as many days. In this case the drawback was the rent being way above his means.

Walking along the Parade, an upright figure in a best suit of brown fustian, boots buffed to a fine gloss, he looked more the schoolmaster he wished to be than the fisher lad Polly knew.

How he longed to see her, to tell her his plans.

Ahead loomed the sea-battered walls and dipping roofline of the Harbour House. Without thinking twice, John turned into the courtyard and entered the kitchen. Instead of Polly's mother, he saw to his surprise a young woman stirring the large iron pot of stew over the fire.

'Good day to you,' John bid her. 'I wonder if I might speak with Polly?'

'Polly, is it?' she said, straightening, her plain face alight with the prospect of a choice piece of gossip shared. 'You're too late, mister. Polly's gone. Went in the night, she did. Nobody knows where.'

'Gone?' John looked at her incredulously. 'But she can't have, not with her mama so poorly. Polly wouldn't desert her like that.'

'Well, she has. You should have heard the master when he found out. Stamping and raging, he was, and his good wife scarcely strong enough to lift her head, poor soul. If you ask me, the mistress knows more about Polly's disappearance than she's letting on. Quietly satisfied, she seems to me. As if she's got her own way for once and ... hey, mister! Where are you going?'

John had already slammed out. Crossing the straw and dung littered yard with angered strides, he cursed himself for a fool. If only he had come yesterday. If only he had never broken with Polly. If only....

The sound of Dominic's car turning into the lane brought Thea back to the present with a sense of relief. She was tempted to tell him about her experiences – anything to lighten the burden of what was happening to her. But how could she describe them? They were not dreams as such; they were more like flashbacks to a previous age.

Not only did she see and hear what was happening, she could tell what the people were thinking. It was freaky and yet it intrigued her. But were the characters figments of her imagination or had they really existed?

There were ways of finding out. She had considered it before but had baulked. Already she felt at the mercy of events beyond her comprehension. Who knew what else might be stirred up by delving too deeply into the past?

'Hello, there,' Dominic called, cutting across the grass towards her, the setter bounding in demented circles around him. 'What a nice surprise. How are you?'

'I'm fine.' Thea bent to fuss over the dog. 'Hi, Trina. Good girl. What a good dog.'

'Spoiled rotten, so she is. Trina, will you leave us in peace! I've just come past your place, Thea. The workmen are back, I see. And here's me thinking the renovations on the Harbour House were done and dusted.'

'Oh, there was some tidying up still to do so I told them to go ahead and finish. Might as well have it looking respectable, for what it's worth.'

'It's a thought.' Dominic's smile was understanding. 'Poor old you. It hasn't been your year, has it? Have you decided what you're doing with the house?'

'Not really. It's turned out to be something of a white elephant. I'm sometimes tempted to take it on myself but ... you know.'

'Too many memories? Don't I know exactly how you feel!'

'Do you, Dominic?' She looked at him closely. 'Do you really? What a puzzle you are sometimes. Could we make a pact? I let you in on something really weird that's happened to me, and you tell me what you meant by what you just said.'

'It's a long story.' The amazingly blue eyes never left her face. 'And not a very nice one.'

'Still, I'd like to hear it,' she said evenly.

He seemed to consider, then grinned suddenly.

'Sure, it'll have to wait while I feed Trina, or won't she be ringing up Justice For Dogs with a complaint of neglect?'

Thea didn't raise a smile but waited. She was growing wise to Dominic Shane. A funny remark was usually a ruse to get out of a tight corner, and this time she wasn't playing.

'OK, fine,' Dominic said, relenting. 'Tell you what, Thea, me girl. Let's see to Trina and then what if you and I can go to the pub for a bite to eat? I don't know about you, but my revelation could need fortifying with something stronger than the lighter beverages.'

This time Thea allowed herself a grin.

'You're on,' she said.

Richard's head swam. They had arrived at Limerick only to find that the original venue for the gig had been double booked and he and the boys had spent the best part of the day looking for an alternative. Quite by chance – or so Richard thought at the time – they had bumped into Aisling Cleary.

Having valuable contacts in the Irish jazz scene, she had made a few calls on her mobile and presently they were unpacking their equipment at a lugubrious-looking but seemingly popular premises on the outskirts of the town.

They had an hour to prepare before the club opened. While

Tracey was getting ready in a cramped little dressing-room behind the stage, the boys tore around setting up microphones and loud-speakers. Richard had to be everywhere at once, checking for sound quality and the lighting.

On stage, the drummer's long, sinewy hands executed triplets and paradiddles as if his very life depended on it.

Aisling, perched elegantly on a tall stool by the bar, watched the proceedings covertly, her long-lashed smoke-grey eyes not missing a thing. Richard looked up from wrestling with a mike that refused to adjust and sent her a friendly wink.

Whatever Tracey's opinion, tonight they owed a lot to the glamorous Irish girl. To show his gratitude Richard had awarded her a prime slot in the guest spot. The smile she'd bestowed on him had said it all.

'Right, lads,' Richard shouted, his eye on the clock over the entrance. 'That's about it, here. We've got ten minutes to change. Let's move!'

They made it with seconds to spare, leaping on stage as the doors burst open and the punters came pouring in. This was a different audience from the more cosmopolitan Dublin and Wexford crowds. Jeans and cycle jackets of battered black leather predominated, with hair spiked and dyed a myriad of hues.

All this Richard took in at a glance, before the PA system uttered a warning stutter, the house lights slowly dimmed and the usual stomach-grabbing hush descended. Raising his saxophone to his lips, Richard blasted out the first phrase of notes and, as the group came in gratifyingly on cue, gave himself up to the music.

'Sure, you were great. Just great,' Aisling praised when the buzzing, up-tempo night was finally over.

'You weren't so bad yourself,' Richard returned with a grin.

Tracey, at his side, nodded her agreement. She still hadn't exactly warmed to Aisling, but potential disaster had been overcome and they had her to thank for that.

They had all gone for a meal after the show. Now, the other members of the group had claimed utter exhaustion and taken themselves off to the hotel they had booked into, leaving Richard and Tracey, as always, to mull over the performance. Aisling looked to have no thoughts on following the rest of the band's example.

Richard was just beginning to unwind. Accepting the coffee Tracey handed him, he looked at Aisling.

'So what are your plans now? In fact what are you doing over here anyway? I thought you worked in Dublin.'

'I did,' she replied, shrugging laconically. Every movement she made was measured and graceful.

When she had first turned up at the Dublin club her sultry appeal had intrigued him. Now, a few weeks along the line, he was able to see through the glitz to the determined and manipulating creature beneath. He could even find it in him to tease her a little.

'Did? You mean they've given you the push at Ferlann Ridge?'

'Indeed they did not! Wasn't I the best admin officer they had on the floor! Sure, I left of my own accord to follow a singing career. I'd been offered a contract for a permanent spot at the Dublin Club and there'll be others. The money's good and I enjoy it. Besides, it was never the same at Ferlann Ridge after Dom went.'

Tracey looked at her sharply.

'Dominic Shane, you mean? He's a vet in the Wirral.'

'That's right. I'd heard he got another job pretty quickly. Well, he would. He's a brilliant vet. You'll know about the trouble.'

Richard looked blank.

Aisling lowered her voice to a confidential tone.

'We were getting married, had the house, furniture, everything. I don't need to tell you how expensive all that is....' She shrugged. 'I ... well, let's just say I'm not one for doing things on the cheap! The chance to make a quick buck came along....' She grinned ruefully. 'Didn't come off, as it happened. Then the balloon went up. Doping isn't the done thing in the racehorse trade.'

'Dominic was accused of horse doping?' Richard was incredulous. 'Heck! I bet the press had a field-day!'

She nodded.

'It did get a bit nasty. The only way Dom could hold on to his career was to get out and start again, go somewhere else where he wasn't known.' Aisling hesitated, as if she were weighing up her words. 'The thing is, I need to see him. It's a private matter but it's in his interest. I've tried to contact him but it's hopeless. He doesn't reply.

'You'll be going back to the Wirral when the tour is up so you're sure to see Dom. I wondered if you could put in a word for me?'

Richard thought fast. What was she up to? Something about the story just didn't ring true. Tracey looked about to speak but he silenced her with a glance.

'Aisling, we haven't made any specific plans beyond the tour,' he said carefully. 'There could be something in the pipeline for us, so we may not be going home.'

Finishing his coffee, he sent Tracey a nod.

'Don't know about you, but I'm bushed love. Shall we go?'

They all stood up and Aisling, who was staying with friends in Wicklow, reluctantly took her leave.

'That was a clever cop out,' Tracey said as they walked hand in hand to their hotel.

'Well, you can't be too careful. We don't want to be dragged into anything we mightn't like, especially as Thea seems to have hit it off with Dominic.'

'Has she? It's true the engagement's off, then?'

'Yes. I'm not really surprised. Geoff's a great guy but there was no spark there, somehow. Thea and Dominic? Well, maybe. Anyway, I don't want to be the cause of trouble. I wouldn't put it past Aisling to go tearing over there with whatever scheme she's cooking up.

'We don't even know the full picture. All we heard was her side of the story, and even that seemed evasive. Frankly, I suspect there's more to it than she's letting on.'

'She's cunning, that one. Dominic's well rid of her. I can't think why he took up with her in the first place.'

'Can't you?' Richard looked amused. 'But she's done him no favours. I can't honestly see Dominic getting mixed up in a doping scandal, can you? He's far too ethical for that.'

'Oh, it'll be her. She's the sort who can't stay out of trouble for long. Funny business, all the same. Dominic Shane had it made here. Something pretty dire must have happened for him to settle for a job at Parkgate. I'd love to get to the bottom of it all. I don't know, all these mysteries! And talking about mysteries, what's this about "something in the pipeline"? Or aren't I supposed to know?'

''Course you are.' Richard dropped a kiss on the top of her tawny head. 'I got a text from the agent so I called him back during the interval. Remember the album? Apparently it's getting great reviews, even better than the guy thought. He wants us to do the round of the London clubs – maybe Germany later on next year.'

'Wow!' Tracey flung her arms around Richard and hugged him in glee, all thought of Aisling Cleary and shady dealing fled. 'That's fantastic, Rick! Come on, let's break the news to the boys!'

'That's more than my life's worth! No, the morning will do.' An arm around her shoulders, he ushered her along to her room, grinning down at her.

'Good, eh? Wait till they hear back home. If there's anything that'll make Dad see things our way, it's this.'

Geoff eased the cattle wagon up the exit from the M53 and signalled for Heswell and home. It hadn't been a bad day at the market, considering. The calves had fetched more than he expected, and a chap with an interest in pedigree Friesian stock had approached him about purchasing a promising young Roseacre bull they had been running on.

Wasn't afraid of paying the price, either. Wait till he told Dad!

It was drizzling rain, dusk drawing down, the wipers hissing busily, though the road was fairly quiet. Ahead, just before the interchange for Thornton Hough, Geoff made out what looked like a breakdown and slowed his pace accordingly.

As he overtook, the old grey car looked familiar, as did the slight, worried figure bent over the engine.

Geoff gave the horn a blast of greeting, chuckling to himself. Trust Bryony to choose her moment!

He pulled into the kerb and stopped, winding down the window.

'Run out of petrol?'

'Oh, Geoff, it's you! Thank goodness! No, of course it isn't the petrol. The wretched thing just died on me.'

'Could be the electrics. Let's have a look.'

He jumped down and, getting Bryony to train the torch, tinkered with the engine. As he worked the rain decided to come down all the heavier. After a few moments he gave up.'

'Look, you're getting soaked and you've no coat. I'll take you on to the farm and come back in the truck with the towing ropes.'

'But I need to get back to the flat,' Bryony said. 'Liz will be furious if I'm late. We're supposed to be going out tonight.'

He shook his head.

'It's not looking likely. Best thing would be to ring her from the house and tell her it's off.'

'I'm not being towed,' she said stoutly. 'I've never done it before. I'd be useless.'

'Now there's a surprise!' He grinned at her good-naturedly. With her hair in rats' tails about her face and her mascara running down her doleful face, she still looked chocolate-box pretty.

'Not to worry. One of the lads will do the honours. Grab your bag and any other valuables you don't want to leave in the car and let's go. Look at it, belting down! Give me the keys and you get in the cabin. I'll lock up here and be right with you.'

Bryony's spirits rose visibly as they chugged along to Roseacre.

'I was so relieved when I saw the wagon. I thought it was you, but I hardly dared hope!'

'Knight of the road, me.' He grinned. 'For some obscure reason, that stretch is notorious for broken-down vehicles. I'm always rescuing damsels in distress. The last one was ninety if she was a day! She screeched at me to get a move on because she had to get home to feed her cats!'

Bryony giggled.

'It's true. Ah, here we are. This rain's in for the night.'

He paused, frowning towards the main yard to the big dairy

farm. All the lights were on and there seemed to be a lot of undue hustle and bustle. Geoff swallowed hard, his mouth suddenly dry with foreboding.

'What's going on here? I don't like the look of it....'

Parking the wagon in the big open-ended barn, they got out as the back door of the farmhouse opened and Geoff's mother emerged. Her face was very troubled and Bryony went immediately across to her, gripping her arm.

'Mrs Sanders, what is it? Has something happened?'

Tears brimmed in Helen Sanders' eyes but she seemed incapable of speech, her eyes seeking her son. At last, the words stumbled out.

'Geoff ... it's your dad. He – he was found unconscious in the parlour. He *would* start the milking himself when I told him not to! I told him!'

'Where is he now?' Geoff asked gently. 'How was he?'

'Jim Stokes saw to him while I called the ambulance. They left about five minutes ago. Oh, Geoff! If anything happens....'

Jim Stokes, the cowhand, hovered uncertainly in the background.

'Might be best if you went with the missus, Geoff,' he said quietly. 'I'll see to things here for you. If I'm honest, lad, it didn't look too good....'

Chapter Five

'I'll need my bag!' Helen Sanders gasped, panicking. 'And my keys. Where are they? Oh, poor Mike! Will he be all right!' She looked anxiously from one worried face to the other.

The ambulance had vanished into the stormy November dusk. Geoff had hurried off to fetch the car from where it was parked in the barn, leaving Bryony and Jim Stokes, the cowman, on the rain-swept farmyard with Helen.

Agitatedly she turned towards the farmhouse where light spilled out from the spacious pine-furbished kitchen, then changed her mind and, oblivious to the deluge, began turning out the pockets of her lightweight trouser suit in a desperate search for the missing keys.

The rain continued to hammer down, dowsing the three of them thoroughly, whilst from the milking parlour came the forlorn bellows of cattle anxious to be rid of their burden of milk.

'I'd best get back to the cows,' Jim muttered, before making his escape.

Bryony, gathering her wits, took a firm grip of Helen's arm.

'Mrs Sanders, let's get out of the rain and wait for Geoff. That's right. Look, here are your keys on the table. Now, why don't you sit down for a moment and let me fetch whatever you need?'

'Thank you … so kind.' Helen allowed herself to be guided to one of the tall ladder-backed chairs and subsided into it. Her skil-fully made-up face began to pucker.

Bryony fetched a box of tissues from where it lay on the dresser and left them to hand.

'Try and keep calm. Mr Sanders is in the right hands. Is your handbag upstairs? I'll get it, shall I?'

'What? Oh, yes, please, if you wouldn't mind. It'll be on the chair by the bed. My coat's there too. Perhaps I should put a few things together for Mike.'

'I wouldn't right now,' Bryony soothed. 'Just get yourselves to the hospital. Geoff can always slip back later for whatever you need.'

The sound of the car drawing up outside galvanized Bryony into action. She fled out and up the wide, soft-carpeted staircase, located the Sanders's bedroom and Helen's coat and bag, then sped back down to the kitchen again.

A blast of the horn outside had Helen jumping to her feet. Bryony hastily helped her on with her coat, handed her the bag and keys and ushered her back out to where Geoff held open the passenger seat door of the big family saloon.

''Bye. Best of luck,' Bryony bid them as Geoff bundled his mother into the car. 'Don't worry,' she told Geoff. 'I'll stay here until I get some news.'

Geoff sounded brisk and in control.

'Thanks, that's brilliant.'

Moments later he was pulling out of the farmyard, rain lancing in the powerful beam of the headlamps, muddy water from the swimming yard spurting from under the tyres. Bryony, watching them go, then turned and ducked back through the downpour to the house.

Pewter, the Sanders's sleek grey cat, lay comatose in front of the Aga, its long tail curled neatly around its paws.

Taking a few long breaths to calm her racing pulse, Bryony shook the raindrops from her springy blonde curls, removed her sodden jacket and put it on the Aga rail to dry, and glanced round. Helen Sanders had obviously been preparing the evening meal when disaster had struck. Half-peeled vegetables, a bottle of the coarse red wine generally used for cooking, and a freezer pack of what looked like diced beef lay abandoned on the worktop, beside an attractive country-ware casserole dish.

'Better get on with that,' she said to the unresponsive cat. 'They'll need something to eat when they get back. Oh, heck, I nearly forgot. We were going out tonight … I'd better phone Liz.'

She delved into her bag for her mobile and called her friend's number.

'Bry?' Liz answered almost immediately. 'What's going on? I thought you were getting back early?'

'Sorry, Liz. Something's cropped up. My car packed in and Geoff came along and we ended up at the farm. It was panic-stations here, Liz. His Dad's been rushed to hospital. Geoff's just gone there with his mum. She was in such a state! I felt really sorry for her. Anyway, I said I'd stay here for now – well, you never know. I don't think things looked too bright.'

'That's awful. What about your car? D'you want me to phone the garage?'

'No, the chap who works on the farm's here. He might be able to sort it out for me. Look, I must go. You might as well carry on without me. I could be here ages.'

'Well, if you're sure. Cheers, Bryony. Good luck.'

Bryony clicked off, slipping the phone back into her bag. The kitchen seemed very quiet. Wondering how Geoff was getting on at the hospital, and trying not to think the worst, Bryony picked up the sharp little kitchen knife and began to peel the vegetables.

Cooking wasn't exactly her best skill, but she did her best, adding a generous dash of the wine and a couple of bay leaves from the spice rack on the wall. She put the dish into the Aga, then filled the kettle.

Outside, it was pitch black but the rain had stopped. Bryony ran across to the parlour where Jim Stokes was finishing the milking.

'Any news?' he enquired, his blunt, middle-aged face full of concern.

'Not yet. Kettle's on. Would you like tea or coffee?'

'Tea, please. Milk and two sugars. The missus generally does toasted teacake or something as well.'

'Will biscuits do for now?' Bryony told him about her car, left apparently dead on the side of the road.

'Don't worry about that,' the cowman said kindly. 'My lad's a mechanic. He'll get it sorted. I'll give him a bell.'

'Thanks, Jim. Have you any idea what the cat has to eat?'

'There'll be something in the cupboard, no doubt. The missus is right fond of that cat.'

'I'll see to it,' Bryony said. 'Tea in, say, fifteen minutes?'

She was coming in from having shut in the hens for the night, gratified that the casserole she had thrown together now seemed to be simmering fragrantly from the oven, when the phone began to ring shrilly.

She snatched it up.

'Bryony? It's me, Geoff.' His voice sounded strained. 'It's not good news, I'm afraid. The hospital did all they could but it was hopeless. Dad's gone, Bryony. I've just spoken with the doctor. She said it was a massive coronary.'

Bryony swallowed hard.

'I'm so very sorry, Geoff. He was a lovely man. He always used to tease me and make me laugh. Look, I'll stay here till you get back. I'll light the fire in the lounge, shall I? Your mum might be glad of it.'

Ringing off, feeling suddenly older and rather worn down, Bryony went out to tell Jim the news.

'Mike Sanders – gone! I can't believe it,' Mae said to Chas. 'Poor Geoff. And poor Helen. They'll both take this very badly.'

Chas, just in from the fields, went to the sink to wash his hands.

'Aye, it's a bad do. Are you going round there?'

'I feel perhaps I should.' Mae was thinking aloud. 'Sending a card seems so inadequate, somehow. There might be something I can do to help. I'll go after lunch. I could take Helen one of my fruit cakes and pick up some flowers from the market garden on the way.' She shook her head again. 'Poor Helen....'

An hour later she was driving through the lanes to Heswell, some of her delicious home-bakes in a basket on the seat beside her. Mae was surprised, on reaching Roseacre with its wide concreted yards and mixture of ancient and modern cattle housing, to see a familiar little car parked in the yard.

Standing there, undecided whether to go round to the front door of the big stone-built farmhouse or use the back, the decision was taken out of her hands when the door opened and Bryony emerged.

'Mum!' Her daughter's face registered surprise, and then started to crumple. Unable to conceal her relief, she sprang forwards and gave her mother a hug.

'Darling! What a lovely surprise.' Mae kept a firm hold over her emotions and with great effort managed to give the impression of calm. 'Are you all right?'

'Yes thanks. Oh, Mum. Isn't it awful about Mr Sanders?'

'Terrible,' Mae agreed. 'I know he wasn't a well man but it still comes as a shock. I've brought a few things for Helen. How is she?'

'Oh, you know. But she'll be glad to see you. Mum, I'm sorry but I'll have to go. I slipped out during my lunch break to bring some shopping Helen wanted from town. They've been fantastic at the shop about letting me off early and so on, but I don't want to push things.'

'Of course not,' Mae said, noticing that the formal address of Mrs Sanders had given way to the more familiar use of the woman's first name. She thought her youngest girl had a maturity about her that had not been evident a few weeks ago when she had left home.

'You run along. My love to Liz. 'Bye for now, Bryony.'

She dropped a kiss on her daughter's cheek and went on to the house. As she rapped on the door, Mae found that her hand was shaking.

Helen Sanders seemed pleased at the visit and was touchingly grateful for the offerings Mae had brought.

'That's so good of you,' she murmured. 'People are so kind.' Her face, bereft of make-up, looked pale and wan.

'I have to say what a boon Bryony has been. I really don't know how we would have coped without her.'

'Really?' Mae stammered, her eyes widening in surprise. She heard how Bryony had comforted the older woman and kept house and even given Jim Stokes a hand with the milking whilst Geoff saw to the hundred and one formalities required.

Mae, astounded and bursting with pride, couldn't wait to get home and tell Chas.

'I always said she was the one with the most heart,' Chas agreed later. He had greeted her news quietly and had been thoughtful for a while. The evening meal was now over and they sat in front of the television set, curtains drawn against the inclement November night.

'How did she look? Spiked hair and nose-bobs like her friend, what's-her-name ... Liz?'

'Not at all. She was dressed for work and you know how particular they are on appearances at the shop. She seemed ... well, older somehow.'

'Did she mention coming to see us?'

'Not as such. Chas, there was hardly time. I told you. She had to get back to work.'

Chas grunted, though Mae had not missed the pride that had sprung to his eyes when she had repeated Helen's accolade about their daughter. It was now replaced by the bleakness that had been so much in evidence this autumn. Bryony's rejection of her family had gone deep.

'Did Helen mention what their plans were for the farm?' he asked abruptly.

'We didn't touch on it. Geoff will take over, I suppose. He was doing the bulk of the work anyway during the latter months. Mike wasn't fit to do more than potter, and Helen sees to the secretarial side of things. They'll manage, I'm sure.'

'It's a shame Thea and Geoff couldn't make a go of it,' he grumbled. 'Thea could have turned her hand to anything on that farm, including all the blasted red tape and paperwork.'

'But Thea has her own career,' Mae pointed out fairly. 'Talking of Thea, have you any thoughts on what is to become of the Harbour House?'

'Should I have? It's not my concern any more. The property was made over to them by the solicitor, all square and legal. It's up to Thea now what she does with it.'

'I expect she'll have to buy Geoff out. As I understand it he put quite a lump sum down on the house.' Mae's brow creased. 'Oh dear. It's all so complicated. I'm none too happy over Thea, either. She's lost weight. She works too hard, all those extra hours she puts in at school, then the ponies and the history group to run. It all takes its toll.'

'Hard work never hurt anyone, love. It's stress that causes the problems. Thea will be all right. She's going through a sticky patch but she'll cope.'

At that moment the phone rang from the kitchen.

'Who can that be at this time of night,' Mae grumbled, getting up to answer it.

She heard the television set being turned up as she left the room and Chas flicking through the channels.

She lifted the receiver.

'Hello? Woodhey Farm.'

'Mae? It's Roz. Jam stall next to yours at the Heswell Market?'

'Oh, Roz, hello.'

What now, Mae thought, her heart missing a beat.

'Have you heard the news?' The woman's voice throbbed with excitement. 'Remember that petition we got up contesting the threat to close us down? Well, it's worked! The town committee have allocated us a new venue off the main road. It's more spacious than the other. There's adequate parking and the rent's not so high. Better all round, in other words.'

'Well, that's marvellous!' Mae said. 'I thought for a moment you were about to tell me something awful had happened!'

'Not this time.' Roz laughed. 'Nice to have a bit of good news for a change, isn't it? We've the customers to thank as well. Apparently they made a huge fuss when word got out that we were going. Good, eh?'

'I'll say. What a relief. And here I was wondering whether to put my name down for one of the other markets, Nantwich or Whitchurch. Either would be a long way to drive and heavier on the expenses. Now, I won't have to. Fantastic!'

'I thought you'd be pleased. I know I am. No doubt we'll be

hearing officially from the market committee in due course. It was the woman who headed the Heswell shoppers' protest who told me.'

'So when do we start at the new place? Not immediately.'

'Oh no. It won't be until the contract runs out at the end of the year. We'll start at the other venue in January.'

'Fingers crossed until all is signed and sealed then.'

'Well, I can't see a problem, myself. I'd better ring the others. 'Bye, Mae, see you Tuesday.'

'Yes, and thank you.'

Mae couldn't keep the smile from her face. She rang off and hurried to tell Chas the glad tidings.

'Whoa, pony. Steady. Now walk on.'

The young filly tossed her head skittishly and Thea tightened her grip on the lead-rope. It was early yet, a hazy Sunday morning towards the end of November, mist wreathing up over the mudflats, the roads and lanes reasonably quiet. At least, that was what Thea had hoped when she had opted to do some road-work with her latest show prospect. So far, that was the third vehicle to have gone past and she hadn't yet reached the main highway.

The showing season was long over and the ponies, looking rotund and snug in their thick growth of winter coat, had been turned away until early spring. A spacious wooden shed in the corner of the grazing gave shelter against the worst of the weather.

Generally, however, the hardiness of their native breeding prevailed. Only extremes of weather sent her small herd seeking refuge, and even then Thea would find them standing in the lea of the building rather than inside it, their noses against the outside wall, tails tucked in against the offending elements.

The approach of yet another driver brought a wary flick of the ears from the pony.

'Steady, Merry. Walk on,' Thea commanded.

Up behind them came a car but this one slowed down sensibly and crawled past. Thea recognised Dominic's vehicle. Driving on a short distance, the vet pulled in and stopped....

'Thea, hello there,' Dominic called, jumping down. 'You're out early.'

'I could say the same for you. Or is it more a case of working late?'

'You've said it!' Dominic quirked his lips ruefully. 'A misplaced calf-bed. The vet on duty was already out on a call so I did the honours. Why do they always manage it in the middle of the night?'

'You tell me,' Thea countered with a laugh.

Dominic ran an experienced eye over the pretty grey pony.

'Nice filly. How old is she?'

'Just coming up to twelve months. She's a handful. I need to get her going on the long reins but it's difficult on your own.' She coloured. 'Well, Geoff or my brother could sometimes be persuaded to help at this stage.'

'Strong arm stuff, is it?'

She nodded.

'It's amazing how wilful they can be. If Merry decided to take off I doubt if I could hold her.'

'Want a hand now? Give me half an hour to get cleaned up and I'll be right back.'

'Are you sure? You must be exhausted....'

'Oh, I'll be glad of the fresh air. I know how tricky these young-sters can be. A pony back home once took off with me across the peat bogs. Halfway to Galway we were before I could stop him!'

'Go on!' Thea giggled. 'You're making it up.'

'Now would I do that?' His blue eyes twinkled. 'Half an hour, then? She can graze the verge for now. Don't go away. I'll be right back.'

Throwing her a wink, he returned to his car and drove off. Thea, feeling suddenly less anxious, allowed the filly enough rope to crop the roadside grass and turned her thoughts to the Harbour House.

'Why not consider renting it out?' her father had suggested only last night. 'It would bring in a good income.'

'I know. It's the thought of someone else enjoying the fruits of my hard work that stops me. Silly, really.'

'I'd take it back off your hands myself, but I'm afraid funds won't stretch to it right now.' Chas sighed.

'I know, Dad. I wouldn't dream of putting you to the expense. I've considered living there myself. Well, it would give Mum my bedroom. It's nice and big. She could take in students. Or do B&B like the Demseys at Ridgeway.'

'I reckon your mother's got enough spare bedrooms if she wants to do that,' Chas replied. 'Anyhow, she's got enough on her hands as it is. Think about renting, though. Let me know what you decide.'

'OK, Dad.' On impulse Thea had given her father a hug. The year that had begun with such promise hadn't turned out well for her parents. Thea was saddened to have added to their burden. Sorry, too, over the sadness at Roseacre. Her first instinct had been to go and see Geoff and Helen.

But then she had second thoughts. They'd only have been embarrassed, and Helen was such a stickler for correct form. In the end she had penned a warm little missive of condolence and left it at that. What Bryony had been doing there she had no idea.

Thea sighed, giving the pony a little more rope to reach a particularly lush clump of wayside grass.

Dominic's return put paid to more musing. Spruce in clean cords, Aran jumper and padded jacket, his dark hair slicked back wetly from the shower, he looked wide awake and ready for work.

'No Trina?' Thea enquired.

'Trina's had a romp round the garden and is now sleeping off her breakfast. Let's concentrate on one thing at a time.' He took the pony's lead-rope off her. 'Right then, we'll do the lanes and come back along The Parade. That should get the tickle out her feet. Come on, Merry, me girl! Walk on!'

The morning was almost over by the time they returned, Thea feeling much more relaxed, to Woodhey, where the Sunday roast sizzled mouth-wateringly in the oven.

'Stop and have some lunch,' Chas said to Dominic. 'It'd be nice to have company. I could show you that winter wheat crop you were interested in.'

'Yes, do stay,' Mae agreed.

Dominic accepted the invitation readily.

'My car's down the lane. I should fetch it. And there's the dog.'

'What if I pick up your car and fetch Trina?' Thea offered. 'That'll leave you free to walk the fields with Dad.'

After the long trek on top of the broken night, it was probably the last thing Dominic wanted and Thea hid a smile.

'Good idea,' he said manfully. 'While you're there you might as well pick up those house deeds you were interested in.

Thea's face lit up.

'You've got them? Great!'

'The solicitor sent me the whole batch. Apparently all land records are now going on electronic files, so there won't be cause to keep those old documents any longer.'

'So what happens to them?' Mae asked.

'I expect they'll be destroyed.' Dominic shrugged. 'My solicitor said I could keep mine. It's tough on future history fans. No more boxes of old papers to rummage through!'

He handed Thea his car keys.

'Large padded envelope on the kitchen table. You can't miss it. Watch Trina doesn't have a go at you!'

'That'll be the day!' Thea said with a smile.

She left her mother making coffee for them all and went back into the sharp wintry air. The sun had come out and her spirits, already lifted, rose still higher. Sprinting down the lane, long plait thumping on her shoulders, she came to where Dominic had left his pick-up and drove on towards Parkgate, enjoying the handle of the bigger vehicle after her own small car.

She was given a rapturous welcome by Trina. Fussing her, Thea picked up the bundle of papers, pausing. Lunch would be an hour yet. Where better to read about the house but there, in the very place where Jessica Platt had been born and raised?

Sitting down at the table, the setter at her side, Thea took the papers out of the envelope and found the one she wanted. The central heating was on, humming away soothingly, the house warm and quiet. After the exercise in the bracing outdoors, the contrast was pleasingly soporific.

Thea allowed her gaze to roam round the room. It would be very different now from when Jessica knew it. She looked up at the marks of the crafter's awl on the twisted old ceiling beams, wondering if Jessica had once done the same, yawning....

Jessica opened the letter the post boy had just delivered, spreading it out on the small mahogany writing desk in front of her.

My dearest Aunt Jessica, Polly had written in her neat hand.

I trust this finds you in good health. I have now been at the position you very kindly found for me with the Kendrick family for one whole month, and feel I must let you know how I fare.

My mistress treats me well and the master, too. The children, Miss Amelia and Miss Florence, are wondrous sweet and no trouble at all. There is an older son, Harry, by an earlier marriage, who thinks a lot of himself. Chester is very different to Parkgate, with much noise and bustle. The house on Stanley Place is in a good neighbourhood.

There is no carousing at night as at the Harbour House, and we grow our own fruit and vegetables in the large back garden. I am sure the milk here is watered down, for it looks and tastes thin.

It grieves me to think of poor Mama and how much she will be missing me. Have you visited her? I miss Papa too. I am sure he does not mean to be unthinking and boorish. As Mama used say, 'tis the drink speaking. But there, I am gratified to have found a good place here.

I wonder, Aunt, if you could find me news of John Royle, the fisherman's son from Hoylake?

My deepest regard always,
Your affectionate niece, Polly Dakin.

Jessica sat back in her chair, musing. Her niece painted a commendably vivid picture of her new lifestyle. She hoped the older son of the house was not giving trouble. Remembering Polly's attitude to George Rawlinson, she smiled. Dear George.

It had not taken him long to recover from his disappointment, she was gratified to note. Her eyes again sought the name of the younger man in question.

Jessica rang the small silver bell at her elbow to summon the maid. She came at once, apron strings fluttering, frilled cap askew.

'Yes, ma'am?'

'Ah, Agnes. Your cap, girl. How many times do I have to tell you? Agnes, do you happen to know a young person by the name of Royle? I believe he comes from Hoylake.'

'Would that be John Royle, ma'am?' The maid's perky young face broke into dimples. 'Yes, I do. Everyone knows John. His father heads the fisher-fleet and John has his own boat.

'"Tis said, though,' Agnes went on confidingly, 'as John wants better things in life. He's what some would call a scholarly lad. I've heard he's looking for premises to start up his own school.'

'Really? How very ambitious of him!'

'Yes, ma'am. 'Twas believed he was very smitten with Polly from the tavern. Went there looking for her, he did. But Polly had gone. It must have been to do with that business of Innkeeper Dakin wanting Polly to wed—'

'Yes yes!' Jessica brushed all this aside. 'Where would I find this John Royle?'

'Young John, d'you mean, ma'am? Only his sire goes by the same name.'

'Yes, of course. Does he trade here in Parkgate?'

'Yes'm. John supplies the Harbour House and comes round the houses every Thursday. The fish you eat comes from him. Well, it's always fresh.'

'I see. Thank you, Agnes. Oh, one more thing. I'm thinking of giving a dinner party. Just a small gathering to brighten up the winter. Let us say … six in all.'

'Yes, ma'am.'

'I can name the guest list for you. Mr George Rawlinson—'

'That'll mean fillet steak on the menu, ma'am. Loves his fillet steak done in red wine, does Mr Rawlinson.'

'So I've observed. Pray do not interrupt, Agnes. As I was saying. Mr George Rawlinson. Now, who else? The rector and his daughter, Susanna. Oh, and we'd best include the rector's sister, Miss Charlotte Marsdon. I know she's with them on a housekeeping basis but she is family when all's said and done. It would help if she were less shrewish, but we shall cope.'

'And let us have my nephew from the Harbour House.'

'Master Edward, ma'am?'

'Yes, of course Master Edward. Whom did you think I meant? My nephew is turning out a very personable young man. He tells me he has leanings towards becoming a solicitor. Such a dry occupation for one so full of fun, though I daresay it takes all sorts. Anyway, Edward will bring a touch of life to the company.'

'Yes'm.' Agnes bobbed a curtsey. 'Will that be all, ma'am?'

'I think so. Oh, and Agnes' – Jessica proffered as the agitated maid was about to vanish from the room – 'next time young Royle is due with a delivery, you might let me know.'

'I will, ma'am,' Agnes said.

That afternoon, Jessica donned her cape and bonnet with the intention of visiting her sister. She was picking her way delicately over the straw on the tavern yard, avoiding the passengers who had just disembarked from the Chester Flyer, one of the new fast stage coaches, when she was halted by a voice speaking her name.

Jessica turned and found herself face to face with the rather odd character known as the village wise woman, Meg Shone. She had clearly been gathering seaweed for her potions, as her basket was full to the brim. She came closer.

'Glad to have come across you, mistress,' she said in her flat, low tones. ''Tis about young Polly. I'd be grateful if you'd pass on a message.'

'Oh? And what makes you think I'm in a position to do that?' Jessica queried.

The woman gave a rusty cackle.

'You don't have to pretend with me, mistress! Nobody has any secrets from Meg Shone.' Her black eyes glinted. 'A grand girl, is Polly. That girl saved my life. Near drowned. I did! Tell her Meg Shone never forgets a favour.'

'Very well. I shan't forget.'

'Oh, I knows that. Meg Shone knows who she can trust and who she cannot. I'll bid you good-day, mistress. May you get all you desire.'

Bestowing a gap-toothed smile, the woman hurried on her way. Jessica carried on thoughtfully into the tavern. Loud snores directed her to the tap-room, where her brother-in-law was sprawled in a drunken stupor, his head cradled in his arms, an empty flagon on the table beside him. Halting, Jessica delivered him a sharp prod with her parasol.

'Wake up, lout! Have you no shame? Barely mid-afternoon, and you already in your cups!'

Wallace Dakin opened bleary eyes, took in the woman before him and closed them again, groaning. Jessica, unsympathetic to his plight, again enlisted the use of the parasol to rap insistently on the table top for the girl in the kitchen, provoking another groan from the suffering landlord.

The girl appeared reluctantly, wiping greasy hands on her gown.

'Bring some coffee,' Jessica snapped. 'Black and strong and plenty of it. And look sharp about it.'

The coffee duly delivered, Jessica set about sobering up the tavern-keeper.

'Wallace, you must listen to what I have to say,' she began, once it became apparent that she had his attention. 'It's come to my knowledge that we are shortly to be paid a visit by the coastguards. Do I make myself understood?'

He stared at her, his once handsome face working stupidly.

'Aye, that's perfectly clear. It is correct, I suppose.'

'Indubitably. I think perhaps it might be wise to take stock of what lies in your cellars. Mind me?'

He nodded.

'And while I'm here I want a word regarding my sister. Marion is failing, Wallace. You are aware of that?'

Another nod, stricken this time.

'You will do her a favour by smartening yourself up and laying off the drink – or at least, cutting back on it. Show her a little consideration, man. Let her see that you care for her. It's the very least you can do.'

Pressing her lips tightly together to indicate an end to the conversation, Jessica left the room, taking the stairs to the bedchamber above. Marion lay propped up on pillows in the vast bed, her eyes closed in her wan face. Jessica caught her breath. Her sister seemed to have deteriorated in the few days since she had last seen her.

'Marion, it is I. Are you awake?'

Marion opened her eyes with effort.

'Why Jessica, how robust you look. Is it windy outside? You have a fine colour in your cheeks.'

Aware that her heightened colour stemmed more from the altercation with Wallace than from any idiosyncrasies of the weather, Jessica could not help but smile.

'It's very fine for the time of year,' she remarked, going to sit in the chair by the bed, her back ramrod straight, skirts spread out around her.

'You're about to ask if there is anything I require,' Marion continued in her new, unfamiliar, weakened voice. 'There is but one thing. Jessica, I want to see my daughter one last time. Could it be arranged?'

Jessica did not answer. Spiriting Polly away had been far from easy. She knew, and Marion knew, that the girl was better off where she was. What her sister asked was a heartbreakingly impossible request.

Trina's cold nose in her hand brought Thea awake with a jolt. Disoriented, she threw a glance around at the unfamiliar surroundings and laughed shakily when realization dawned. Whatever would Dominic think if he knew she had dozed off in his kitchen.

Sitting back in the chair, stretching lethargic limbs, she allowed her mind to trail back over the scenes and conversations she had just witnessed. People today were not so very different, she concluded, with their loves and problems and loyalties. She glanced at the clock on the wall.

'Come on, Trina,' she said to the dog, scooping up the documents before her. 'Mum will be wondering where we are. Let's go. With luck you might get a nice juicy bone as a special treat.'

The rest of the day passed agreeably. After lunch, she and Dominic took Trina for a walk across the fields and along the sandy lanes that criss-crossed this part of the Wirral. It seemed natural for Dominic to take Thea's hand in his as they strolled along.

'It's been a grand day, Thea,' he said in his lilting brogue. 'Just grand. All being well, I'm free again next Sunday. Will you be needing some more strong-arm stuff for Merry?'

She was aware of her rapidly thumping heart and the warmth of Dominic's hand against hers. She looked up, her clear grey-blue eyes meeting his.

'Yes, I'd appreciate your help, Dominic.'

Regrettably, it was not to be.

At break at school the next day, Thea was taking her turn on playground duty when the mobile phone in her pocket started up. She answered it hastily, her attention fixed on the playing groups of children under her care.

'Thea? It's me, Richard. Look, I know this isn't convenient so I'll be quick. Will you be seeing Dominic Shane today?'

'I could be – any particular reason?'

'Well, yes. I haven't mentioned this before but we've come across his ex-girlfriend, the lovely Aisling Cleary. I don't know how much you know about his problems here, we only know Aisling's version and Tracey says she doesn't trust Aisling any further than she could blow her. Thea, she's coming to look for him.'

'Aisling is?' Thea's voice rose to a squeak. 'But why?'

'Oh, some idea she's cooked up about wanting to make amends and all that. I wouldn't have thought Dominic would be too keen to see her. You might warn him, sis. Tell him she's getting an early flight tomorrow.'

'Thea? Are you still there?'

'Yes,' Thea replied, seeing a skirmish in the furthest corner of the yard and making a bee-line for it. 'OK, Richard. I'll do that.'

The troublemakers saw her coming and broke up instantly, leaving Thea with the phone still in her hand and her mind racing.

From what Dominic had divulged of Aisling Cleary, she seemed ruthless, cunning and untrustworthy. Was she coming to claim Dominic back? Now, just as they were on the verge of something new and exciting? Thea bit her lip. It certainly looked that way....

Chapter Six

Thea knew she was too late the moment she drew up outside Dominic's front gate. The house looked shuttered and silent; no smoke rising from the chimney, no window open to the late autumn sunshine, no dog barking a warning. There was nothing to indicate the presence of the householder.

Heaving a sigh, for she had left the school premises as soon as she reasonably could and driven straight here, Thea slid out of the car and went to double-check. She rang the doorbell and, receiving no response, walked round to the rear of the house, her feet crunching on the pebbled path.

Glancing in at the kitchen window, she saw all the signs of a hasty departure; newspaper flung aside, cupboard doors left ajar, the remains of a hurried meal still on the table.

Two plates, she noticed, with a pang that shocked her.

She was about to leave when a voice hailed her from the neighbouring garden. A pleasant-faced woman stood by the fence, a quilted green gilet over a shapeless jumper and trousers, secateurs in hand. Behind her, a rose-bed had been given a rigorous pruning.

'Were you wanting Mr Shane?' she asked politely. 'Only he was called away unexpectedly.'

'I see.' Thea managed a smile. 'Did he say when he'd be back?'

'No, the young woman with him seemed in a desperate hurry. They've taken the dog with them. I think there was some talk over putting her in kennels, but you know how Mr Shane is over Trina!'

'Well, thank you.'

Leaving the woman to her gardening, Thea returned to the car.

On the way home her mobile phone trilled. When she arrived at the farm there was a message.

Hi, Thea, it's Dominic. Remember that business back in Ireland I told you about? Well, something has turned up. It's too complicated to explain here. I hope to be back before long and will be in touch. Trust me.

Sitting in the car, frowning a little, she played it back again. No mention of the woman responsible for his sudden departure. Thea had to wonder what Aisling Cleary's game was. Bad news, Richard had called her. It wasn't like her brother to cast aspersions.

Maybe the Irish girl had caused problems between him and Tracey. She'd certainly come between herself and Dominic – and just when the friendship had subtly changed.

The chugging of a tractor made Thea look up and moments later her father drove into the farmyard, the huge double wheels spewing clods of mud across the concreted surface. Parking the vehicle in the barn, he reappeared, sending her a salute of greeting.

Thea collected her bag of schoolwork and left the car to go and speak to him.

'Hi, Dad. What a mess on the yard. I hope it's not my turn for hosing down.'

'Think it is, actually. He grinned. ''Course, if you're pushed I don't mind taking over.'

'I wouldn't say no.'

As a rule she enjoyed doing her bit on the farm. Right now she had too much on her mind.

'Thanks, Dad. Oh well, suppose I'd better get changed and see to the ponies before it gets too dark.'

'You sound a bit out of sorts, Thea. Bad day?'

'No, not really, it's this time of year. You know, winter coming on, spring a long way off. I should have sold that mare and foal when I had the chance. It would have been less to do.'

Chas looked his daughter over carefully but made no comment. At the back door of the farmhouse they parted company, Chas to seek out the new farm hand, Thea to run upstairs and get into working jeans and a warm jumper. She remembered as she came down again that it was her mother's day at the farmers' market, which meant the making of the evening meal fell on her.

'It'll be curried something,' she muttered, then felt an immediate stab of guilt. Curry wasn't her father's favourite dish; his dinner could well end up in the bin.

Dusk was drawing down rapidly as she hurried to the fields with hay and a bucket of dry feed. A cold wind swept in off the estuary, stinging her cheeks and making her eyes water. The small herd of ponies were gathered around the gate watching for her, their eyes bright under their shaggy forelocks, bodies rounded and snug in the thick winter coats they were growing.

'Hello, you lot,' Thea called, dishing out their usual treat of Polo mints. One of the foals pushed in and gave her an impatient nip.

'Bad pony!'

Thea rubbed the tender spot on her arm. It hadn't broken the skin but would leave a bruise.

Animals fed, she hastened back to the house to start the supper, only to find Mae home and in the process of cooking their evening meal.

'Honestly, Mum,' Thea began, 'you must be shattered after being on your feet all day. You don't have to scrub potatoes and clean masses of vegetables like this. Something light would do.'

'Not for your father, it wouldn't. He's been out on the fields and deserves a decent evening meal. Anyway, chops and two veg is easy enough. Put the kettle on, will you, love? I'm gasping for a cup of tea.'

Thea obliged. Handing the tea to her mother, she made instant coffee for herself and went to thaw out by the range.

'Did you see anything of Helen Sanders at the market?'

'Yes, I did. She was having some friends round so she bought quite a lot of stuff. I thought she looked a little better.'

Mae deftly milled some rock salt over the prepared vegetables and transferred the steamer to the hob.

'Bryony still features a lot in the conversation. Helen can't praise her enough. D'you know, your sister's even turned a hand to the milking.'

'Then miracles do happen,' Thea murmured, sipping coffee.

'Oh, Thea. Bryony always was a helpful little thing as a child. It's just the teenage stage that was … well, a little fraught. And when is it not?'

'I suppose you're right,' Thea said, relenting.

When Chas came in, the conversation turned to his farming day and whether to spend the evening filling in the welter of agricultural forms that were piling up on the dresser, or go to the Thatch for a game of darts.

Meal over, Thea took herself off to the sitting-room to do her preparation for tomorrow's lessons.

'Not herself,' Mae mouthed to Chas, directing a meaningful look at the closed door.

'I noticed. It wouldn't have anything to do with that young vet she's been seeing a lot of lately?'

'Dominic, you mean?' Mae switched on the dishwasher and went to sit opposite her husband by the range. 'Why d'you say that?'

'Well, I was having a word with the lad' – Chas's usual way of addressing farm hands, young or old – 'and he said they'd taken on a relief vet at the practice because young Shane had been called back to Ireland.'

'Really? Did Jason say what for?'

'No, but it'll be unfinished business, I suspect. I always thought there was more to that fellow than met the eye.'

'Oh, Chas!' Mae threw her man a glance of amused affection. 'You say that about everyone you haven't known from being a boy.'

She broke off, frowning.

'I hope this isn't a disappointment for Thea. She's not had it easy this year.' She bit her lip. 'Oh, dear. She seemed quite taken with Dominic, and he obviously likes her. But then what young man wouldn't? Thea's lovely … I do so want her to be happy, Chas.'

'Me, too.' Her husband nodded, then glanced at the clock. 'I might tackle some of that confounded paperwork, then slip down to the Thatch for an hour.'

'Why not, love? I'll just read a few chapters of my library book, then,' Mae said comfortably.

Much later, schoolwork done, Thea shouted goodnight to her mother and went upstairs.

A soak in the bath failed to work its usual relaxing therapy, and as Thea climbed into bed, Thea knew she was in for a disturbed night.

Taking a while to glance through the new copy of her equine magazine in the hope of a distraction, she eventually switched off the bedside lamp. She dropped off to sleep at once, moaning softly as the images took shape behind her closed lids....

'No, Puss! You must stay in the cradle where I put you!'

Florence was a pretty six-year-old with a bright crop of golden ringlets, china-blue eyes and an angelic expression that totally belied her forceful nature.

Her sister, Amelia, a year younger and of a quieter disposition, took pity on the cat and, after a slight hesitation, grudgingly removed her doll from a second toy cradle.

'Here you are, Florence. Let Puss go and have Mary Rose instead.'

'No, I don't want your stupid doll! Dolls are for babies. I like cats best.'

'I'm not a baby.' Amelia pouted.

'Yes, you are.'

'Not!'

'You are. Babies play with dolls and that's all you ever do!'

'Girls, girls,' Polly cried, sweeping into the nursery with an armful of freshly laundered linen. 'What's all this? You're never squabbling over poor Puss again?'

The cat seized its opportunity and fled to the high window-sill, where it sat twitching its tail in injured affront. The two little girls, dressed identically in white muslin, their faces shining and rosy with recent washing, immediately forgot their differences and found their most fetching smiles.

'Here you are at last, Polly!' Florence said. 'Are we going to the park now?'

'Please, Polly. You promised,' Amelia added.

'I know I did and yes, we shall go at once while the sun's out. It will do us good – and I daresay Puss will relish a bit of peace.'

Bundling her small charges into their outdoor clothes, Polly thought how happy she was with her situation here in the tall house on Stanley Square. She adored the little girls.

Their mama, Dorothea Kendrick, had turned out as generous as she was beautiful, giving Polly her cast-off gowns to make over for herself. Jerome Kendrick, the master of the house, was involved in politics and absent a good deal.

Polly knew him as a distant figure, tall and distinguished-looking, with mid-brown hair and a handsomely twirling moustache. There was a son by an earlier marriage – Harry. But Polly didn't want to think about Harry.

Feeling very trim in her dark blue nurse's gown and matching bonnet, Polly ushered the girls out into the bright summer day. Weather permitting, most afternoons were spent thus. They either walked in the park or by the River Dee, or took the governess cart for a drive around the leafy lanes that surrounded the city.

Although Polly's day began early, lighting the nursery fire and dusting, and ended late, since she was often required to attend her mistress when she returned from a dinner engagement or a visit with friends to the theatre, Polly was well satisfied with her lot.

She still fretted over leaving her mother and missed John Royle with a fierce ache that would not go away. But she knew her Aunt Jessica had been right. She was better away from the dangers and insecurities of the Harbour House and the daunting prospect of a loveless marriage.

After spending a pleasant couple of hours taking the air, the little party returned home for the children to have their afternoon nap. As a rule, Polly made use of this quiet time to catch up on some mending or personal sewing. Today, finding herself short of coloured thread, she slipped down to the kitchen for more.

'A letter's just arrived for you, Polly,' Cook, a comfortable body who was also the housekeeper – this being a small household – informed her.

Seeing the Parkgate postmark, Polly stowed the letter away in her apron pocket to read later and lingered for a few moments to chat. Returning by the back-stair, booted feet tapping smartly on the uncarpeted oak treads, bundle of thread clutched to her, she reached the top and was about to cross the shadowy landing when a hand shot out and held her fast.

'Ho, there, Miss Polly. Where are you off to in such a hurry?' Harry Kendrick's voice rasped in her ear.

'Master Harry! Let me go or I shall scream!' Polly struggled against his grip, bobbins of thread bouncing to the floor and rolling away in all directions. 'Let go of me!'

'Not until I've had that kiss.'

'I'd sooner kiss the pony,' Polly retorted. 'Stop this at once or I shall tell the mistress!'

'It'll be your word against mine, Polly my sweet. What a feisty creature you are! One little kiss, Polly, then you may go.'

Spirit-laden breath seared Polly's nostrils and the hands on her shoulders tightened frighteningly. But Polly hadn't lived all her days in a tavern for nothing. Twisting her head away, she delivered her tormentor's shin a sharp kick with the pointed toe of her boot. He let out a howl of anguish, swiftly checked.

His hands fell away and Polly ran for it, not stopping until she gained the safety of the nursery quarters. Shutting the door, she shot the bolt and leaned her back to the solid wooden frame, fighting to control her gasping breath. She realized she was shaking.

This wasn't the first time Harry had made a nuisance of himself and she wasn't sure what to do. He was a good-looking youth who knew how to wield the charm. Would the mistress believe her word against that of her stepson?

'Polly?' A drowsy voice beckoned from the darkened bedroom beyond. 'Polly, I'm thirsty. I want a drink of water!'

The simple request did much to restore Polly's scattered wits.

'Coming, my dear,' she called, and pouring water from the jug on the side table she went through to where her charges were tucked up in their beds. 'Want a drink of water – what, young lady?' Polly asked in mock severity.

'Please,' Florence obliged, dimpling.

'That's right. What a good girl. Now drink it up, then have another little sleep. It's muffins for tea, Cook tells me. Won't that be nice?'

Much later, Polly took out the letter from her aunt and, squinting her eyes in the flickering light of the candle lamp, began to read....

My dearest niece, Jessica wrote. Polly pictured her, seated at her small writing desk, a morning cup of hot chocolate steaming fragrantly at her elbow. *I was gladdened to hear that you are settled in your new post. I keep in excellent health as ever, though I am saddened to report that not the same cannot be said of your poor mama. She is failing, Polly. Today she told me that you are constantly in her thoughts.*

Polly's heart quailed. Somehow she must try to visit her mother. How could she manage it? She wanted desperately to go but the terms of her employment were clear. No leave granted until she had been with the family for twelve calendar months. Polly had only done six as yet.

Even so, perhaps she should contemplate approaching her mistress for leave. Polly pulled the spluttering candle closer and read on.

Now to more cheerful news. I have decided to give a dinner party, Polly – just one of my little gatherings, you know. You will never guess who is on the guest list. None other than your brother Edward and his love, Susanna Marsdon! I have made it my duty to observe the progress of this romance, Polly, and am delighted to see that Susanna has had an agreeably sobering influence on your wild and wilful sibling. Not that I had doubts that he wouldn't sort himself out in time. I like to see some spirit in a lad. But there. Edward has now abandoned his former ways and tells me he is looking to the legal profession as a career.

Polly read the letter to the end, smiling a little at her aunt's witty narrative, biting her lip anxiously as she read again the news of her mother's decline. Too consumed with anxiety to seek her bed, she fetched writing materials and began to pen a letter of response.

Here, too, was a chance to share the problem over Harry Kendrick. Jessica would know what to do.

At Parkgate, Jessica studied Polly's missive with interest. Her niece had a sparky turn of phrase and her anecdotes on the small girls and their escapades brought a chuckle. It stopped when she read of the amorous elder son. That Harry! Waylaying pretty nursemaids was not his only weakness, if what she had heard was to be believed – his appetite for gambling and carousing being rife.

It was high time his father took him in hand. Jessica only hoped that Polly had the wit to avoid trouble.

Putting the letter aside for now, she rang for her maid. After several moments the girl appeared, very out of breath, her cap askew as always.

'There you are, Agnes. Straighten your cap, child. And look at your apron. It's very soiled.'

'I'm sorry, ma'am. I was peeling the potatoes and—'

'In your housemaid's apron? How often do I have to tell you? You wear your drugget one for kitchen tasks and save your other for wearing out of the kitchen.'

'Yes'm.' The maid bobbed a curtsy. 'Sorry, ma'am. It'll try to remember, but all this chopping and changing puts me in a twist. Yesterday, I changed that many times I clean forgot where I'd put my good pinny, and by the time I'd found it and put it on the caller had given up and gone!'

Mustering patience, Jessica continued with the task in hand.

'Have you delivered my invitations to dinner, Agnes?'

'Yes'm. Mr Rawlinson was in the garden when I turned up so I handed it over to him personally. Very pleased he was with it, too.'

Jessica suppressed a smile. Her little sojourn with George was progressing splendidly. He had sent her a carafe of Rhenish the other day. Before that it was a length of Italian silk for a gown. She did not need to enquire from whence the bounty came.

Most folks hereabouts benefited from a little quiet trafficking and she was no different.

'And Master Edward? Did he receive his?'

'Oh, yes'm.' Agnes put her hand to her lips and giggled. 'A real tease, is Master Edward. There's no harm in him, though,' she added hastily.

'I should hope not indeed! Agnes, about that the young fisherman who calls....'

'He's due later today, ma'am. Will I tell you when he arrives?'

'Please do, Agnes. That will be all for now.'

That afternoon, Jessica met up with John Royle. The pleasant-looking, quietly spoken young man was not what she expected.

'I shan't beat about the bush,' she told him. 'It has come to my knowledge that you wish to exchange your present trade for a venture into the teaching profession.'

'That is correct, Miss Platt,' John said mildly.

'And have you any qualifications in this area?'

'As many as the next man. I spend much time studying. I have a knowledge of Latin, a smattering of other languages and am an able mathematician and scriber.'

'I don't doubt it,' Jessica murmured more to herself.

'Ma'am?'

'Oh, 'tis nothing. An irritating habit of mine. Irritating to others, that is. Mr Royle, do you mind my asking if you have obtained premises for this school?'

'Not at all, though I'm afraid the answer is no. I must have made enquiries into every available property in the district, all to no avail.' He looked wry. 'No one is prepared to deal with a common fisher lad. I shan't give up. One day something will come along.'

'Then I wish you well in your quest, John Royle.'

'Thank you, ma'am.'

Long after the young man had gone Jessica sat at her desk, deep in thought. Perhaps she had been too hasty in removing Polly. She had liked John Royle and saw what an admirable couple they would have made. Oh, there was that absurd matter of the betrothal between Polly and George, but that could have been dealt with. Jessica was altogether fond of her niece. She was saddened to have been so mistaken.

Thea woke with a start. Her throat was dry, her head heavy. She felt as if she'd been up all night instead of sleeping in her bed. Realizing it was Saturday, with no immediate hurry to get up, she rolled on to her back and let her mind drift. Her 'dream' characters, she thought ruefully, were going through as bad a patch as herself.

Or was it all fiction? Were the curious sequences that came to her as she slumbered a result of her own troubled state of mind? At Dominic's suggestion, she had acquainted herself with some reading on what was termed 'waking dreams'.

Thea was prepared to accept them for what they were; scenes from the past visiting the dreamer with extraordinary accuracy. But why her? And why now?

Giving up, Thea rose and headed for the shower.

'Darling, you look dreadful,' Mae cried as Thea came into the kitchen, her eyes shadowed in her pale face. She had shampooed her hair and bundled it up turban-like in a towel, which did nothing for her strained appearance.

'Thanks!' Thea shot her mother a pained look. 'I had a bad night, Mum, that's all. Nothing to worry about.'

'But I am worried. Is it Dominic? You can tell me not to pry if you like....'

'As if I would.' Thea smiled ruefully, accepting the tea and toast her mother handed her with a quick smile of affection. She buttered it thoughtfully. Trust me, Dominic had said, but how could she?

'Yes, you're right about Dominic, Mum. Something's going on

... I don't know the details. Just that an ex-girlfriend has arrived on the scene and she's ... well, what Richard would call a bit of a stirrer. Very glam, too.'

Her voice trailed off.

Mae sank down opposite at the table.

'Oh, dear.'

'Quite. Dominic has a past he doesn't talk about.' She shrugged. 'All I can say is it was something to do with a doping scandal and it turned nasty.'

'Dope? Racehorses, you mean?'

Thea nodded.

'You know he was resident vet at Ferlann Ridge. Well, his girl-friend – they were engaged then – was somehow involved. Dominic was cagey over her part in things. It shattered the rela-tionship, anyway. At least, so he said. And then she turns up again and off he goes with her.'

She sighed.

'I suppose that's men for you.'

'Darling, Dominic doesn't strike me as being the fickle type.'

'Me, neither, but it's scary how manipulative some women can be. Look at Bryony. I wouldn't mind betting she had designs on Geoff all along.'

'Thea, surely not!'

'Well, she was always prinking and preening when he was around. We used to laugh about her. Not that it makes any differ-ence now.'

'No,' Mae agreed. 'Though I think you're being too hard on your sister. She may have been infatuated but she I'm sure she wouldn't have deliberately set out to steal Geoff from you.'

Thea wasn't so certain. A permanent rift between herself and her sister wasn't what she wanted, but following the events of the past weeks she had to wonder if she could ever trust anyone again.

'Honestly, Geoff, it's not on,' Bryony fumed as they crossed the spacious yard at Roseacre. Yesterday, she had bumped into her mother during her lunch break and been kept for ages on the bustling pavement while Mae unburdened her worries. 'All Mum could talk about was Thea and how stressed out she is! Some things never change. Thea always was the shining light.'

'I don't think that's quite the case,' Geoff said gently, pausing in a patch of mellow November sunshine to stand and smile down at her. The cattle were up for the winter, and from their quarters issued an urgent lowing that suggested milking was imminent.

'I was always aware of how Mae spoke with equal affection of all of you. Chas was different. You could do no wrong in his eyes!'

'Good old Dad! Bryony chuckled. 'Someone has to champion the lost cause!'

'Hey – stop putting yourself down.' He looked seriously at her. 'Bryony, isn't it time you made it up with your folks? My mother's never said as much, but I'm sure it worries her that you never go home.'

'Woodhey isn't home any more,' Bryony said evenly. 'Too much has happened.'

'Of course it is! They're your kin and they love you. These things happen in the best of families, but with a bit of effort on both sides they can usually be resolved. Will you think about it, at least?'

It was an issue Bryony had purposely avoided. Chatting to Mum in town now and again was fine, but the prospect of facing her whole family was daunting. The longer she put it off the harder it became. Then again, she supposed Geoff was right. She'd have to think of an excuse for dropping in … some time.

Geoff was looking at her very hard and Bryony, holding his gaze, gave a hesitant nod.

'That's my girl!'

In the cattle byre the cows increased their complaint and Geoff glanced up.

'We'd better get on with the milking. What if we go out for a bite to eat afterwards? It's a fine day. We could drive to Southport.'

Bryony's heart leaped. It would be great to go out with Geoff and linger together over a meal.

'That would be lovely,' she said. 'But what about your mum? Sunday lunch at Woodhey was always a big thing with my parents.

I expect it was the same here? We can't very well leave her on her own just yet.'

'You know, you're right. I'd forgotten there's sure to be a roast on the go.'

Geoff rubbed his face wearily with his hand. Bryony's heart softened. She knew how hard the difficult recent weeks had been for him. A few hours' respite away from the farm would have been no bad thing.

'So what do you suggest?' he asked eventually.

'We eat here with your mum as usual – and maybe go for an Italian one night in the week? Thursday might be best. It's Helen's WI evening so she'll be out as well.'

'You're brilliant! Did I ever mention what a great PA you'd make?'

'Not in so many words, but I'm always open to flattery!'

'Cheek!' His mood lifted noticeably. He gave Bryony a playful shove. 'Get along with you, woman. Fetch those animals across before they bust the doors down!'

Laughing, Bryony went to do as he asked. Her flatmate and best friend Liz thought her plainly mad to tie herself down at weekends like this, but if she were honest, she liked nothing better. Working alongside your man, knowing your animals were well looked after and the farm running smoothly, brought a deep satisfaction she could not fathom or even understand.

It had never been like this at Woodhey.

Gaining the doors of the cattle shed, Bryony bit her lip. Only, Geoff wasn't her man, was he? She only pretended he was and had almost convinced herself that it was true. If only things were different....

Rain splattered against the windscreen and Dominic, decreasing his speed slightly on the windswept coastal road of south-east Ireland, flicked the wipers to full strength.

'This had better be worth my while,' he said, with a sideways glance at Aisling.

'It will be. Do you think I'd drag you back here otherwise?'

'I'm not sure, exactly. I just wish you weren't always so damned mysterious, Aisling.'

'I'm not. I just think it's better for you to hear it for yourself.'

In the back of the hire car, Trina whined worriedly.

'Hush,' Dominic murmured to the dog. 'Nearly there. At least, so I hope. Why Wexford, anyway?' he asked Aisling.

'Because the guy we're going to see is a Wexford man. Don't question me any more, Dom. Just wait and see. It'll be in your interest.'

'So you keep saying,' Dominic muttered.

The past twenty-four hours had been gruelling. Yesterday, just before morning surgery, his boss had called him through to the office for a word.

'I'll come straight to the point, Dominic,' Freddie Barnes had said. 'Something has come to my attention that could be bad for the practice. You know Bob Perrit?'

'Sure I do.'

He had been called out to the man's racing yard many times.

'He rang me last night. It was over that doping scandal at Ferlann Ridge last year.' Freddy paused significantly. 'You never mentioned you were involved.'

'That's because I wasn't. My name happened to be dragged through the mud along with several others, but I had nothing to do with it and I saw no reason to bring it up.'

'I see. The thing is, Perrit has strong connections with the Irish racing scene. If he should start spreading rumours it could make things very difficult for us. As you know, a good chunk of our profit comes from the equine side of the practice. People are always quick to take their custom elsewhere if they scent trouble.'

'Yes,' Dominic agreed, with a horrible sinking feeling inside. The past always caught up with you. Maybe he should have stuck out for getting his name cleared. If it hadn't been for Aisling he'd have done just that.

'Is that all?' he said in a voice tight with bitterness.

'For now. As things stand, Perrit's made the point that he doesn't want you anywhere near his horses in future. It's to be hoped others don't follow his example.'

Dominic was silent. He had believed himself settled here. He had a job he enjoyed, a decent home and a good social life. And there was Thea. Her quiet face and slow smile rose in his mind and he swallowed.

He didn't want Thea involved in any of this. On the other hand, he wasn't prepared to go without a fight.

'So what am I expected to do?' he asked his boss. 'Give in my notice, just because a single client has come up with some gossip guaranteed to be a string of lies?'

'No, of course not. I'm simply putting you in the picture. You're doing a good job here, Dominic. I wouldn't want to lose you.'

'But if it's a choice between me and losing clients to a rival practice, we both know what the outcome will be....' Dominic finished grimly.

Freddie Barnes had spread his hands in a way that was open to interpretation, and the discussion had come to a close.

As if that hadn't been enough, Dominic had arrived home that evening to find Aisling waiting for him – as heart-stoppingly fetching as ever. At first he had wanted nothing to do with the garbled story she had flung at him regarding new evidence, and a pressing need to put matters right.

But after a while he detected a quiet resolve in Aisling that made him give her the benefit of the doubt. Following the morning's developments, it had been a simple matter to ring his boss and, with a few well chosen words, arrange some leave.

'We turn off here,' Aisling said suddenly. 'Ahead on the right.'

Frowning in puzzlement, he indicated and turned into the narrow by-road and then through a stone-pillared gateway, drawing up outside a tranquil white-walled building in grounds that were obviously newly landscaped.

The Hospice of St Theresa, a noticeboard in subdued green lettering on a buff background informed. Dominic quirked an eyebrow enquiringly.

In a graceful gesture Aisling arranged a gauzy scarf over her dark hair, turning to him.

'Dom, I should warn you this could be an ordeal. I certainly found it so when I came. You can bring Trina. They don't mind dogs here.'

They clambered out of the car, the dog leaping around, glad to be free. Dominic called her to him and clipped on the leash. The rain had eased, a fitful sunshine washing the landscape in watery light. Overhead, sea-birds wheeled and called. The familiar air of Dominic's homeland was soft on his face.

'Right then,' he said to Aisling. 'Lead the way.'

Chapter Seven

'**M**urty?'

Dominic gazed in disbelief at the figure in the easy chair, shock ripping through him despite Aisling's hinted warning. Short, whippy, with a wind-scrubbed red face, Murty Miles had been the essence of robust good health as he laughed his way past the winning post of more jump races than Dominic could name.

Now, all the eager vitality was gone. Murty's clothes hung on him and the skin that stretched over the high cheekbones was pale. But the well-remembered glint of humour was still there in the grey-blue Irish eyes.

'Dominic, lad. It's grand to see you,' Murty greeted him, his deep, lilting voice strangely weakened. He sent Aisling a nod, his eyes twinkling. 'And Aisling, me darlin'. Lovely as ever, so y'are.'

'Ah, go on, you old rogue. Sweet-talk is all I've come for, and well you know it!' Aisling quipped, effectively easing the moment of awkwardness.

She set about arranging the chairs around a low table and Dominic sank into one gratefully, glancing around him. The day room of the hospice was bright and welcoming. A nurse bustled in with flowers in a tall vase, giving Murty a cheery word in passing, clicking her tongue to the dog who had accompanied the visitors.

Trina, her copper coat gleaming in the pale Wexford sunlight that poured in through the big windows, had relinquished her favourite pink ball at Murty's feet and now grinned up at him hopefully.

'Not here, you daft animal,' Murty told her. 'Sure, is it trying to get me thrown out you are?'

Stroking her, playing absently with her silky ears, the jockey launched straight into the reason for summoning Dominic to his side.

'I'll not have to tell you what I'm doing here, Dom, it's as plain as the nose on your face. Point is, my days are numbered and there are certain issues that need to be put right before I go.'

'Would it be to do with the doping case?' Dominic guessed.

'It would.'

Murty continued to fondle the dog, whilst Dominic fixed his gaze unseeingly on the grounds beyond the window, rerunning in his mind the chapter of events that had led up to his disgrace – Aisling entering the home they were putting together, her face a quixotic mix of anxious optimism, excitement and doubt.

At Ferlann Ridge that day she'd been approached by a guy who had offered 'to see her right' if she'd slip a titbit to a horse in a specific race.

'He said it's harmless, Dom,' she'd told him. 'It'll just slow the horse down a bit, that's all. No one will think anything of it. They're used to seeing us feeding titbits to the horses.'

Dominic had stared at her – incredulous, accusing.

'You're not serious? Do you honestly believe I'd have a part in something like that? Aisling, this a doping mob you're talking about. It's trouble.'

'Oh, come on, now, don't be getting all high-handed! It's only this once, and it's big money, Dom.' She named a sum that made him blink. 'Think what we could buy for the house.'

'Forget the house!'

He'd gone ballistic, demanding to know if she realized what she was getting herself into, and what the consequences of discovery would be. Not just for herself, but for him too.

Did she in fact know him at all to think he'd ever consider such a dangerous practice? He was a vet, for heaven's sake, committed to the health and well-being of animals, not to harming them in any way.

The verbal battle that followed had been short and rancorous. He'd turned on his heel and slammed out. As it turned out, Aisling had then had a last-minute fit of conscience and backed out.

'Well, I remembered seeing a horse in a bad way after having dope,' she'd admitted sheepishly. 'It wasn't a pretty sight.'

How very clearly Dominic remembered her words. But had she told him the truth?

The horse had reacted. A stable hand reported having seen Dominic feeding treats to the animal in question and a disciplinary hearing followed.

Dominic, protesting his innocence, half-suspected Aisling, resolved to keep her name out of it and ended up taking the blame.

Now having a black mark against his name with the Irish Jockey Club, his career as a Ferlann Ridge vet in ruins as well as his future with Aisling, Dominic had fled to England and the post in the quiet backwater of Parkgate, to lick his wounds and piece together a new life.

Many were the nights he had woken in a cold sweat, wondering, puzzling, on the verge of pinpointing some vital clue that would lead to the truth of the matter. Always it eluded him, and again the finger would point at the beautiful girl with the long, curling hair.

He recalled how Aisling had sobbed out her innocence. He'd tried to believe her, wanted to. It was a conundrum that had eaten into him. The real truth of the matter had never come to light. Until now?

'It was meself that gave the horse the stuff,' Murty said now.

Dominic, brought shockingly back to the present, waited for the man to continue.

'Sure, now, I wasn't to know the trouble it'd get you into, Dom. All I can say is how sorry I am and that I'm prepared to come clean about what happened. Officially, you know? I've a letter drawn up. Well, these things can drag on and time's running out for me. It's all been legally done and witnessed. All you have to do is set the thing in motion.'

It was obvious that Murty was tiring. He left off stroking the dog to reach into his jacket pocket and withdraw an official-looking envelope. Without a word, Dominic took it from him.

'Will you shake on it, Dom, lad?' Murty said humbly, extending a hand that had reined in some of the best thoroughbreds on the Irish racing scene. Dominic was aware of Aisling sitting tense and silent beside him, heard the faint exhalation of relief that passed her lips as he took the jockey's quivering, fleshless hand in his strong grip.

'Thanks, Murty. I'll look into matter immediately.'

From the corner of his eye he saw the nurse bearing down upon them and stood up.

'Are you ready, Aisling? Come, Trina. Cheers then, Murty. I'll be back.'

Outside once more in the sweet, damp air, Dominic stood a moment and waited for the world to stop reeling and rocking around him. It was as if a weight had been lifted from his shoulders, leaving him with a curious feeling of lightness and optimism.

'Poor old Murty,' he said abruptly.

Aisling nodded.

'It was a shock when he got in touch with me. I nearly didn't follow it up but I'm certainly glad I did. And I was right to have brought you here. You'd never have believed any of it from my lips, would you?'

It was true. He couldn't have trusted her word. With Aisling, even the truth was questionable. Innocent, but with reservations. She'd always been fond of animals. He couldn't see her deliberately harming a horse. But then there was the money. And Aisling loved her little luxuries.

'What now?' Aisling asked when he didn't speak.

'Oh, I'll stay on here and get this thing sorted. Ring my boss and explain. Get an extension of leave.'

Ring Thea.

Dominic's heart warmed at the thought of her and he smiled suddenly, causing Aisling to slip a hopeful hand into his. Gently he disengaged it and, whistling up the dog, indicated that they move on to the waiting car.

*

Thea tucked her mobile back into the deep pocket of her coat and stood a moment in the open entrance to the ponies' field-shelter, contemplative. She had been tossing them some hay when it rang and had answered impatiently, biting her lip when Dominic's voice sounded in her ear.

He wanted her to join him in Ireland for the weekend as he had a matter of importance to discuss with her. She could get a flight to Dublin and he'd meet her at the airport, he said. Her heart had skipped a beat at the prospect, but caution prevailed and she didn't give an immediate answer.

She couldn't just drop everything and leave, she'd told him, hitting on the most plausible delaying tactic. What about the ponies? She'd have to ring him back.

It was a still night, no moon but the sky was bright with stars. Thea wondered, a trifle self-consciously, if Dominic was looking up at the same glimmering canopy and thinking of her.

And where in this uneasy scenario was Aisling Cleary?

'I don't know, Dancer!' she murmured to her little mare who had left off munching the hay to put a questing muzzle in Thea's palm in the hope of titbits.

'What can Dominic have to say that he can't tell me over the phone? Why doesn't he just come back here? Why all the mystery?'

At her voice, the rest of the ponies stopped feeding and threw up their heads, small ears pricking, wisps of hay hanging from their mouths. The big wooden structure of the field-shelter hammered suddenly to the thud of hooves as they came plodding up, pushing and nuzzling impatiently at Thea's pockets.

Thea dug out the mints they knew she had for them and shared them out, chuckling as the ponies crunched them up.

'Gannets! Now get on with your supper. I'm going in.'

She checked that they had fresh water and went trudging back across the field, her booted feet squelching in the soggy ground. In the farmyard, Chas was hosing away the day's mud, so Thea took up the spare hose and helped finish off, her mind on Dominic and his unexpected phone call.

Mouth-watering smells met her in the kitchen, where Mae was

preparing for tomorrow's market. An additional order for fancy cakes meant that supper was delayed, and by the time Thea had helped wash up and gone over her lesson notes for the next day, it was well past her usual bedtime.

In bed at last, she lay wakeful, her thoughts still on Dominic. He had sounded different, not excited exactly, but with a positive note to his voice that was new.

Thea closed her eyes and slept, spinning headlong into her tangled world of dreams.

Harry Kendrick paused outside his stepmother's room. The door was ajar and there on the dressing-table her favourite diamond pin glinted in the mellow afternoon light. The room was empty. Harry cast a furtive glance up and down the corridor, and assured that no one was about, he seized his chance.

Slipping silently into the room, he picked up the pin and left, making a stealthy way up through the house to the nursery quarters. He had seen Polly leave earlier with the children on their daily walk.

Miss Hoity-toity! *He'd* show Polly Dakin what was what!

In the nursery, all was quiet. Opening the door of the room next to the children's where Polly slept, he looked around. The small bedchamber was clean and neat and smelled sweetly of the lavender cologne that Polly wore, and for a moment Harry faltered.

Polly had something, a quality that made her a cut above the other servants. He knew how well thought of she was by his father and stepmother, and realized how clever he'd have to be to convince them of her lack of trustworthiness.

Hardening his heart, he entered the room and concealed the diamond pin under the linen in the chest of drawers. Then he left, closing the door softly behind him.

That evening, Polly was sitting sewing by the nursery fire when there was a peremptory knock on the door and the housemaid entered. She looked agitated.

'Such a hue and cry, Polly,' she said. 'The mistress can't find her diamond pin anywhere. She wants to speak to you.'

'Me? What for?'

'I'm not sure. Maybe the mistress thinks you'll know where it could be.'

'In the china dish on the dressing-table, most likely. That's where it gets left as a rule. I've told Madam to put it away safely in the jewellery box but she doesn't listen. Well, she wears it a lot so I suppose it's understandable.'

'The master's there. Seems everyone on the staff is being questioned. Cook's in a right state over it, I can tell you. Leave that, Polly. Master says you're to come at once.'

'Oh, very well.'

Heaving a sigh, Polly set aside the day gown she was making over for herself from one of her mistress's cast-offs and followed the girl out.

In Dorothea Kendrick's sitting-room, the master stood with his back to the window. His face was grave. Dorothea was seated on the day bed, her eyes swollen and red from weeping.

'Come in, Polly,' she said, dabbing her cheek with an embroidered handkerchief. 'Dear me, what a to-do!'

'Close the door, Polly,' the master ordered. 'Now then. You will know why you have been summoned here. Can you tell us precisely when you last saw your mistress's diamond pin?'

'Why, yes, sir. I saw it this morning when I dressed Madam's hair. It was on the dressing-table dish with the roses round the rim. I mentioned to Madam that it would be better put away … sir.'

'So you did, Polly.' Dorothea's voice broke. 'Oh, how I wish I'd taken notice.'

'It's sure to be here somewhere, ma'am,' Polly said comfortingly. 'Maybe it's become caught up in a shawl and put away. Will I take a look for you?'

'Polly, the room has already been searched with a fine-tooth comb.' Jerome Kendrick's stern expression did not waver. 'Tell me truthfully. Was the pin still there when you tidied up after the mistress had left for town?'

'Why, yes, sir.' Polly looked in puzzlement from one to the other. 'I clearly remember seeing it when I replaced the hairbrushes and pin-boxes on the dressing-table. After that I went to see to Miss Florence and Miss Amelia. Why ... why, sir. You surely don't think *I* had anything to do with the fact that's it's gone missing?'

'No, Polly. Of course not,' cried Dorothea from the couch. 'The very idea, Jerome! One could trust Polly with the crown jewels!'

'In which case Polly should have no objection to her room being searched. Well, Polly?'

'No, sir, of course not.' Indignation burned on Polly's cheeks. 'But you won't find anything!'

'Nevertheless, since you were the last one to set eyes on the wretched object it might be just as well.... Oh, do not weep, my dear. It's not the end of the world. If it doesn't turn up I'll buy you another pin.'

'It wouldn't be the same, Jerome,' Dorothea sniffed. 'It was your engagement gift to me. It has a sentimental value that cannot be replaced.'

The room was duly searched, the pin found.

'Polly. How could you?' her mistress said, injured reproach in every line of her elegant figure. 'And after all I've done for you too!'

Polly, her eyes wide and imploring in her white face, could not believe it.

'But Madam ... I didn't do it,' she protested. Beneath the bodice of her gown her heart was beating a frightened tattoo. 'Please believe me. It must have been planted there. Maybe for a joke. But I did not do it!'

'That's enough, Polly.' Jerome Kendrick's voice was cutting. 'You will pack your bags and leave the house first thing in the morning. There will be no references, of course, but I shall make sure you receive whatever wages are due to you.'

He drew himself up to deliver his last, stinging remark.

'Needless to say, you will have no further contact with my children. As soon as you have gathered together your belongings you can remove yourself to the kitchen. One of the maids can take over here until a substitute is found.'

As the door shut behind them, Polly subsided on to the narrow iron bed, arms wrapped around herself, rocking to and fro.

'I didn't do it,' she whispered vehemently into the enclosing darkness. 'I did not!'

In the grey hour before dawn next morning Polly left the house, her bundle of belongings under her arm. As she crossed the silent square, Harry Kendrick was just returning from a night carousing with his friends. Polly met his gaze squarely, noting the shiftiness of his pale eyes, the weak mouth and set of jaw in an otherwise handsome face.

Harry was the first to look away and Polly, giving a small, bitter smile of understanding, straightened her back and walked on under the lightening sky.

At the ancient walls that surrounded the city she paused, gazing out over the grassy stretches of the race-course known as the Roodee, towards the river. The oily slap and swish of the water lapping the banks carried over the quiet morning air, bringing to mind her trysts with John Royle on the estuary wharf at Parkgate.

How she missed John, his kindly face and steady grey gaze. Perhaps she should have made an effort and got in touch. Now, it was too late.

No sweetheart, no home, no job in a fine house and, without the necessary letter of recommendation, no hope of finding another. She had lost everything.

Hitching her bundle of clothes more securely under her arm, she started to walk, heading out of the town, a small, solitary figure that was soon lost to view.

Swimming up out of the deep mists of sleep, Thea opened her eyes. Her long hair had come loose from its plait and lay in a tangled dark-gold mass across the pillow.

Too late. Too late! Polly Dakin's thoughts hammered on her senses. Maybe Polly had been trying to tell her something. She had lost her own love, it seemed irretrievably. Was Thea in danger of doing the same?

A late-November darkness pressed against the window. Thea glanced at the bedside clock. Six-thirty. Early yet, though not too early to ring. Sitting up in the bed, she reached for her mobile and punched out Dominic's number. His voice when he answered was wakeful and alert.

'Thea?'

She felt a rush of sudden indescribable joy.

'Hi, Dominic. Is the weekend still on?'

'Indeed it is. You're coming then. Terrific! I'll find out the flights for you and be in touch.'

'Great.'

'Can I ring you at school? Around lunchtime?'

'I guess so. Make sure and call after twelve. I'm in class until then.'

'I won't forget. I've lots to tell you, Thea.'

'Really? I'm looking forward to it. It's been ages since I was in Ireland. I certainly didn't expect to be going there right now. What a guy you are for springing the surprises.'

They talked some more and then rang off. Half-smiling, half-wondering if she was doing the right thing, not really caring, Thea leaned back against the pillows and allowed herself the luxury of planning what clothes she would take with her … always supposing she could coax Dad into looking after the ponies for a couple of days.

'Dad!' Bryony had seen her father coming out of the subway and ran to catch him up. 'How are you? It's been ages!'

'Bryony, lass!' Chas beamed at her, unable to keep the smile from his face. 'I'm fine, love. All the better for seeing you.'

'How's Mum? And Woodhey? Did you get the ploughing done before the wet weather set in?'

'Just about. You know how it is. You never get all you want done on a farm, the next season always creeps up on you. Your Mum's all right. A bit quiet, but that's to be expected. She's taken on a lot of extra work with these farmers' markets.'

Beside them the rush-hour traffic chugged past, the drivers

finding a way through the congested roads of Birkenhead as they made for home after the long working day.

'So, what are you doing in town?' Bryony asked.

'Seeing the accountant. It's been a better year this time. At least some good has come of it. Bryony, lass ...'

'Yes?' Bryony throat went dry. Here it comes, she thought. The moment she was dreading. The outpourings of reproach and how gutted they all were over what had happened. All her fault....

'When are you coming to see us?' he asked abruptly. 'This weekend mightn't be a bad time. Your sister's going away and she's lumbered me with the ponies. If you came on Sunday you could have some lunch with us and do the honours. You know how good you are with little pests. Ponies always see me coming!'

'Don't I know it! Remember when old Pixie nipped your backside? You couldn't sit down for a week and Mum couldn't stop laughing!'

Bryony felt an overwhelming relief. Here was the excuse she'd been waiting for to make it up with her parents, and it would be a lot easier without Thea there. Especially now with the subject of Geoff like an elephant in the room.

Bryony swallowed. Mum might know what to do about Geoff, who continued to treat her like a kid.

'I'd love to come, Dad,' she said. 'And consider it a deal over the ponies. I expect they're turned out on the pasture right now, so there'll be the field-shelter to muck out and fresh straw to lay. I'll help Geoff with the early milking as usual, then come straight on to Woodhey afterwards. It'll be a good opportunity for Helen to have Geoff to herself for a while.'

Chas rubbed his pinkly-shaven face with his hand.

'Did I hear correctly when you said "early milking"? I don't rightly remember you ever seeing Sunday morning at Woodhey. Still in the land of nod, you were.'

'Things change, Dad,' Bryony sniffed. 'I've got used to being up before six. The only thing that's no different is the car.' She pulled a woeful face. 'I'm still never quite sure if it'll get me places or not!'

He looked concerned.

'Well, we'll have to see about a replacement – can't have you breaking down on the road. Like I said, there's been an improvement with finances this year....'

Chas consulted his watch.

'Well, I'd better be off. See you on Sunday, Bryony. I'll tell your mum to rustle up an apple pie. It's still your favourite?'

''Course it is. With oodles of yummy custard done the way only Mum can make it. Mmm, I can't wait!'

She fetched her father a kiss on his cheek and watched him go striding off, still smiling; a good-looking, robust, country man in sludge-coloured cords and warm winter jacket, the farm's audit papers in a battered brown leather briefcase swinging from his hand.

Everything comes to she who waits, Bryony thought, and wouldn't Geoff be chuffed when he heard she was doing the right thing over the rift in her family at long last?

Nevertheless, that Sunday, Bryony felt her stomach tighten when she drove into the yard of her home. Everything looked the same – the hosed surfaces, the big green tractors standing neatly side by side in the big barn, smoke huffing from the tall chimneys of the squat old farmhouse that was so different from the classic proportions of Roseacre, but strong on character all the same.

Across the fields, Thea's ponies were enjoying a headlong flight round and round the pasture, kicking their heels against the cold wind that surged in off the estuary. They'd be a handful when she crossed the field to tackle the work in the shelter.

The kitchen door opened and Mae came out.

'Bryony! You're nice and early. Coffee's on. Come on in and get warm. Dad's gone to the newsagent for a paper. We'll have the chance for a chat before he gets back.'

'Great,' Bryony said, pleased there was no awkwardness, no hint of recrimination. It was going to be all right.

Later, ponies seen to, lunch eaten and the sitting-room fire stoked up to a good blaze, the three of them sat down and relaxed.

'I shouldn't have had that second slice of pie but it I couldn't resist it,' Bryony said to her mother.

'It always was a toss-up as to who got the last piece, you or your brother!'

Bryony laughed.

'Talking of Richard, have you heard his CD on the radio? Jazz Today played two tracks this morning – Geoff has music on while he milks. The cows like it.'

Mae sat up in her chair.

'Richard's band was playing?'

Bryony nodded.

'Tracey was singing on the first track. Sounds great! The album's out in the shops so I got you one.'

She delved into her bag and brought out the CD with Richard and the band smiling on the cover. Chas sat stony-faced in his armchair, but Mae reached out and took the disc.

'Thank you, darling. What a lovely thought. Don't the boys all look handsome? And look at Tracey. She's a lovely girl....'

'I'll say!' Bryony tugged at her own wildly curling hair – a bequest from her father and her bane – and gestured at her jeans and jumper.

'Tracey Kent makes me feel like something off the back page of "Farmer's Weekly"!'

Mae burst out laughing.

'Bryony! You're much prettier than anything I've seen there.'

Mae didn't mention that Richard had already sent a copy of the CD for them, and that it lay hidden in the dresser drawer out of her husband's sight.

Bryony contemplated her father's silent figure.

'So, what do you think, Dad? Isn't it great having a famous name in the family?'

She was aware of her mother holding her breath and mentally crossed her fingers. The day had gone well so far; she didn't want to spoil it but Dad was taking this grudge with Richard too far.

'Aye. I reckon so,' Chas grunted at last. The air lightened considerably. Mae raised an eyebrow in gratitude at her daughter.

'I'll put it on, shall I?' Bryony rose, taking the CD, dropping her father a kiss on the top of his greying mop of hair. 'Dear old Dad. I love you all the more when you act grumpy!'

'Not so much of the old,' Chas protested, but his mouth was twitching, and when the cheerful and heart-tuggingly familiar sound of the Richie Dene Band blasted out into the still corners of the beamed and flagged room, he didn't tell Bryony to turn it down.

'I should think there's hope for Rich yet. That must be a relief, Mum,' Bryony said to her mother afterwards, when they had gone into the kitchen to make a pot of tea, leaving Chas snoozing off his dinner.

'There could be,' Mae replied. 'Oh, I do hope so. This year has been so difficult, what with one thing and another.'

'I haven't helped, have I?' Bryony said in a low voice. 'Sorry, Mum. I don't know what comes over me sometimes. But then, I always was the black sheep, wasn't I?'

'Not at all!' Mae was shocked. 'It isn't easy being the youngest in a family, love. I should know. There are five years between your Uncle Jake and myself and my sisters were almost a different generation. Anna and Lucinda always seemed so grown-up to me. They used to tease me mercilessly.'

'Did they? I never thought of you being the youngest, Mum. Did you all get on?'

'Oh, more or less. Funny to think of us all so spread out now ... Anna in Australia with a family, Lucinda a career woman in the States and Jake in New Zealand. I'm the only one to have stayed on home ground.'

Mae slid the big black kettle on to the hob and grinned affectionately at her daughter.

'You look different. More ... grown up? A bit tired around the eyes? I hope Geoff's not working you too hard at Roseacre. You've got your own job to cope with, too, remember.'

'I doubt if Geoff would notice if I wasn't around.' Bryony sighed. 'He'd just ring for a relief milker and tell Helen they'd better step up the search for another farm hand!'

Her young voice was bitter and Mae looked up sharply.

'Oh? But I thought the three of you were getting on so well at the farm.'

'Oh, we are! I mean, we don't fall out or anything and Helen's been marvellous to me. Mum, I – I think I'm in love with Geoff. But to him I'm just Thea's pesky little sister. Sometimes I can't bear it!'

Hearing the throb of tears, Mae took her daughter's hand.

'Darling, I don't think you're seeing things clearly. Geoff's just lost his father. Mike Sanders was a huge presence in his life – in both their lives. The farm revolved around him. He made Roseacre what it is today.

'Right through the recent farming problems, particularly in the dairy trade, Mike kept their heads above water. They survived when others went under. Geoff's got a hard job stepping into his father's shoes. He's got a lot on his mind, love. I should imagine it's given him a few sleepless nights. Don't you think?'

'I suppose so,' Bryony said slowly. 'I hadn't really thought of it that way. Geoff's so good on farm. It doesn't seem a strain to him, though putting it that way, you could be right. Helen once said something similar but I'm afraid I didn't take it on board. You know me!'

'Yes, I know you!' Mae laughed. 'I should go on as you are doing, being at Roseacre and not making any demands. Give him time. One day he'll see you differently and, believe me, it'll be illuminating for him.'

Bryony's voice dropped to a whisper.

'And Thea?'

'Your sister's got other things on her mind at present.'

'Like Dominic Shane? Have you heard the rumour that's going round? Apparently there's a question mark over his integrity. Something to do with doping when he worked at Ferlann Ridge?'

'There'll always be talk, you know what people are. They get hold of a story and then it grows feet and legs. I like Dominic. He seems genuine enough to me.'

'Me, too and Geoff won't hear a word against him. Says he's a brilliant vet and you know how careful they are at Roseacre as to who looks after their cattle. No, it's the horse people who are spreading the gossip, namely Bob Perrit.'

Mae frowned.

'I do hope this doesn't mean trouble for Dominic – and for Thea. Oh, dear. You do have to wonder about Dominic Shane though. He could be one of those unfortunates who attract trouble no matter how clever or hard-working they might be. It's what your Gran Dene calls the black dog of fate snapping at the heels.'

'I hope not. It'll be tough on Thea otherwise. I think she really likes him....'

Bryony drew in a breath and let it out again in a long sigh.

'Mum, I don't want Thea to think I've fallen out with her. Not that she could be blamed for believing the worst about me and Geoff. But I behaved like an idiot.'

'No,' her mother said stoutly. 'You did your best. Call it growing pains. We've all suffered them one way or another. Ah, the kettle's boiling. Fetch the cake tin, please, Bryony, there's a chocolate sponge. What a good thing we Partingtons don't run to fat or we'd never be able to fasten our waistbands!'

Thea hadn't quite known what to expect of Ireland. On the Friday evening, Dominic had been waiting for her as the plane touched down. They had driven through the brightly lit streets of Dublin, Dominic pointing out places of interest, Thea craning her neck to see the enchanted city she'd always wanted to visit.

'We'll come back another time and I'll show you round properly,' Dominic promised. 'Look, there's the Liffey. Doesn't the water look black under the sky? That's how Dublin got its name. *Dubh lin* is the Gaelic for black water.'

Thea felt a little shiver touch her.

Soon they were out of the city, leaving the bright lights and heaving traffic far behind, driving through suburbs that were seemingly endless. Then, ahead, Thea saw the glitter of the sea and stretches of pearly sand spiked with dark rocks. Rain pattered on the windscreen and water gushed beneath the speeding tyres.

'The watery song of Ireland!' Dominic laughed. 'Don't worry. It'll clear up. Tomorrow is going to be fine.'

'I'm more concerned about here and now Dominic, where are we heading?'

'A little place on the Wexford coast I thought you'd like. It's an old fishing lodge turned into a hotel. I've made it my base for now. Anyway, I had to find somewhere that would take Trina.'

Thea looked over her shoulder at the dog who lay sprawled on the back seat, dozing blissfully.

'She seems in her element.' She looked back at the man by her side. 'Dominic, what's all this about?'

'Patience, girl.' He smiled. 'We're nearly there. Let's get you settled in and then I'll explain.'

They pulled into the forecourt of a quaint white-walled building where lights spilled out on to the wet flagstones. Inside, sound was muted, faces welcoming. Over a delicious meal in the low-ceilinged dining-room to the lilting background of an Irish harp, Dominic told Thea about his meeting with Murty Miles.

'Murty's a great fellow. No one could condone what he did but … well, money's a great temptation to anyone and at the time he was in desperate straits. And now there's his health problem. He's in a bad way, Thea. You have to make allowances.'

Thea gave a slow nod.

'So what now?'

'I've already spoken with the Irish Jockey Club. They've agreed to put things in motion. It'll be more a formality than anything. My name will be officially cleared and I'll be free to come back here to work if I so wish.'

'I see. And … Aisling?'

'Thea....' Dominic reached out and covered her hand with his. 'Whatever Aisling and I had, it's over. She's accepted it. There's no reason why we can't stay friends and one day I'll introduce you. But not just yet, I'm thinking. Meanwhile....'

The deep blue eyes that held hers spoke volumes.

'Let's get this business with the Jockey Club over with,' Thea said, a little breathlessly. 'It'll be easier to think straight then.'

'That's true.' Smiling, Dominic withdrew his hand and sat back in his chair. 'So, have you heard anything from that brother of yours lately?'

'We keep in touch.' This was safer ground. Thea fought to

control her treacherous emotions and won. 'Mum and I miss Richard lots. Dad too, though he'd never admit it. According to the reviews in the jazz columns, the band's going from strength to strength. Have you heard their album?'

'I'd have a job not to.' He grinned. 'Every time I turn on the car radio some DJ or other is playing a track from it. Tracey Kent looks like having a hit with that number of hers.'

Thea nodded.

'"Stardust". She used to sing it back at the Parkgate club.'

'I know.'

'The band is still here in Ireland. Somewhere.'

'I know,' he said again, pausing, laughter in his eyes. 'What if I were to tell you there's another reason for dragging you out here rather than staying in Dublin?'

Picking up the house menu from the table, he turned to the back page and pointed. *Special Entertainment*, Thea read silently. *Saturday, November 25. The Richie Dene Band and Tracey Kent.*

'That's tomorrow!' Thea cried. 'It never entered my head I'd see Richard while I was here. Oh, wow!'

Chapter Eight

Thea sat in the window embrasure of her hotel bedroom, gazing quietly out into the silent Wexford night. An almost full moon bleached the landscape of colour. To the right, the forest was a black line etched against a sky scattered with stars, whilst on her left, the sea broke gently on to the pebbly shore.

She had forgotten how evocatively beautiful Ireland was and felt moved to wonder how Dominic could ever have walked away from all this. It couldn't have been easy.

It dawned on Thea, suddenly and with a tug of pleasure, that in the few short hours she had been here she had fallen deeply in love with the country.

With Dominic, too. But that had been a more gradual process, an unfurling. First had come attraction, then friendship, and now this heady feeling that left her breathless and not altogether in command of her emotions.

Below, within the hotel grounds, lights spilled from some of the windows of the row of timbered cabins where guests who had their dogs with them were accommodated, the main premises being kept for those who did not.

'Cosy we are, Trina and myself,' Dominic had said as they lingered, relaxed and replete after an excellent meal, over liqueurs and coffee in the hotel lounge.

'Just as well, as it's turned out. I could be over here for quite some time.'

Thea had been astonished at how his words had affected her. Parkgate and no Dominic seemed an unthinkable prospect. No coming across him walking the dog along the estuary, no willing help to be had with one of her wayward ponies ... no looking out for his tall figure at the History Society meetings.

Dominic now felt very much part of her life and all at once the weeks stretched bleakly ahead.

'I'll miss you,' she'd said impulsively, and Dominic had smiled, little creases appearing round those amazingly blue eyes.

'That's great! But what's to stop you from coming out here at weekends?'

'Well, a number of things,' she replied ruefully, her heart lifting that he wanted her here at his side.

'I couldn't expect Dad to keep seeing to the ponies. He's not all that comfortable with them and he's bound to grumble. Mum's fine with them and I know she'd stand in if I asked her, but it wouldn't be fair. She's got enough on her plate.'

'Pity that little sister of yours isn't around,' he mused. 'Still, I dare say we could find a way round that.' Dominic held her gaze, lighthearted, teasing.

'So what else is keeping you at Parkgate?'

'School. The Christmas term is so demanding. Plays, children's parties, carol concerts – you know. I often wonder how we fit it all in but we do, somehow.'

'Do you like teaching?'

'Well ... yes, I suppose.'

Even to her own ears she sounded doubtful and made an effort to be more positive.

'Yes, I do. The day-to-day routine can be tedious, though that can be said of any job. I wouldn't mind a change of school but ... I don't know. It's convenient where I am. I remember how thrilled I was at getting the post. It's five years ago now. Seems longer.'

'Would you consider going away?' Dominic asked. 'A teacher friend of mine went out to Canada on a twelve-month exchange. He liked it so much he stayed.'

Thea swallowed. That wasn't exactly what she had thought he was going to say and the sense of despondency and disappointment that ripped through her was disturbing. Did he want her around or didn't he? The uncertainty was agony.

'No, I wouldn't go down that route,' she said. 'I know there are great opportunities to be had overseas, but I wouldn't walk out on Mum and Dad right now. It would be too much after what's happened with Richard and Bryony. The time to do it was straight after finishing university.'

'Have you any regrets?'

'Perhaps, just a few. At the time the decision seemed the right one. Geoff was around then of course. And I was able to have the ponies and do the showing circuit – something I'd always wanted to do. Anyway, I've liked being at home. I've never been very adventurous!'

'Depends how you define adventurous.' Dominic laughed. 'I'd call tackling the pony showing circuit enterprising. Anything to do with horses is. Speaking for myself, I've had enough "adventure" to last a lifetime!'

Thea looked at him, her blue eyes full of empathy.

'What happened to you was one of those horrible quirks of fate that takes matters entirely out of your control. But it'll get sorted, Dom. Then you'll be free to start again.'

'It was my belief that I'd already done that. I like the Parkgate job, get on fine with my colleagues and the work's interesting. It's a growing practice. There could be a partnership in the offing if I play my cards right.'

'You'll stay on, then? You may feel differently when your future is more … settled.'

'Think so?' he'd said obtusely, sending her a burning glance that had brought a wave of colour to her face and made her thankful for the concealment of soft lighting and flickering firelight.

They'd stayed on, talking and sharing viewpoints, touching on subjects Thea had never before aired or even thought to. What surprised her was how in tune they were. It had never been like this with Geoff. That had been a relationship based on mutual liking, familiarity and similar backgrounds. That was all.

Marriage with Geoff would have been predictable and safe.

She'd have done her best to be a good wife to him. They'd have settled into the same comfortable routines she had recognized and admired in Geoff's parents and in her own.

This – Dominic – was something entirely different and so exciting she wanted to hold her breath lest it should be suddenly snatched from her.

The clock had chimed the witching hour and Dominic, saying he should give Trina a last run before retiring, had kissed her good-night and left.

Thea had come straight up to her room and prepared for bed. Now, sitting at the window, washed by wintry moonlight, the memory of his kiss burned on her lips.

Catching the end of her long plait of hair, she twirled it absently. So much had been said over the course of the evening … and so much left unsaid. She hadn't spoken of the snatches from the past that dogged her sleep, sapping her energy and making her wonder if she were losing her wits.

Once, several weeks ago now, she had been going to tell Dominic about the dreams. They had gone to the Thatch at Raby with the intention of each spilling out their innermost problems. Dominic's confession had turned out so startlingly serious that by comparison the dreams – or 'timeslips', or whatever they were – had seemed harmless and rather insignificant, and she'd glossed over them.

But not before Dominic, with the reassuring insight of the true Celt, had put it simply.

'You must listen to the dreams, Thea. Sure, they could be trying to tell you something.'

A cloud sailed over the moon, flinging the sea and land into shadow. Yawning, Thea rose and went to bed. She had thought that here, away from Woodhey and all it represented, she would get some respite from those startling glimpses into the past. But the dreams came as they always did, plunging her back to when Parkgate had a thriving fishing community and the Harbour House was the tavern which served it.

*

With deft, powerful strokes, John Royle guided the boat in to slide against the Parkgate quayside. Heedless for once of the catch of mackerel and herring in the hold that comprised his livelihood, he seized the painter and sprang ashore.

With the tide almost at full, the boat rode barely a couple of feet below the quay and John, pausing only long enough to loop the painter round a bollard and secure it, headed off towards the tavern, leaving the boat – and the fish – bobbing idly on the water.

It was no good. Throughout the long hours of the night as he emptied his nets and recast them, John's mind had dwelled on Polly and what a fool he had been to let her go so readily.

Never once had he balked at wrestling against the sea at its most rough and dangerous, and yet when it came to the girl he loved and the prospect of her being given in wedlock to a man he considered his better both socially and financially, his nerve had failed him and he had backed down.

Polly had upped and fled and now he had no idea where she could be. But he'd find out. He surely would!

In the tavern yard, the stagecoach had arrived and the lad was changing the team. The new horses, fresh from the stable, snorted and stamped as they were hitched to the carriage, keen and ready to be away. In the doorway of the tavern, a handful of disgruntled travellers looked equally anxious to be gone, if for a different reason.

'Disgraceful! The worst night's lodging I have ever experienced,' muttered a middle-aged man whose coat of fine grey worsted, plain cravat and smoothly fitting breeches and highly polished footwear declared him not short of a coin or two.

'I shall not be stopping at this establishment again.'

'Nor will I.' His travelling companion, an older fellow in a tattered periwig, beribboned coat and breeches and high boots, gave a disparaging sniff. 'Man and boy, I've stopped off at the Harbour House on my way to Chester. Never again! The food! Not fit to throw to a dog! And as for the bed....'

He scratched suggestively at his wrist.

''Tis said the landlord's wife is sick to dying,' a gentle-faced lady

proffered. 'One must make allowances, I suppose. But dear goodness me, how glad I shall be to get home!'

'Passengers aboard!' the coachman hollered, and the small body
of people surged forward and boarded the vehicle, pushing ill-
temperedly in their eagerness to be free of the place where they
had spent such an uncomfortable night.

Waiting till the coach had rumbled out of the entrance, John
crossed the straw and dung strewn yard and entered the premises
of the tavern by the rear door. In the kitchen, a scarlet-cheeked
maidservant was stirring a large black cooking pot that hung over
the blazing fire.

Piles of dirty platters and pots littered every surface and the
floor was thick with trodden-in mud and spilled food. From the
tap-room beyond issued a loud lamenting from whom John rightly
judged to be the landlord.

'Listen to him!' The maid sniffed. 'Madam's taken a turn for the
worse, and it's only now hit him that she's bad. And not likely to
get over whatever it is that ails her, poor lady! Have you brought
the fish?'

'I'll see to it later.' John had stopped in his tracks. 'Mistress
Dakin is worse, you say? Have they sent for Polly?'

'No, nor is it likely. Don't know where she is, do they? Morning,
noon and night the master's bewailing the fact. But he's only got
himself to blame. I'd have done the same in her shoes and made
myself scarce.'

'Surely someone here must have an inkling as to where Polly is?'
John pressed.

The girl shook her head and a few greasy strands of hair came
adrift from her cap. She shoved it back, scratching absently.

'She could be dead and gone for all we know. Never a word has
there been. Never a word!'

At that moment the cooking pot boiled over with a hiss that
threatened to put out the flames, bringing the girl's attention
abruptly back to the matter in hand. Seizing a cloth, she pushed the
pot off the fire.

'Landlord's through there if you want him,' she said, with a jerk of her head. 'Not that you'll get much sense out of him. Don't forget the fish, will you? I'll need it for the stew.'

Moving on to the tap-room, John stood in the doorway and surveyed the scene before him. The low-beamed and flag-floored chamber, whilst displaying a masculine rough-and-readiness, had always been spick and welcoming, with a good fire burning and clear evidence of spit and polish.

Now, it was in a similar state to the kitchen. Used tankards littered every surface and a great deal of the floor space. A dismal fire struggled for life in the wide inglenook. There was a sour smell of strong ale. At a low table smeared with food and drink, Wallace Dakin sat with his head in his hands, mumbling and groaning and seemingly oblivious to all around him.

John cleared his throat, causing the man to glance up blearily.

'Who is it? Oh, it's you, Royle. What d'you want?'

John regarded the landlord with a mixture of pity and exasperation.

'Man, look at you! This won't get you anywhere, will it?'

'So what would I care, eh?'

Wallace picked up a jug at his elbow, righted an overturned beaker and poured a generous helping of the liquor, slopping it carelessly.

'Sit down, lad. Have a drink. It's good French brandy. You won't get better.'

'Ssh!' John cautioned, casting a furtive glance around. At this time of the morning the place was deserted, but voices carried and anybody could have been passing.

Common knowledge though Wallace's sideline was, such talk was dangerous. Those who benefited were adept at turning a blind eye; others knew better than to open their mouths. A few – a very few, it was true – had no such qualms. Tempting gains were to be had for certain information. John could have named one or two who'd have no qualms at seeing the Harbour House go under.

'Dakin, you must have more discretion. Put that jar out of sight. Here, let me.'

He took up the telltale beverage and tucked it away behind

some dusty vessels on a shelf next to the bar. Then, retrieving a fallen stool, he set it down opposite the landlord and sat on it.

'I've come about Polly. Can you tell me where she is?'

Wallace, frowning for a moment, hiccupped loudly and launched into a maudlin litany on how he hadn't set eyes on his beloved girl in months and what'd he'd give to be able to find her.

'Her mother's dying. Dying! She calls for Polly day and night and it does no good. Did you know how lovely my Marion was? I hardly recognize her. Wasted away, she is. Can scarcely raise her head and—'

'Stop this and listen to me!' John would never normally have spoken so out of turn to a customer, even one in his cups, but desperation drove him on.

'I'll willingly fetch Polly for you, if only you'd give me some clue as to where she is. Anything, no matter how slight. Do you understand what I'm saying? Come on, man, stir yourself! Look at it from Polly's point of view. She'd want to be with her mother at such a time, wouldn't she?'

'Aye.' Swaying unsteadily on his seat, Wallace raised his hands in a gesture of hopelessness and let them fall again to his lap. 'Can't say where she'd be. I've thought and thought but I can't come up with anything. She used to go tripping off now and again. It'd be that Fernlea woman that encouraged it. Stuck-up creature!

'Never had any time for me, that one. Too high and mighty to be associated with a common tavern keeper, brother-by-marriage or not. It must have vexed her sorely when I won the hand of her sister!'

Wallace let out a titter of remembered glee, stopping abruptly, his eyes narrowing.

'I wouldn't mind betting she's the one behind Polly's disappearance – always were thick as thieves, those two.'

'Do I take it we're speaking of Miss Jessica Platt?' John's face sharpened. 'Well, it's a start. I'd better see what can be done. And landlord, mind what I said. Not a word on certain issues. Understand?'

Without waiting for a reply, deaf to the pleas from the kitchen where the maid began a panicked shouting for her fish, John rose to his feet and hurriedly left the premises.

Outside the tavern, he paused to breathe in some fresh air and mull over what he had learned. Thinking about it, there could be some substance behind what Dakin had said. There was a marked similarity between Polly and her aunt and he could imagine them getting on well together.

On the one occasion he had met her he had taken to Jessica Platt. Unlike most of her class she had not treated him as an inferior and had seemed genuinely interested in his views and career aspirations. Very much her own woman, she had appeared to him.

Talk was that she and George Rawlinson had been seen out together more than once in the Rawlinson carriage and pair. There was always talk, but maybe Jessica had had her own motives for spiriting Polly away. He'd have to take care how he approached this....

Glancing down at himself, John grimaced. Unwashed, unshaven and stinking of fish, he was hardly in a fit state for calling on a lady, but when needs must.... He smoothed down his thickly waving, wind-tousled hair, brushed off his rugged fisherman's gansey and salt-encrusted trousers and, satisfied that he presented a fairly reasonable appearance, he squared his shoulders and started off for the house in the centre of the village.

A sudden clatter of hoofs from the rear made him look back. Turning into the yard of the Harbour House were two men clad in the unmistakable scarlet and black of officialdom.

John's stomach clenched. So his caution had come too late. He wondered where Polly's brother could be, Edward being more in command of his wits than his sire. There was nothing more he could do – except to convey the news to Miss Platt. But not before he had made his enquiries.

Spurred by the hope of finding his love, John continued on his way, whilst overhead the clouds began to release their cold burden of rain.

*

Thea woke up to raindrops pattering lightly against the window and the shushing of waves on the shore. She glanced at her travel clock. Not yet six. Late though she had been coming to bed, the habit of early waking was deeply ingrained. Swinging her feet to the floor, she padded across to the refreshments tray provided by the hotel, switching on the kettle.

She'd give herself the luxury of a cup of tea in bed, then shower and get into the snug needlecord trouser suit that had cost the earth and she'd never, until now, had occasion to wear.

In spite of the chilly rain showers it turned out to be a jewel of a day.

'All serious topics are strictly taboo!' Dominic ordered, ushering her into the car where Trina was already ensconced on the back seat. He got in beside her, fixing the seat-belt, and smiled roguishly.

'Today's purely for pleasure. Bit of sightseeing, lots of loitering in good eating places – maybe a stroll later on the beach. Have you ever walked with the wind fresh off Newfoundland on your face and the Atlantic breakers at your feet? No? Well, woman, you haven't lived!'

'Oh, really?' Glancing askance, laughter in her eyes, Thea entered readily into the banter. 'We've got mudflats! What more could you want?'

'I'm telling you, once you get acquainted with the coastline here you'll wonder what you ever saw in the sands of Dee. Who was the old gloom-monger who wrote that verse? I never can remember.'

'Charles Kingsley – I thought you liked the poem.'

'So I do. I'm just not in the mood right now for ghostly cater-wauling. Ready? Off we go, then....'

The day went by much as Dominic had suggested. Thea couldn't remember when she had last enjoyed herself so much. That evening, wind-blown, bright-eyed and happy, she changed into a long woollen skirt and soft cashmere jumper, and went downstairs to where Dominic was talking to a familiar bunch of musicians.

Richard had his back to her but turned as Dominic looked past him and directed her a smile.

'Thea!'

'Richie! Oh, it's so good to see you!'

Brother and sister embraced warmly, and then Tracey was there, a glowing Tracey, proudly displaying a hand on which sparkled an elegant diamond ring.

'Let's break open the champagne. It's actually happened. We're engaged!'

'Oh, I wish you every happiness, both of you. It's no great surprise but terrific all the same.'

'Isn't it just?' Richard put his arm round Tracey, smiling down at her. Happiness shone out of them, as if there had been a magical sprinkling of golden dust.

''Course, she's still got to sing for her supper. Did you know she's had offers to go solo?

'Couldn't have that, could we, you guys? This was the only way I could get her to stay with the band!'

Tracey shook her head helplessly, tut-tutting.

'Isn't it time you lot got tuned up? Or am I mistaken in believing that the crowd in there have come to be entertained?'

And entertained they were, with a fast and furious floor-thumping sound that went on long after the allocated time and had the audience leaving light of heart, a catchy tune on their lips.

For Thea, it turned out yet another late night. After the performance Richard wanted updating on the home front, which brought a sobering quality to the atmosphere.

'They're all fine, truly,' Thea said. 'Let's not spoil a great night with a fit of the mopeses.'

This was a phrase from childhood used by Mae if any of them looked glum, and Richard brightened accordingly.

'You're right. You will be sure and give Ma my love? Tell her about Trace and me?'

'I won't forget. Um … Richard?' Thea bit her bottom lip. It was no good. She had to ask.

'Have you seen anything of Aisling Cleary?'

'That little stirrer! No, I haven't. Why?'

'Just curious.'

Dominic had gone to replenish the glasses but Thea kept her voice low all the same.

'She does the jazz circuit, doesn't she?'

'The Irish one, yes. Maybe she's realized she's outnumbered and opted out for once. Or else Dominic's given her short shrift. Saying that, she's been amazingly upfront with him over this new light on the doping scandal.'

'He's told you about that, has he?'

'Briefly. That's what we were discussing when you came down. Good news, eh?'

'Very good. You couldn't fault Aisling's hand in resolving it, could you? It's just that … well, is she really as glam as she seems?'

'Probably. To quote Tracey, "she's the sort of female other women hate on sight". Oh, come on, Thea. Let's not talk about her.'

'You're right. Where are you heading for once this tour is over?'

'France, then Germany. We're due back in England in the early spring. My agent's got us a gig with a London club. Not bad, eh?'

'That's terrific.' Thea beamed at her brother and the dark moment passed.

On Sunday the weather turned appreciably colder, with a wintry nip that reminded Thea of home and the flight she would take that afternoon. The brisk wind that whipped up flecks of foam to sting their faces and tug Thea's hair from its plait to send it streaming wildly did not stop them from taking another long walk along the shore.

Huddling together, laughing, Thea and Dominic braved the bracing air and declared, back in the warmth of the hotel, hands cupping steaming mugs of frothy chocolate, that winter actually had a great deal going for it!

All too soon she was winging homeward, her mind reeling with images of a joyful time shared. At the airport, Dominic's lips had pressed possessively on hers.

'See you next weekend? I shan't let you go till you promise!'

'I promise,' Thea said eagerly.

Now, settled in her seat by the window, she watched the clouds beneath them and closed her hand over the small white pebble Dominic had picked up on the beach.

'A keepsake,' he'd said. 'One day we'll get it polished, shall we?'

It seemed a token for the future – of sorts.

Mae, putting out the festive sprigs of holly alongside the trays of cakes and pastries on her stall, paused to place her frozen finger-tips to her temple. The headache she had woken with that morning hadn't gone away. She only hoped she wasn't in for one of those debilitating migraines that had dogged her since she was a teenager.

It was early yet but the farmers' market already heaved with shoppers. Some of her home-bakes had sold even before she'd had time to put them on display – all to the better, since with Christmas rapidly approaching and the start of the additional Thursday market, she had come with enough stock to fill two stalls.

About to delve into her shoulder bag for the painkillers, Mae was suddenly confronted with a large queue and her attempt to stave off the discomfort of a throbbing head had to be abandoned.

It was a long morning, not helped by the flurries of snow that swept across the shopping area and the lowering sky that spoke of worse to come. Not helped, either, by the gossip that flew around the stalls.

'Heard about the new vet? The good-looking Irish guy, you know.'

'The one that's been struck off because of a doping scandal?'

'I don't think it's come to that yet, but it could. Freddie Barnes won't want trouble in the ranks. There are plenty of other practices. Customers have the right to switch if they're not satisfied – or don't go along with the type of staff being taken on.'

This last voice, belonging to the wife of Bob Perrit, who was responsible for starting the rumours, rang with vindictive glee.

'You use the Barnes practice, don't you Mae?' she called across the aisle. 'What does Chas think of it all?'

'Not a lot,' Mae replied neutrally. 'We don't have any stock now so we don't need the services of a vet as much as we used to. My daughter's had Mr Shane out to one of her ponies. We all liked him very much. Thea was well satisfied with the treatment he gave the mare.'

Her words effectively put an end to some of the talk, but Mae couldn't forget how viciously it had blown up. At around eleven-thirty a lull in trade gave her the opportunity she needed to swallow the tablets in the hope of some relief from the pain which had worsened.

The flask of the coffee she usually relished remained untouched. The thought of the cheese rolls she had hastily put together brought a wave of nausea.

'Good morning, Mae. Cold, isn't it?'

Mae looked up to see Geoff's mother, Helen Sanders, trim as always in a long green coat over elegant trousers and boots, a fur-trimmed hat on her neatly-coiffed hair. Mae, in thick cords and jumper, heavy jacket and woolly ski cap, felt at an immediate disadvantage.

'Helen. Good morning. Yes, it's a bleak one, isn't it? Seasonal, though.'

'Indeed.' Helen looked closer. 'Are you feeling quite well, Mae? You look a bit peaky.'

That really was the understatement of the day, Mae thought uncharitably. Peaky. Now wasn't that a typical Helen expression!

'Headache,' she murmured. 'It's nothing, it'll pass. What can I get you? Mince pies? There should be one of those lemon sponges that you like here somewhere. I've had a run on those this morning … ah yes, here it is.'

'Lovely, thank you. Now, what else shall I take...?'

Small red dots were appearing before Mae's vision and her heart sank. This was it. The forerunner of a real humdinger of a migraine.

'Have you heard the news about Dominic Shane?' Helen went on blithely. 'I find it very hard to believe myself.'

'Me, too,' Mae said, more sharply than she'd intended. 'I've no time for that sort of thing. Witch-hunting! It's untrue and damaging to the person or persons involved.'

'Quite.' As she chatted, Helen was making her selection of the goods on the stall. 'There, I think that's it. A dozen mince-pies – so delicious, I really don't know how you turn out such perfect pastry every time. The lemon sponge and two plum cakes for keeping. Well, you never know who might come this time of year, do you?'

Mae didn't answer. She picked up her calculator and tried to total the goods, but the figures danced crazily before her eyes.

'Mae?' Helen's voice came as if from a long way off. 'You really don't look yourself. I think you should go home. A little rest might do the trick. Look – I don't mind taking over here for you, if you'd like.'

'What?' Mae couldn't believe her ears.

'Your stall. You've worked terribly hard to put all this food together. It would be tragic for it to go to waste and besides' – she smiled, rather self-consciously – 'between you and me, I've always wanted to try a hand at running a stall.

'Mike used to say it would do me good to join the ranks here but I could never find the time. Or the courage! It was your Bryony who brought the subject up again. "You're a brilliant cook," she said. "Why don't you and Mum get together? You do the savouries and Mum can carry on with her yummy cakes and stuff".'

She smiled suddenly.

'But there, I'm rattling on.... Tell you what, I'll ask one of the other ladies to run you home. We'll sort something out here, Mae, don't worry.'

Through tight bands of pain and an explosion of coloured light, Mae found herself giving in to Helen's suggestion. All she wanted was home, the peace and quiet of a darkened room … and bed.

'So your foundation stock were all show champions,' Bryony asked, having sorted her way through a confusion of documents on Friesian bloodlines that went back to when Mike Sanders first started his herd.

'That's right.' Geoff took up one of the hard-backed volumes, opened it and pointed. 'Dad took photos of all the prominent animals, just for the record. But you must be bored to tears with all this.'

'No, I'm not. Really, I'm interested. Thea does much the same over the ponies. 'Course, I grew up with them so I know them – and it's on a much smaller scale than this.'

'True, though I wouldn't mind betting that, given the opportunity, Thea would go in for showing ponies in a bigger way.'

Bryony kept her head down and continued turning over the pages of pedigrees. It was rare for Geoff to mention Thea's name and she didn't quite know how to respond. When she looked up, however, Geoff was smiling at her steadily, his mild brown eyes unperturbed and reassuring.

'It's OK, Bryony, you don't have to feel awkward. Thea's your sister and you spend a lot of time here. Her name's bound to crop up in the conversation.'

'You … don't mind? You've got over it, the whole Thea thing?'

He nodded.

'She was right to back out when she did. Naturally I was upset at the time and my pride took a hammering.' He grinned. 'But maybe it was all for the best.'

'Free now to move on, and all that?'

'Absolutely,' Geoff said. 'And I have you to thank for helping me sort out these books. Dad knew exactly where to put his hands on certain numbers when he was writing out the papers for stock being sold. But I'm not so familiar with it all and I can't risk making mistakes. Cataloguing it properly is the answer.'

'A computer job, then.'

'Might be best. I've made a start, but this lot was in such a mix-up I gave up.' He paused. 'You never mentioned how the visit to Woodhey went. Was everything OK when you went home?'

'It was fine. Thea was away so I did the ponies for Dad. He's utterly useless around them and don't they know it!'

'Chas has got my sympathy. I was never much good around horses myself.'

'I know. Thea used to laugh about it. I can't see the difficulty, to be honest, but I guess we all have our strengths.'

She grinned, impish, her curly blonde mop framing her pretty face.

'Did they nip you?'

'All the time! They never, ever tried it on with Thea as far as I recall. She made handling them look so easy.'

'The way you do with the cattle. It's like I said. Every person to their own thing.... What is it?'

Geoff had picked up the local paper that was lying on the table and was studying it with interest.

'Remember that night club in Liverpool they spent so much money refurbishing? The Pink Parrot? It's opened up. D'you want to go?'

'Oh, do I!' Breathless, Bryony grinned at him across the table, all else forgotten. 'When?'

'Saturday? I could pick you up around eightish? That should leave plenty of time for you to get ready.'

'Make it half-past. Saturday's always frantic at the shop. Customers make such a mess of everything and it's Christmas party time. They try on every dress and trouser suit in the place and leave them out any-old how. I have to tidy the rails and vacuum the whole place before going home!'

'OK, eight-thirty it is. I don't know what time we'll get back, though. If I nod off over the milking on Sunday it'll be your fault.' He grinned.

All Bryony could do was smile at him incredulously. Geoff had actually asked her out! They were going clubbing! Wait till she told Liz....

'So he's come out of his gloom at long last?' her friend said later. She hurled herself on to the battered sofa, a slim girl with endless legs and shaggy hair, coloured this week her favourite shade of ruby, and stretched her arms in a parody of laconic boredom. 'Wow!'

'Oh, you! Geoff's not been down – and even if he has it's only to be expected. A farm like Roseacre is a big responsibility. You should see the pedigrees of the cattle, Liz. Dozens of show champions, and every one of them home-bred.'

'Amazing!' Liz affected a yawn, ducking neatly as the patchwork cushion in vivid primary colours came hurtling her way. Retrieving it, she dusted it down with studied care.

'This is one of our more respectable items. You should have more consideration. Didn't your mum teach you how to behave around the house?'

Bryony was saved a retort by the phone ringing. She snatched it up.

'Dad? Hi, there. Are you OK?'

'So-so. It's your Mum, Bryony. She's come down with one of her migraines. She was so bad I got her to the doctor. It seems her blood pressure is up. Doc Gillian said she's to have several days' rest and no messing. You know Gillian. You don't argue.'

'Come to think of it, Helen mentioned Mum having to skip the market and go home. I never thought anything of it. She was so made up with taking over the stall neither Geoff nor I could get a word in. Oh, poor Mum! It must be awful being stuck in bed, and at such a busy time, too.'

'I don't think she's in any fit state to care at present, love. That's why I'm ringing. You know how useless I am about the house. Could you come over this weekend and look after things, d'you think?'

'Me?' Bryony's world seemed to turn drastically, horrendously, upside-down. 'But what about Thea?'

'She's away on one of those special training courses teachers do. It's only a two-day effort but tomorrow she's going straight on to Ireland from Aberystwyth – that's where the course is being held.'

'Ireland?' Bryony queried, ignoring the rest. 'What, again?'

'Seems this is more than a casual weekend away. It's to do with Dominic Shane and this problem he's got. You'll have heard.'

'Yes,' Bryony said impatiently. 'Dad, I don't know if I can. There's work and … things. I'll have to get back to you, OK?'

'No, it isn't, Bryony. Your mother's health is important, and you're needed here.

'We're going to have to think up something to lighten your mother's workload. She's overdoing things. Right now, though, what with the house, your mum and those ponies on top of my own work, I don't know which way to turn.' He sighed.

'Thea said she'd skip the course and come back if need be. But I'm not having that. Her job is crucial.'

And mine isn't, Bryony thought woodenly.

'What about the weekend?'

'She can't give Ireland a miss. I told you, it's important. Oh, I think I heard your mum calling. Better go, Speak to you soon.'

The line went blank. Bryony replaced the receiver and turned a woebegone face on Liz.

'You heard?'

'I got the gist of it, yes. What are you going to do?'

'I can't miss this date with Geoff, Liz. I just can't! But ... poor Mum. She sounds bad and the doctor's been laying down the law.' Bryony picked up the coat she had just discarded. 'I'm going over to see her.'

'You can't go out again in this, it's blizzarding down and it's forecast for the night. Pity your old man didn't think to ring earlier. You could have spent your day off at Woodhey, instead of slogging your guts out at Roseacre.'

'I haven't been – oh, never mind. Liz, what am I to do?'

'About Saturday? Well, you've got your own life to lead, Bry. It's Friday tomorrow, anyway. Why not take a couple of days off work and look after your mum, but go out with Geoff on Saturday as arranged? Simple!'

'But it isn't,' Bryony said gloomily. 'Geoff'll throw a wobbler if he knew I was breezing off out and leaving Dad to it. He's like that. So terribly upstanding and always having to do the right thing. He'll say we can do the club another time and that would be that.'

And he'd be right, she thought with a horrible sinking feeling. Why did Mum have to be sick right now?

'I could always do Saturday night for you,' Liz said.

'What? Go out with Geoff?'

'Don't be daft. I meant fill in at the farm. I'm a good nurse – and your dad and I get on just fine.'

Bryony looked bemused.

'But that means you'll have to give up whatever plans you had yourself.'

'No problem.' Liz's direct green gaze was challenging. 'The offer's there, anyway. It's up to you.'

A few weeks ago Bryony knew she wouldn't have thought twice. Now, she was in a quandary. Should she go, and risk dropping several notches in Geoff's esteem? Or put him off till another time – if indeed there would be another time.

Chapter Nine

Frowning and a bit restless, Bryony prowled across the small living-room of the upstairs flat to draw the curtains against the snowy December night.

'If this keeps up, our date will be off anyway. Geoff will be hitching up the snow-plough! He likes to keep the lane to the farm clear in case of emergencies.'

Her friend, Liz, stretched out on the shabby sofa, ruffled her fingers laconically through her spiked, ruby-tinted hair, metal bangles jangling.

'I wouldn't get in a state about the weather, Bry. Snow never lasts all that long here. This could all be gone by morning. Like I said, I don't mind doing a Saturday stint at Woodhey. It's up to you, but I'd certainly go for it.'

'Thanks, Liz. I must confess I'm tempted, only— Oh, I don't know!' Bryony threw herself into an armchair by the radiator. 'Why does life always have to be so complicated?'

'It isn't. It's people who make the complications,' Liz pointed out reasonably. 'Would a cup of coffee help with the great decision? I'll make it if you like.'

'No, I'll do it. Anything to keep occupied.'

She was in the small galley kitchen, waiting for the kettle to boil, when the phone rang. Bryony snatched it up.

'Hello?'

'Bryony? It's me, Geoff. Just checking you got in all right in this weather.'

'Yes, I was fine, thanks. It was only flurrying when I drove home.'

'It's coming down heavens hard here. What's it like with you?'

'The same.'

'I've stepped up the cows' rations. Got to keep them warm and happy.'

'Yes, you do....'

There was a pause, in which the kettle boiled and clicked itself off.

'Bryony, are you all right?' he said at last. 'You seem quiet.'

'Well it's—' Hooking a stool under the breakfast bar with her foot, Bryony yanked it out and subsided on to it. 'It's about Saturday night. Dad rang just after I got in. Mum's come down with a migraine and apparently Thea's arranged to go away for the weekend. It can't be put off and Dad wants me at Woodhey to take over.'

'So? Where's the problem?'

'Saturday? The Pink Parrot – remember? I thought I'd come straight to Roseacre after work and get changed there. I could help with the milking then,' Bryony added in a rush. Anything to encourage things along – and it was a task she enjoyed in any case.

'Oh, I think we can safely leave that to Jim Stokes. I've already arranged with him to switch his hours. What's this about Mae? Is she very poorly?'

'Well, Dad says the doctor went on about strokes. It scared him a bit.'

'I'm not surprised. What a worry for you all. It isn't like your mum to be off-colour, is it? But I suppose with Thea being away Chas has got the ponies to see to on top of everything else.' The smile was obvious in Geoff's voice. 'That'll please him!'

'Oh, I can do the ponies, Geoff, if I fall in with what Dad wants, Liz has offered to stay at Woodhey for me on Saturday night.'

'Has she? That's decent of her. Though, thinking about it, what with the weather and now this, it might be best to postpone going out till the following weekend.'

Bryony's grip tightened on the phone.

'We will go then, though? Promise?'

'Of course. The snow's bound to have cleared by then. When

were you planning to go to the farm? After work on Friday? Why
don't I pick you up from the shop and run you over there? That'll
save you risking the byroads in your car. The pick-up's brilliant in
these conditions.'

'Are you sure?'

'Sure I'm sure!' He laughed. 'We can't have you coming to grief
on the ice, can we? Chin up. Do your bit for the family and we'll
have a great night out on Saturday week instead. It'll be good to
have some time at Woodhey, won't it?'

A good opportunity to get relationships back on an even keel, he
means, Bryony thought ruefully. On the heels of this came the realization that Geoff was right. Far from the disappointment she
expected at missing out on the yearned-for date, she was aware of
an overwhelming sense of relief.

Doing the daughterly thing wouldn't be at all difficult now that
Geoff had pointed out there'd be the following weekend to look
forward to.

'Yes, it'll be fine,' she replied. 'What d'you bet the place will be
a mess? Dad's hopeless at keeping house.'

'Maybe, but you won't find a better farmer anywhere on the
Wirral,' Geoff returned succinctly. 'Right, then. Get the bus into
work tomorrow and I'll meet you at around six. OK?'

'Thanks, Geoff.'

'No problem. Take care, love. See you.'

The line went dead. Bryony sat on, smiling dreamily at the
receiver, coffee long forgotten. Geoff had been so dependable and
reassuring ... and he'd called her 'love'. He wasn't normally given
to endearments. As far as she could remember, he'd never referred
to Thea by anything other than her given name even when they
were going out together.

This, surely, had to be significant?

Thea flicked on the windscreen wipers against the sleety rain that
fell, and slowed her pace accordingly. Trust the weather to turn
nasty, and just when she was running late anyway! What with her
class of six-year-olds on a high due to Christmas approaching and

the usual ends to tie up in the classroom before she could happily leave for the weekend, it truly had been one of those days.

Thea frowned, the little wrinkle that was all too obvious of late appearing between her brows. She'd hated leaving Mum so poorly, looking pale and worn, the bedroom darkened because the daylight hurt her eyes, the scent of the lavender oil the girl in the health shop had recommended drifting on the air.

But Mae had insisted Thea went ahead with the arrangements for the weekend.

'I'm feeling better, really. The painkillers the doctor prescribed are working. I slept well last night and I do believe it's done me good. Such a nuisance. I haven't had one of my heads for ages.'

'You've been overdoing it, Mum. Why don't you make it easier on yourself and drop one of the farmers' markets? Maybe just do Neston, as it's the closest to home.'

Mae closed her eyes wearily.

'Oh, please, not now, Thea. I've already had your father saying as much when he knows what a boon the extra cash has been.'

'Sorry.' Thea bit her lip on the argument for the time being. 'Anyway, I've taken a casserole out of the freezer for Dad's evening meal. All he has to do is pop it in the microwave. I'll grab a sandwich at the airport, rather than risk being late by coming back here.'

'Very sensible. What about the ponies? Dad gets in such a frazzle over them.'

'I know, and there's absolutely no need. I've left them a deep straw bed and there's plenty of hay in the shelter. All he has to do is check the water troughs for ice and give them some concentrates.'

Thea glanced at her watch.

'Mum, I must go. It's my turn to take assembly and I need to read through my notes first. Are you sure you're all right? Do you want anything?'

'No, thank you. I might have another sleep.' Mae managed a small smile. 'You get off now, darling, and be careful on the lane with all this snow.'

At least the snow had almost gone, Thea consoled herself as she dropped a gear for the junction ahead. Another vehicle was approaching, and Thea pulled as close as she could to the verge to let it pass on the narrow country road.

Slushy ice showered up from the wheels as the car swished by with a cheerful acknowledgment of the horn. In her dipped headlamps Thea glimpsed her sister's blonde curls and Geoff's serious profile. They looked inordinately chummy and Thea's heart twisted.

She wondered where they were heading and what they'd been talking so animatedly about that neither one had taken in who she was. Neston, probably, where Bryony had her flat-share.

Shrugging, she drove on to the junction and made the turn, setting her sights on the M53 and ultimately, Liverpool Airport.

Several hours later, after a delayed and turbulent flight due to the inclement weather conditions, Thea arrived at Dublin with only one thought in mind; to be enfolded in Dominic's embrace and be whisked away to his snug retreat on the coast.

This was the fourth time she had made the journey and the airport at Dublin was now familiar territory. As she disembarked from the plane into the rainswept darkness of the wintry evening, her eyes sought the bright lights of the exit terminal and Dominic's tall figure amongst the huddled crowd who were waiting to meet people off the flight.

He wasn't there.

Not especially alarmed, since none of the planes seemed to be running to schedule, she assumed he'd have whiled away the time in the passenger lounge with a coffee and a newspaper. She murmured a greeting to a cheery member of the ground staff and, weekend bag in hand, pushed her way through the milling throng.

But he wasn't in the waiting area or any of the cafés.

She checked her mobile for a text, but that, too, was frustratingly blank. A call to his number told her that he was not available at present, which meant there was a chance he had been held up and was on the way here.

Meantime, Thea went to reception to see if there was a message.

'Sorry, miss, nothing from a Mr Shane.' The girl behind the desk flashed a professional smile. 'Can I get you a cab, perhaps?'

'No, that's fine, thanks,' Thea replied. 'Something must have happened for him not to have met the plane. I'll go for a cup of tea and see if he turns up. If he doesn't, could you recommend a hotel for the night?'

'Sure, no problem at all. Will I take your name? Then I can direct him when he comes.'

Giving her details, Thea picked up her luggage that seemed all at once to have grown heavier and, regretting the whim that had caused her to pack extra jumpers for those bracing winter walks along the bay, she headed for one of the airport cafés from which there was a clear view of the entrance.

Half an hour later there was still no sign of Dominic. By now it was gone ten, too late to make the journey to Wexford. She decided the best thing would be to take advantage of the receptionist's offer and spend the night in Dublin.

Tired, hungry, her concern over Dominic's unprecedented desertion mounting, Thea was glad to reach the small but pleasant hostelry on a quiet square, and the impersonal warmth of the single room to which she was directed. Dinner was long finished.

Availing herself of the refreshments provided, Thea made yet more tea and put an order through for yet another sandwich, after which she tried again to get in touch with Dominic. It was hopeless. Either he wasn't answering the phone or he'd left it somewhere by mistake … an all too frequent occurrence.

Midnight had begun striking from the many church clocks of the city as Thea climbed wearily into bed. After a particularly arduous day and having so much on her mind, she knew she was in for a disturbed night. She wasn't far wrong. The last resounding chime had barely died away before Thea was plunged into vivid dreams.

'I need to see your mistress,' John Royle told the maid who answered his summons at the door of Fernlea. 'Tell her it is a matter of utmost urgency.'

About to protest, the maid took a closer look at the caller's troubled face and nodded.

'You'd better come in. I'll tell Miss Platt you're here.'

John entered the house and stood impatiently in the panelled hallway. It struck him latterly that it had not occurred to him to come by the usual tradesman's entrance, but then this was no usual call.

In the general surroundings he was more aware than ever of his workaday appearance and the obvious reek of fish that hung about his person. Half wishing he had delayed long enough to get into some decent linen and his Sunday suit, John heard the distant female interchange from a room beyond and willed the girl to hasten.

Moments later the maid came bustling back along the carpeted passage towards him.

'The mistress will see you immediately. Please follow me.'

John was shown into a pretty drawing-room where Jessica Platt sat at a polished writing desk. Aware of the door closing behind him with a discreet click, John sketched a bow.

'Miss Platt. Good morning. My apologies for having disturbed you, but—'

His words were waved aside.

'Get on with it, man. No doubt you have good reason to be here. Tell me what it is.'

'I was actually on my way to see you over another matter entirely, but something rather alarming has happened and ... I'd better start at the beginning. I had reason to call on Wallace Dakin at the Harbour House. As I was leaving, two excise men turned into the inn yard. Mistress, I won't beat about the bush. The Harbour House's involvement with the contraband folk is no secret hereabouts. What I've just seen did not look good for your sister and her man.'

Jessica Platt's mouth tightened.

'What you say doesn't surprise me one jot. I make no secret of it, John Royle. Words cannot express how often my brother-by-marriage has been reminded of his indiscretion in these matters.

But there you have it. The man's a fool and a drunken one at that.'
She lifted her chin.

'What happens to him is no more than he deserves. However, my sister is a different case. Rest assured, should anything unto-ward occur at the tavern, her well-being will be taken care of. I hope with all my heart that this visit you saw was not an official one. Marion is in extremely poor health. Such trauma would do her absolutely no good at all.'

'But – begging your pardon, ma'am – it looked uncommon offi-cial to me.'

'Then we shall have to hope and pray that you are mistaken! It could well be that they were passing and felt in need of some liquid refreshment. If not, there is nothing can be done about the excise men in their working capacity. It might be best to forget what you saw, John Royle.'

John's deep-grey eyes narrowed. He felt he could be treading troubled waters here. How much did the lady of Fernlea really know of the illicit trading that went on in the dark of the moon? Was she involved herself? He wouldn't have been at all surprised.

Jessica Platt cleared her throat.

'You mentioned another matter. Am I to know what it was about?'

'Yes, ma'am. I wish to speak of your niece. Polly and I have a – a fondness for each other. I wanted to ask for her hand, but unhap-pily the move was thwarted.'

'Well put, man. So what now?'

'I think you may know of Polly's whereabouts.'

'I?' The strong black brows rose archly. 'Fie, sir. What gives you that idea?'

'I know how Polly confided in you. Her removal was too swift to have been done under normal circumstances. Someone who could pull strings had to have had a hand in it. Begging your pardon, ma'am, but that someone could only be yourself.'

In his need, John unwittingly twisted his cap in his salt-rough-ened hands.

'I love Polly and want her for my wife. Please, ma'am. Could you let me have her current address.'

For a few trying seconds Jessica hesitated. Then she gave a little shrug and turned back to her desk. Taking up a sheet of writing vellum, she dipped the quill into the inkwell and wrote what he requested, sanding it lightly to dry the ink.

'There you are, young man. You will find Polly at this house. I must add that she is settled in her new life and not unhappy. Giving it all up will not be undertaken lightly. But then mayhap true love will prevail.'

Her tone was wry and slightly mocking. Taking the sheet of paper, John folded it neatly and stowed it away in his trouser pocket.

'My thanks, ma'am. I assure you that in this case, it will.'

She smiled at that, her fine dark eyes twinkling.

'I believe you, John Royle. May God go with you. Mind you give Polly my deepest regards when you see her.'

Next instant she had summoned the maid and John was being shown out.

He put a fair distance between himself and the house before glancing at what she had given him.

Polly Dakin, c/o Jerome Kendrick Esquire, 3, Stanley Place, Chester.

The elegant copperplate danced before his gaze. So that's where Polly had vanished to! She had gone into service with one of the Chester gentry and would be working all hours as a kitchen maid, or perhaps a nursemaid if she were lucky. At least he could now go and seek her out.

All thought of the running tide and the catch that awaited fled. First he would go home and spruce himself up, then he would hire a horse from the livery yard and be on his way.

Within the hour he was doing just that, trotting the hired hack smartly down the village street. Passing the Harbour House, he ranged the yard for any signs of upheaval. All seemed undisturbed. Mollified, since he had a certain affection for the old rogue of an innkeeper, John applied his heels to the horse's sides and pressed on.

He was approaching the Chester Road when a fellow rider came cantering towards him, pulling up sharply in a cloud of dust from the unmade country lane.

'Ho, there, John! Where are you bound in such a hurry?'

The rider was Edward Dakin.

John and Edward had been boyhood pals. As youths their way had parted somewhat. John had had a living to make and the hardship of battling with tide and weather had swiftly made a man of him, whilst Edward, the only son of a thriving establishment and never short of a coin or two in his pocket, had enjoyed the sort of freedom most young men could only dream of.

Until Susanna Marsdon had come along. Edward's enchantment with the parson's pretty daughter had pulled him up short and the drinking and carousing had stopped. Now Edward, by all accounts, was joining the rigid ranks of the legal profession.

John reined in his horse.

'Edward – good day to you. Your horse is in a lather. Is all well?'

'Aye, but there's been a spot of bother at the tavern. I had to ride into Neston to check out some details at the firm of solicitors I'm with. All sorted now, fortunately.'

'I'm glad. Would it have been to do with a certain visit from the authorities? I chanced on them earlier.'

'Did you, indeed? Well, it stands to reason you won't be blind to what goes on there. Nobody is. Father's got away with it this time. By the skin of his teeth, I might add.' Edward lowered his voice. 'The cellar had been cleared of certain goods only last night, happily for all concerned. Father must watch his tongue, though. That's how there came to be an inspection.'

'I did try to warn him.'

'Did you? You're a good man, John. Polly missed her chance with you.'

'Not entirely.' John's eyes glimmered. 'I've just come from Fernlea.'

'What – you bearded the lioness in her den?' Edward gave a shout of laughter. 'Brave man! Jessica's a woman one doesn't care to cross. Though she's not a bad sort once you get to know her. What happened?'

'I wanted to know where Polly was biding.'

'And?'

John patted his top pocket, where the sheet of paper giving Polly's abode rested.

'I'm on my way to see her.'

Edward looked impressed.

'Well, I'd best not hold you up any longer. Just one more thing....' His face sobered. 'Mama is failing fast. When you see Polly, you might tell her not to linger.'

'I'm sorry, Edward.'

'Yes, well, Mama never was strong.' Edward gathered up his reins. 'Best of luck, John! Give Polly my fondest love and tell her I hope to see her soon.'

A farewell salute, and they went their separate ways. John's heart sang as he spurred his horse along the open highway to Chester. Not long now and he would see his Polly again.

He was not to know that Polly was trudging homewards, weary and footsore, having left the main route with its many hazards for the unwary traveller, and was taking instead the quieter sandy lanes that wove across country towards Parkgate.

'Oh, no! You'll miss each other! You must turn back!'

Thea jerked awake, her cry strangled in her throat, the rattle of iron-shod hooves on the gritty road becoming the strident buzzing of a telephone at her elbow. Fogged with sleep, it took a moment or two to realize where she was. The phone rang on. Thea reached out to answer it.

'Miss Partington?' The broad Irish brogue of the hotel night attendant was harsh in her ear. 'Sure then, if there isn't a Mr Shane here, asking to see you. Hold on a minute, please. I'll put him on the line.'

It was pitch dark. Pushing her heavy weight of hair back from her face, Thea struggled up in the bed and switched on the bedside lamp. The room sprang into brightness. Squinting, she saw with a groan that her small travel clock indicated five-twenty in the morning. Next instant, Dominic's voice came over the line.

'Thea, are you there?'

'What? Yes, of course but ... Dominic, what's going on? Have you any idea what time it is?'

'Getting on for six, I should imagine. Thea, I need to speak with you and I don't have much time to spare. The hotel is rustling up coffee and something to eat. Could you come down? I'll be in the foyer.'

'Oh but ... oh, very well. How did you find me?'

'You left a message at the airport, remember? I came straight over here. Thea, this is urgent. I need to get back but I must see you first.'

'Give me five minutes to get dressed and I'll be there.'

She rang off, feeling horribly disoriented and uncharacteristically out of sorts. She never had been one for dramatics and Dominic, with his impulsive ways and apparent knack for landing himself in the thick of trouble, really was pushing his luck this time.

But he had made an effort to see her, a small inner voice reminded. And emergencies could crop up in any place and at any time. The least she could do was go and hear him out.

Leaving the still-tempting comfort of the bed, she splashed her face with cold water to wake herself up, scrambled into some clothes and left the room.

Dominic was seated in a secluded corner of the hotel foyer, a tray of steaming coffee and hot toast on the table beside him. He rose as she appeared and went to greet her, taking her hands. His face was unshaven, his hair tousled, his eyes troubled and shadowed, and some of Thea's exasperation dispersed.

'So there you are.' He gave her an eager smile. 'Thea, I'm sorry about yesterday. Something cropped up and— Come and have breakfast and I'll explain.'

Without a word she sat down and let him pour the coffee. Dominic helped himself to toast, spreading butter and marmalade, eating hungrily, whilst she sipped the hot, reviving beverage and felt its warmth spreading through her veins.

'It's Murty,' Dominic began. 'Murty Miles the jockey? I was on my way to meet you yesterday as usual when I had a call from the hospice. He'd taken a turn for the worse and wanted to see me. What else could I do but double back?'

'You never thought to put a word through to the airport? Text me? Ring as soon as you had the chance?' All Thea's indignation rose once more. 'I was worried sick. I thought you'd had an accident or something.'

'Thea, I can't apologize enough. I did try and get in touch but you know me. By the time I'd reached the hospice the wretched phone needed charging, and then it was all systems go and I didn't get the chance again to ring. I've been with Murty most of the night.'

'Is he…?'

'I'm afraid so. He passed away peacefully just after three this morning.'

'Oh, I'm sorry.'

'He just slipped away, Thea. I promised him I'd make the necessary arrangements. He's no folks of his own so what else could I do? *Had* no folks of his own, I should say.'

Dominic pushed the plate of toast away as if it suddenly tasted of cardboard, burying his face in his hands.

'What a dreadful end for a rider like Murty! I keep seeing him at the track, going all out for the winning post, the crowd roaring fit to burst your eardrums and the horse doing its utmost for him. Murty was like that. He could get the best out of the most difficult ride of the bunch.'

With mute sympathy, Thea pushed his coffee closer. Rubbing his face wearily with his hands, Dominic sent her a brief smile and picked up the cup.

'I suppose,' Thea said slowly, 'you'll need to get back and deal with the official side of things. Do you want me to come with you?'

'No, thanks all the same. I'll manage, It wouldn't be fair to drag you round with me.' He sighed. 'Not the sort of weekend we had planned, is it? I feel bad at having to desert you like this but, being as you're here, why don't you join your brother and the band? They were going on to the Midlands, weren't they? Roscommon, if I remember rightly. You'd love it there.'

'I'm sure, but is it worth the hassle? I'd need to hire a car and I'd have to be back in Dublin tomorrow for the seven o'clock flight to Liverpool.' Thea shrugged dismissively. 'It's not really on. And another thing. Mum isn't very well. So perhaps it's best to shelve things for now.'

'Mae's poorly?' Dominic was all concern. 'What's wrong? Is it serious?'

'I hope not. Mum's been prone to migraines in the past and this one struck just at her busiest time. I don't suppose my sister has any idea about it – Bryony's pretty useless at coping anyway. That leaves just Dad at home to look after everything.'

'Ponies and all?'

'Ponies and all! Initially I was tempted to put this weekend off. I only carried on with the arrangements at Mum's insistence – and because you'd mentioned having some positive news about the case with the Jockey Club.'

This provoked a grin, a rueful one.

'Went right out of my head, so it did! It seems the solicitor I'm using believes it should be a cut and dried case. It's more a matter of putting the record straight, ending with an automatic granting of a pardon on my part, rather than a full scale legal procedure. Good news, isn't it'

'Excellent! Did he say how long it would take?'

'He thought weeks rather than months. Meantime I'm free to get back to England and carry on as before. Well, there's nothing to keep me here now Murty's gone. The old rogue! One heck of a load of trouble he made, and all I can do is anguish over his passing!'

Dominic looked suddenly bleak again and impulsively Thea reached out and took his hand.

'It's maybe for the best. Look at it this way. He'll likely be up there riding his winners!'

'I don't doubt it for one moment.' Dominic drew in a long breath and let it out again in a gush. 'So, what would you like to do? Get an early flight home? I could take you to the airport.'

'It might be best,' Thea said.

*

During the flight back, Thea did a great deal of thinking. Exhausted and upset though he was, there was no doubting Dominic's feelings for her.

'Thea, I promise I'll make it up you,' he had told her at the airport. 'I'd really wanted to make this weekend special. Perhaps now isn't the time to say this but I'm going to anyway. Thea, I love you. I think – hope – that you feel the same way about me. No, don't say anything now. Let's wait for the right moment.'

'All right.' Her heart had bumped chaotically. 'Will you ring me? Soon?'

'Of course I will. Chances are I shall be back at the Neston practice by next weekend. We can talk everything through then.'

Talk everything through. Now, the words rang in Thea's head. For her part, there were so many loose ends to tie up she hardly knew where to begin.

The Harbour House, standing empty and forlorn despite all the thought and hard labour lavished upon it.

Then there were the awkward rifts in the family – first Richard, then Bryony. Thea still hadn't made things right between herself and Bryony and, if she were honest, she had no inclination to do so.

Then there was the matter of the dreams. At some point she would have to tell Dominic the full extent of them – needed, desperately, to take him into her confidence.

Would he think her deranged if she launched into the pantomime of what had occurred at the Harbour House a couple of centuries earlier?

She had already touched on the subject. And Dominic had been reassuring.

How well she remembered his reaction. He hadn't dismissed the dreams out of hand the way Geoff had done.

But … and it was a big 'but', there were times, like that very morning when she had woken shouting a warning to a man who was long dead and gone, when she truly believed she was out of her mind. So practical, level-headed Thea Partington had, it seemed, been taken over by the past! Or at any rate, her subconscious self had.

Delving into her bag on her lap where she sat in the narrow seat of the aircraft, she closed her fingers over the small white pebble she and Dominic had found on the beach that first time she had gone to Ireland. There was comfort in its smooth shape.

A keepsake, Dominic had said. In the sunlight the surface was shot with crystal and shimmered like a fairy stone. To Thea the object signified a turning point in her life, and she stowed it carefully away again in the side pocket of her bag.

Over the intercom came the announcement that they would soon be landing and they had made good time. Above flashed the lights telling passengers to fasten their seat-belts. Thea did so, craning her neck to look out as the aircraft broke through drifting cloud in its descent, and the great sprawling metropolis of Liverpool spread out far beneath them.

Thea had deliberately not contacted Woodhey to tell them of her change of plans. She thought what a pleasant surprise it would be for them to have her turn up unexpectedly and take over the reins.

Knowing her father, the kitchen would be a tip, dirty pots everywhere, no clean towels, the stove in need of raking out and goodness knows what else. But the smile of welcome on his face would make the homecoming worthwhile.

Thea couldn't wait to be there.

On arrival at Liverpool she was glad to see that the snow had gone from the runways and the sky was clear. Passing through the terminal gates, she collected her luggage and went to pick up her car.

Presently she was speeding along the ribbon of motorway towards the Wirral peninsula and home, coming off on to the quiet roads of her childhood. Snow still lay here in glistening swathes on the verges and fields on either side.

Deciding to put extra straw down for the ponies (spoiling them, Dad would grumble) Thea turned in at the unmade drive to Woodhey that was rutted and potholed from the trundling passage of decades of tractor wheels.

In the yard, all was quiet. Thea parked the car and made for the back door, the two tabby cats streaking up from the barn to be let in. Inside, a shock awaited. Instead of the expected chaos, the kitchen was neat and sweet smelling, lunch dishes dealt with and stacked neatly on the table, saucepans scoured and put away on the rack. Even the floor was pristine from recent mopping.

In the vast chimney breast, the Aga burned in that comforting manner that spoke of diligent refuelling.

Growing more mystified by the second, since this was clearly none of her father's handiwork, Thea went through to the dark-beamed passage that led to the front of the farmhouse. Voices from the sitting-room grew steadily louder as she hurried along it.

'Hi, Mum. It's me ... oh!'

Three astonished faces turned towards her from where the family were gathered round the hearth. Mum – looking much improved, Thea noticed – and Dad, and—

'Bryony! Well, what a surprise!'

The irony in her voice wasn't lost on any of them. Chas began to bluster.

'Aye, well. It was my idea to fetch her over, Thea. Your mum being so poorly and that.'

'And very pleased I was to see her,' Mae cut in firmly. 'I'm feeling so much better. It's nice to be pampered a little.'

She couldn't have said a worse thing. Thea's chin came up fiercely.

'I did offer to give the weekend a miss, Mum.'

'I know you did, darling, but I wouldn't have had your plans ruined for the world. Thea, what are you doing back so early? We didn't expect you until late tomorrow.'

'Obviously. Oh, well, it's nice to be missed! If I'd known how it was here I might have stayed over in Ireland for the duration.'

'Oh, get a grip, Thea!' Angry colour swept Bryony's pretty face. 'Why shouldn't I be here? Woodhey's my home, after all.'

'Huh! What miracle occurred for you to work that out? Let me guess. It wouldn't be due to Geoff?'

Mae put her hand to her still throbbing forehead.

'Thea, please!'

'Come on, Thea, lass,' Chas said with an anxious glance at his wife. 'You're upsetting your mother. She'll be bad again if we're not careful. This isn't like you at all.'

Thea stood, her fists clenched, looking from one parent to the other.

'Dad. Mum ... I'm sorry, but Bryony and I have got to have this out.'

'Then go and do your shouting in the kitchen and stop upsetting your mother,' Chas said in the sort of voice he had used when they had misbehaved as children.

'Good idea.' Bryony stood up. 'Come on, Thea. I guess I had this coming to me. Let's get it over with.'

She stalked out of the room and Thea, who was now calming a little and feeling the first pangs of guilt, made her parents a helplessly apologetic little gesture with her hands and followed her sister out, closing the door purposefully behind her.

Chapter Ten

'So, go on!' Thea faced her sister accusingly across the flagged floor of the kitchen. 'Let's hear what you're doing here after all this time.'

'What's it to you?' Bryony snapped.

Her manner was an irritating reminder of the headstrong girl who had flounced out of the house several weeks earlier, causing so much upset, and only served to rile Thea further.

'Bryony, you make it perfectly clear you want nothing more to do with any of us, then I walk in and find you chatting away with Mum and Dad as if nothing had happened. It doesn't make sense.'

'Of course it does. If you weren't so obsessed with your own life you'd see that.'

Bryony took a deep breath, as if struggling hard for calm, speaking in slightly more moderate tones.

'It was Dad who asked me round. I came once before when you'd gone off for the weekend and saw to the ponies for him – you know how he hates it when they play him up. This time he was worried about Mum. I think it had all got on top of him. Anyway, he wanted me here so I came.'

'I don't believe you. Dad was incensed when you upped and left. He wanted nothing more to do with you or Richard.'

'Oh, come on! Dad's like that! All bluff and bluster. He doesn't mean half of what he says. Once he's had a good shout and got things off his chest he's generally fine.'

'And is that what you counted on? Forgive and forget? Dear little Bryony, Daddy's favourite, the one who could do no wrong?'

The moment the words were out, Thea regretted them. What was happening to her? Why was it that she, the rational one, could no longer seem to keep in control? The very sight of her sister standing before her, the pretty face flushed and defiant and blue eyes sparkling, made her want to deliver it a good slap! In her mind's eye she saw Bryony and Geoff in the café together, when Geoff to all intents and purposes was supposed to be engaged to her.

Their heads had been bent together, close, intimate. And then there had been the gossip Bryony had spread about Thea and Dominic, with no foundation to it at all at the time.

'You're jealous,' Bryony cried. 'Clever, golden girl Thea! Jealous of pathetic little me! What is it, Thea? Are you miffed because you think I snatched Geoff from under your smug little nose?'

'Well, didn't you?'

'Actually, no.'

'Oh, I think so. You always did like him. So at what point did a silly teenage crush become a sly campaign to get him for yourself? It was blatantly obvious what you were up to. Toadying up to him and to Helen. Making yourself indispensable at the farm. Bryony Partington, milking cows? Since when?'

'Hasn't it occurred to you that I might enjoy it? I like working with the stock. And while we're on the subject of animals, take note that I've spent hours today mucking out your ponies while you go off enjoying yourself—'

'Girls! Stop this!'

The two of them spun round to find their father in the doorway. His hands were clenched, his face tight and troubled.

'What's got into you both? You can be heard all over the house. Your mother's weeping. She's not well, or had you forgotten?'

Bryony's face puckered.

'Oh, gosh. Poor Mum. I'm sorry. I ... oh, it's no good. I might as well go. Better push off and get my things together.'

She made a distressed little cry in her throat and shot off, her feet pounding on the bare oak treads of the back-stair. Thea listened to the sound of her sister's departure getting fainter, then the click of the bedroom door closing. Swallowing hard, she faced her father. The silence stretched on and on.

Chad shook his head in disbelief.

'What in the world were you thinking of to lose your rag like that? All that yelling…. Your mother was on the mend, for pity's sake. This is enough to put her right back again.'

Thea struggled with tears.

'I know and I'm sorry. Dad, I couldn't help it. She's caused so much trouble. These past weeks have been dreadful. And then I come in and find her sitting here as if she's done nothing wrong and everything is hunky-dory again. Then she tells me it was you who asked her to come.'

'I was worried sick about your mother. She wouldn't hear of you cancelling your plans and after what the doctor said I needed some support. Bryony happened to be around. That's all there is to it.'

'Is it? Is it really? Oh, don't look at me like that, Dad. What do you expect me to think? If I had been the one causing all the trouble it would have been a different matter! Would you have been as quick to call me home to look after things? I don't think so.'

'Thea, that's not true.' Chas breathed heavily as he struggled to frame the right words. 'You're upset. I accept it's been hard for you lately. My goodness, your mother's told me often enough! But you and Bryony—'

'Are two very different people,' Thea flung back bitterly. 'Don't I know it!'

'I wasn't going to say that. I was about to tell you how much I love and respect you. You're my firstborn. Our wonderful girl who sailed through school and did so well at university. Your mum and I were so proud at your graduation we nearly burst.'

'That was then. And anyway it's all down to type. School and university. It was easy. Bryony's got a more practical nature.'

'Aye, that's right. Isn't that what she was trying to tell you just now? Life moves on, Thea. Your sister's been good to Geoff and his mother when they most needed it. There's nothing wrong in that.'

'Isn't there?' Thea looked at her father and fury washed over her afresh.

'Goodbye to the lot of you!'

Whirling round, she seized her coat, stumbled blindly for the back door and ran out into the cold winter's night. Her breath streamed in the frosty air as she sped across the farmyard and down the frozen lane between bare black hedgerows to the field and her ponies.

Crossing it, she arrived at the big, timbered field-shelter where, fetlock deep in straw, the six mares and three spring-born filly foals stood at the hay-rack, chomping contentedly. Heads turned as she entered, small ears pricking, wisps of hay hanging from their mouths, large eyes flashing a liquid gleam in the dimness.

'Hello, darlings,' Thea greeted, treating each one to a mint from the pack she always carried with her. Soon the air rang to the sound of munching, the smell of mint mingling with the strawy sweetness of the stable.

The foals were growing fast and at an inquisitive stage, and pulled at Thea's clothes for more. Pushing them gently away, she went to sink down on a straw bale by the manger to rest and gather her scrambled wits.

It was warm, with the heat generated by the animals and the thick bedding at her feet. An aching tiredness stole over Thea. It had been a long day. When she had delved into the deep pocket of her quilted coat for the mints she had felt the tiny pebble there, her talisman. Now, she drew it out, curling her fingers round it in a kind of desperation.

Things would work out, wouldn't they?

The ponies had returned to their hay. Soothed by the knowledge that in here all was safe and well and by the comfortable sound of the ponies munching, Thea allowed her eyes to close....

John Royle stood looking about him at the quiet square flanked by gracious Georgian dwelling houses. He had stabled the hired horse at the Bear and Billet, an ancient part-timbered coaching inn on Lower Bridge Street, and walked the last leg of the journey through the bustling streets of Chester to Stanley Place, where Polly now resided.

Finding the number of the house, he mounted the flight of steps to the glossy black-painted front door and pulled the bell rope. His summons was answered almost immediately by a pert little housemaid in a neat, dark-blue gown and white apron and cap.

'Good afternoon,' John bid her. 'My name is John Royle. I believe this is the Kendrick residence. I wish to speak to the master – Jerome Kendrick Esquire?'

'Have you an appointment, sir?'

'I have not.'

'Then I'm sorry, Master Royle. The master isn't at home to casual callers. I'll bid you good day.'

She made to shut the door but John forestalled her.

'I've come to see Polly. Polly Dakin? She is nursery maid here. I've come all the way from Parkgate. I must see her.'

Curiosity vied with the discipline of rigorous training in the girl's round blue eyes, and won.

'Oh, sir,' she blurted out. 'You're too late. Polly's gone.'

'Gone?' John's heart beat faster. 'Gone where?'

'That's the trouble, nobody knows. Look, sir—' The maid darted an anxious glance over her shoulder. 'I mustn't be found talking on the doorstep. Why don't you come round to the kitchen and Cook will tell you all she can.'

She pointed the way and John departed, hearing the door click closed in his wake. His mind churning, he made his way to the rear of the property and the less imposing environs of the servants' quarters.

The maid had not lost any time. In the steamy warmth of the kitchen, Cook launched readily into an explanation.

'This all blew up over a pin belonging to the mistress. It went missing and Polly was accused of stealing it and sent packing.'

'What?' John was astounded. 'Never! Polly's as honest as the day.'

'So we all said at the time. Not that Upstairs would have taken notice of us. It's now come to light that Master Harry was involved in the matter somewhere.' Cook's face tightened. 'He's a wild one,

172

is Master Harry. Anyway, it's too late for Polly. Seems she's vanished.'

'But ... she can't have. Chester's a big city. She must have found employment elsewhere.'

'With no references?' Cook folded her plump arms, head slowly shaking. 'No decent household would take her on. No, my guess is she's made for home. She wouldn't have had much in the way of savings with not having been here long, so she'd not have been able to afford the coach fare. She'd have gone on foot.'

John was silent. Vagabonds, thieves and rogues roamed the highways. What chance was there of a girl alone reaching her destination in safety?

While they had been talking, the kitchen had echoed to the chink and rattle of best china and silver, the maid who had answered the door being employed in setting up the afternoon tea tray.

'Let me take that through,' Cook said. 'This young man here needs help, and I was fond of Polly. A word in the Master's ear might be no bad thing.'

Presently, John was being shown into the library. Jerome Kendrick was seated at a large, polished desk by the window. John stood awkwardly in front of him, cap in hand. Painfully aware of his dishevelled appearance from the dusty ride along potholed highways, he straightened his back and explained the reason for his visit.

'I make no secret of the fact that I think a lot of Polly. I have to find her. Please, sir, if you can give me any clue as to her whereabouts, I'd be grateful.'

'I only wish I could,' Jerome replied.

Picking up an uncut quill, he twirled it absently between his fingers. These past days had not been easy. The children querulous and grieving for their nurse, his wife missing the girl in countless different ways, brought home to him exactly how much Polly Dakin was missed in the Kendrick household.

The devil take Harry, the young pup! All right, a fellow needed a spot of fun. Jerome accepted that. It was all part and parcel of the growing up. He was prepared to make allowances for a little gaming and carousing.... This time, however, the boy had over-stepped the mark.

'This ... misunderstanding that cropped up has turned out most unfortunately, not least for Polly. I have written to her aunt ... you are acquainted with Miss Platt?'

'Yes, I am.'

'Quite. I have sent Miss Platt an explanation as to what happened with my sincere apologies and an offer for Polly to be re-established here if she so wishes. So far there has been no reply. Of course, we have to allow for the idiosyncrasies of the postal service. Perhaps you should wait a few days more.'

'Sir, I cannot. Polly has been gone for over a week. Even if she were to travel on foot, she would have reached her home at Parkgate by now. A lift with a carrier's cart would have halved the travelling time. Only today I have ridden from Parkgate myself and there was no sign of her, neither in the village nor on the road here.'

'Mayhap the girl has not headed home. Have you thought of that?'

'Where else would she go?' John was scathing. 'Sir, I do not like it at all. Where can she be?'

'You might try a different route. There's more than one way to reach the coast' He suddenly leaned forward. 'How did you get here? Hired hack? Hmm, we can do better than that. I can provide you with a decent horse, plus a meal before you leave, of course. Other than that, I fear I am powerless to help. I am sorry.'

John thought fast. The hired nag was slow and hunger gnawed at him. The only other option was a door-to-door search for Polly.

'Your offer would be most welcome. My thanks, sir.'

'Not at all, young fellow. It's the least I can do.' Relieved to have the matter so easily resolved, Jerome rang to have John shown out. 'One more thing. Remember, should you find Polly, you might convey to her my message that she is welcome to resume her position here.'

Sending the man a brief bow in acknowledgement, John left the room.

As he followed the maid back towards the kitchens and the food that awaited, John's thoughts spun. He badly wanted Polly for his own. She had loved him once and might do still. But when he found her he would feel honour bound to tell her what Kendrick had said.

Having glimpsed the sort of life she had led here, the surroundings luxurious compared to what she had known, the master and fellow staff fair-seeming and honest, he now found himself in a quandary.

A husband, and whatever life he could offer her, or this. The choice had to be Polly's. Always supposing he could find her.

Some miles away, Polly stirred on her pallet to the clatter of pots and pans. Her head throbbed, her mouth was dry. Her whole body felt on fire. Forcing open her sweat-slicked eyes, she strove to look about her. But the room swam sickeningly before her gaze and she uttered a small, croaking sob of sheer helplessness.

At once there was the rustle of skirts and the delicious whiff of herbs. A cool, dampened cloth was placed on her brow.

'Easy, my maid,' The voice seemed familiar. 'Easy, now.'

One of the ponies raked an impatient hoof against the manger. The sound reverberated throughout the wooden structure, jerking Thea to wakefulness. Chilled and shivering, at first she thought she was Polly, gripped in the confusing throes of fever. But then she realized where she was and, berating herself for having dozed in such uncomfortable surroundings, she pulled stiffly to her feet.

That was when she discovered that the small white pebble she had clutched in her hand was no longer there.

Anxiously, she searched the straw where she had sat, hoping for the glisten of white crystal. To her sorrow the pebble did not come to light, and giving a hopeless little sigh, she cast the now-resting ponies a final glance and left.

To Thea the loss of her talisman felt monumental. It had been symbolic of her relationship with Dominic, a fragile thread holding them together. Now, that thread was snapped. Could it signify an ending?

Not for the first time the present-day, sensible side of her cautioned of over-reaction, reminding of the crippling effects of mental and physical fatigue … made worse by the ache of unresolved quarrel in her heart.

But that tiny kernel of superstition that is inherent in most told her otherwise, and the message it imparted filled her with dread.

She knew just how John had felt when he believed his love to be lost to him for good.

Above, the sky was pin-pricked with stars. It was so quiet that Thea could hear the distant slap-slap of the estuary as the tide turned. Shaking the last residue of the dream from her mind, she thrust her cold hands deep into her pockets and set off for home.

'Trust Thea! The weekend was going just fine. Why did she have to walk in unannounced and ruin it all!'

After the quarrel, Bryony had bounded up to her room at Woodhey and rung Geoff to come and pick her up. There had been a short delay while she tended her mother who, unable to cope with what had gone on, had suffered a return of the migraine and taken herself off to bed.

Now Bryony and Geoff were driving back through the starlit night to her flat. All the way she had fumed and fretted. Geoff had borne it patiently, concentrating on the road ahead.

Realizing she had at last come to a stop, he drew a careful breath.

'What you have to remember, Bryony, is that Woodhey is Thea's home, too. She's perfectly entitled to "walk in", as you put it, any time she likes.'

'So? That doesn't mean she can turn on me the way she did.'

Briefly, his hand left the steering wheel to give her hand a comforting squeeze.

'No, you're right. But she's got things on her mind. This trouble Dominic's in won't help. I once crossed swords with Bob Perrit myself. He's the one who's stirring things up. He can be an ugly customer if he wants.'

Momentarily distracted, Bryony turned to face him.

'What happened?'

'Oh, some barney over a patch of land. It was when Dad was alive. Dad wasn't too well and Perrit came lording it to the farm saying we were using a field that wasn't our property. Apparently he'd rented some extra grazing next to our boundary for the horses and there was some confusion over the land registry number. It all got sorted eventually. But at a cost.'

'It made your dad poorly?'

He nodded.

'Things had started to play on his mind by that time. He couldn't let it rest and ended up back in hospital.'

'Oh, Geoff ... and was it Roseacre land after all?'

Geoff slowed as an animal shot across the road, a stoat or a weasel.

'Yes, of course it was. At least Perrit had the decency to apologize. He's an oddball. Never happy unless he's got something to gripe over. His wife's no better. Ma says she's the one responsible for spreading much of the gossip about Dominic.'

'Do you think there's any truth in it?'

'No, I don't. I'd trust Dominic with my animals any day. There's two sides to every story, and if Dominic was brought to task over a doping issue, as the talk implies, I'd put my money on his innocence. Vets as dedicated as he is don't fall for that sort of game, no matter what.'

'I suppose you're right. I remember Dad saying much the same thing. Dominic was called out to Thea's ponies once and he was really good with them. Which reminds me—'

Geoff affected a groan.

'We're not back on the confrontation with Thea, are we?'

'I'm still shocked at her behaviour. It's not like her at all. Thea's usually so calm and in control. Today she just lost it.'

They had reached the small township of Neston now. Parking in the street, Geoff hustled Bryony along the slushy pavement and into the dark and empty flat.

'It's none too warm in here.' She shivered. 'Let's have the fire on.

Oh – no lights, either. We're probably out of electricity. It was Liz's turn to buy the cards. Bet she's forgotten! She'll have gone out and won't bother till tomorrow.'

'Actually, I stocked up when I was in town earlier.' Geoff pulled a generous wad of electricity cards from his wallet. 'Let's feed the meter.'

The shabby little room sprang into brightness. Bryony sent him a tremulous smile.

'Thanks, Geoff. That was really thoughtful. How much do I owe you?'

'Not a thing. Be a good girl and put the kettle on. Ma was about to make a cuppa when you rang. I left her to it and came over.'

'Oh. Sorry.'

He grinned.

'I needed petrol anyway.'

He followed her through to the kitchen which the girls had made cheerful with new paint and brightly coloured crockery.

'Picked up something else while I was out.'

He placed a flimsy computer print-out on to the worktop. Frowning, Bryony studied it and her face instantly changed.

'Oh, wow! Two tickets for The Pink Parrot next Saturday! Oh, Geoff – you absolute darling!'

She flung her arms round him and planted a kiss on his lips. She tasted of honey and all things sweet and Geoff, looking down into her flushed face, felt his heart contract.

What a lovely woman she had become! There was none of the flighty teenager he'd once known in her expressions. It was all female, powerful, and Geoff found himself unable to drag his gaze away.

Bryony was the one to break the spell.

'Kettle's boiling. Tea or coffee? Oh, sorry, we're clean out of instant. It'll have to be tea. Milk and two sugars?'

They took the steaming mugs back into the sitting-room and sat down by the fire, sipping the warming tea.

'And another thing,' Bryony said suddenly, setting her mug aside. 'This afternoon I slogged my guts out seeing to Thea's ponies – filling feed troughs, hauling tons of hay in from the store, humping buckets of water. And did I get one word of appreciation? Did I heck!'

'Can't say I've ever heard an animal saying thanks for dinner myself,' Geoff remarked mildly. 'They just tuck in as if it's their due.'

'Very funny … I'm serious, Geoff. It's like she's turned into someone else.'

'Bryony, what happened earlier doesn't count. If Thea wasn't herself there's a reason behind it. So let's leave it there, OK?'

'Why should I? I gave up my plans to fall in with other people, clearing up the house after Dad. It had only been a matter of hours and the place looked as if a herd of cows had stampeded through it. And he hadn't even bothered to take off his wellies first. I had to get down on my hands and knees and scrub it clean – and that was just the start. I was absolutely done in but nobody cares one jot!'

'Yes, they do,' Geoff said quietly. He saw how she noted the difference in his tone, going very still. 'I care, Bryony. I care very much.'

'You … you do?' A guarded look flashed in the blue. 'Why so?'

'Because I love you, you fool!'

Putting down his tea, Geoff took her in his arms and kissed her soundly. The kiss went on and on and both of them were gasping when finally they broke loose.

'Now listen to me,' Geoff said, love, joy and laughter brimming in his eyes. 'Sooner or later, this upset in your family is going to be resolved. Right?'

'Right.'

'We're going to make allowances for people from now on, and that includes Thea. Right?'

'Well … OK.'

'We give it time, be around if we're needed, but we get on with our own lives.' Geoff paused emphatically. 'Love me?'

'Oh yes. I really do.'

'Then let's quit putting the world to rights and give me another kiss,' Geoff said.

Dominic wound his way through the laughing, chattering groups of clubbers, seeking the bar where Richard and Tracey sat with members of the band. It was for the mid-evening break. Drummer, forever hungry, was tucking into a bar snack.

Tracey was sipping a strawberry smoothie. Richard, deep in conversation with the lead guitarist, suddenly caught sight of Dominic and waved him over.

'Dominic! Come and join us. What are you drinking?'

'Half of bitter would be great, thanks.' Dominic settled his long body on a stool and sent the other members of the party a nod. 'Hi, boys. Tracey ... sure, if you don't look prettier every time I see you!'

'Charmer!' She sent him a teasing look under long lashes. 'Save you blarney for Thea. She might take you more seriously.'

The comment made in jest brought an unexpected frown to Dominic's face, quickly checked.

'Congratulations on the album. I hear it's doing well.'

'Couldn't be better,' Richard said.

Dominic's drink arrived. Richard paid for it, shunting the glass across to him. 'So how're things? You look exhausted. Has something happened?'

'Not as such. I needed to chill out and decided to come over here. Heard the end of the first half. You were great.'

'Thanks.'

Tracey and the others had turned away and begun discussing the next half of the programme in loud voices. Richard drew his stool next to Dominic.

'I saw Murty Miles's obituary in the paper. He had an interesting life.'

'He did. Funny thing, it only seems like yesterday I was making the funeral arrangements but it was weeks ago.'

'Well, you've had other things on your mind,' Richard said understandingly. He lowered his voice. 'Any word yet?'

'About the hearing? Not officially. That could arrive any day now. Word came through the back door this morning from my lawyer. I'm in the clear.'

'Dominic, that's great news. Does Thea know?'

Again the swift frown.

'Not yet. I'll tell her soon, of course. But until I get official notice, I'd appreciate it if you didn't broadcast this.'

'No problem.'

'I don't think it's properly sunk in yet, to be honest,' Dominic went on. 'It all went through as the lawyer predicted. Once the true facts came to light, the rest was mere formality. But mud always sticks. I'm not going to live this down right away.'

'No need to look on the black side, man. Your name's cleared. You can hold your head up again – not that you didn't.'

'Hadn't any need. I was simply seething at the injustice of it.'

And there had been the concern over Aisling's suspected part in the whole sorry proceedings. Dominic had been gladdened and relieved to learn that she was innocent all along, but did she have to pursue him the way she was doing? He had made it clear that their relationship was ended.

Once, on the occasion when she had first taken him to see Murty, he had truly thought she had got the message. How wrong he was? Ever since there had been the phone calls, the emails, the turning up out of the blue expecting to be taken out on the town.

Aisling simply wouldn't take no for answer. It had ended in words, a blazing row in which Dominic had pointed out that he now had other plans so would she get right out of his life?

Something in his attitude had struck home. That had been three days ago. So far, the phone had remained mercifully silent.

Aware of the other man's waiting gaze, Dominic downed his drink, brightening.

'Anyway, the worst's over. Tell me now, what are your plans for the band? Will you be staying here a while longer?'

'Couple more weeks, then we need to sort out the next stage in the master plan with our agent. I want to call in at home some time. I've a few things to put right.'

'Mae will be pleased to see you,' Dominic said. 'Chas too. He's a great guy, your da. Oh, I know he likes to have his say but underneath it all he's sound. Do they know yet about you and Tracey?'

He nodded.

'I've kept in touch with Mum and—'

Suddenly, Dominic's mobile trilled in his pocket. Making a slight apologetic gesture with his hand, he dug out the phone and left the bar, heading for outside where the signal was better.

'Hello?'

'Dominic? It's Freddie Barnes here.'

Dominic was immediately on his guard. More trouble, he thought, it had to be.

'Freddie, hello. How're things?'

'Hectic, as always. That's why I'm ringing, Dominic. We've a horse with a tendon problem on the near-foreleg. The owner wants us to operate.'

Dominic's anxiety abated slightly. Work-related issues he could deal with, it was the uncertainties that blew up out of nowhere that got him down.

'Would it be a damaged tendon?'

'Yes – quite bad. She did it while out on exercise. Thing is, this is more your area than mine. If we operate, what are the chances of a complete recovery?'

'Pretty good. The tried and tested treatment is sedation and rest and give the torn tissues the chance to heal. But it's a lengthy business. Surgery won't speed up the healing process any, but it will lessen the risk of the problem recurring. I did it once on a young thoroughbred. It went on to race again, eventually. You have to give it time. In the racing world time's at a premium.'

'I understand. Anyway, any chance of your coming over here and seeing to it for us? It's a tricky operation. I'm not up to it and neither is any other member of the team. It's a valuable animal, Dominic. The client isn't one I want to turn down.'

Dominic frowned, suspicion swirling.

'Who is it?'

'Bob Perrit.'

He knew it! Of all the horse yards on the Wirral, it had to be this one.

'Perrit? You do surprise me, Freddie. I thought I'd heard he'd switched sides to the Neston practice.'

'He did, but apparently they could only offer the conventional treatment. Anything more specialist they refer to Liverpool. Perrit turned that down. He doesn't want the animal traumatized any more than necessary. If we do it she remains at home in her own box for the recuperation period with a groom she knows looking after her.'

'Well, now, there's sense in that.'

'Quite. And this is one of his best mares. He was retiring her from chasing at the end of the season anyway because he wants a foal out of her. Doesn't want to lose the line.'

'Does he know who'd be performing the op?'

'No, and I'm not prepared to say. Who does what in this practice is up to me. I've simply said the operation is available to him. Saying that, the man's no fool. He knows you're the equine specialist.'

'He also believes I'm safely out of the way!'

Dominic sucked in a long breath between his teeth. Every operation carried a risk, some more than others. There never were any guarantees. He'd known a top man once perform this same type of surgery and it had been a disaster.

'Look, Freddie. This is a highly skilled technique. What if—'

'Exactly, and that's why I'm calling on the best man for the job. If you'll do it, you'll be granting me a big favour. D'you want to think about it? Give me a bell when you've reached a decision?'

Dominic drew another breath. So far his own luck with the knife had held – and, yes, he could give himself some credit for flair and expertise. But there was always the chance of failure. He knew what Freddie meant by 'big favour'.

Clients had been leaving the practice left, right and centre and, innocent though he was, Dominic was the cause. No smoke without fire and so on ... and Bob Perrit had been the one fanning the flames.

Besides, he was in the thick of the legalities here, and that, coupled with a separate seriously interesting issue that could be of some import to his future, meant that he couldn't easily spare the time away.

On the other hand, a successful op meant a satisfied client and would go a long way towards redeeming his good name and that of the practice....

Chapter Eleven

'Thea?' Dominic ducked his head against an icy blast and held the mobile tighter. 'It's me.'

'Dominic!'

Even here on the edge of the estuary with the December wind shrieking around him, he couldn't mistake the incredulity in her voice. He braced himself for what might be coming. Contact between them had slowly dwindled and Dominic's guilt was enormous.

'Well ... what a surprise.' Thea seemed to collect herself. 'Dominic, I've been so worried. Why haven't you been in touch? Is everything all right?'

'It's fine. Thea, I'm in Parkgate. I caught the early flight from Dublin this morning. Thought I'd catch you before you left for school.'

'I'm in the car. Another minute and I'd have gone ... why didn't you say you were coming?'

'It was a spur-of-the-moment decision. Freddie Barnes rang, he needs me to operate on a horse. A tendon problem. It's one of Bob Perrit's.'

'Oh, I see....'

'Quite. I couldn't very well refuse.'

'No, I suppose not. When will you do it?'

'Today. Around mid-morning. Thea, I must see you. Could we meet somewhere? The Thatch at Raby might be best.'

'Well, it'll have to be late on. It's the school carol concert tonight. It won't finish till eight and even then I could be delayed.'

Dominic groaned inwardly. What he had to say would not be easy, not for himself or Thea. He needed all the time he could get to explain.

'I understand,' he replied. 'You're right, of course. You'll be exhausted. Do you want to leave it till tomorrow? Straight after school perhaps?'

'Tomorrow's out.' She sighed. 'It's the Christmas party.'

This time he groaned aloud, then cringed at Thea's indignant snort.

'Dominic, this is a hectic time in the school year. With the best will in the world I can't just down tools and come running because it suits you.'

'Ouch!' Dominic said. 'I suppose I deserved that.'

He pictured her, chin slightly raised in that commanding way she had, eyes going steely. Thea, when crossed, was a force to be reckoned with and he loved her for it.

'Tonight, then,' he said, coaxing. 'I'll be waiting there for you at the Thatch.'

'Right. I must go or I'll be late. 'Bye, Dominic ... oh, and best of luck for today.'

'Thanks. I hope the concert goes off OK, too. See you later, then, Thea....'

His words seemed inadequate. He wanted to say so much more but she'd gone. Putting his phone away, scowling at the sudden sting of raindrops on his face, Dominic set off for the modern precincts of the veterinary centre he had left. It seemed an eternity ago. So much depended on the work that lay ahead of him.

Inwardly he was nervous, yet he knew that once he had begun surgery his mind would empty of all thought bar the task in hand. It *had* to turn out a success....

Thea was at the Thatch just before nine, weaving her way through the Thursday night crowd, nodding a greeting here and there, pausing briefly to exchange a word with the barman, who was a friend of her father's.

Spotting Dominic, she came across to the fireside table where he sat, her thick plait of dark-gold hair ruffled by the still-buffeting wind.

He stood up to greet her, noticing the smudges of fatigue shadowing her eyes and the strain on her fine-boned face.

'Thea ... sure, it's good to see you. Come and get warm here by the fire and I'll get you a brandy – no argument, now! You've had a long day.'

He knew he was jabbering and silently berated himself. Thea, however, directed him a brief smile of gratitude and sank down by the crackling logs, holding her hands to the blaze.

'Thanks, Dominic. A small brandy would be great, but plenty of soda, please.'

'Brandy and soda it is, then. We'll have a bite to eat afterwards. Don't go away.'

He strode off to the bar. When he returned with the drinks she had unwound her long white scarf from her neck, taken off her coat and was sitting back in her chair, looking pale but composed.

'Thanks.' Accepting the glass, she held his gaze. 'How did today go?'

'The repair job? All according to plan, I'm glad to say. It's early days yet, of course, but the mare bounced round from the anaesthetic, and that's always a good sign.'

He settled down opposite her with his own drink, feasting his eyes on her. How lovely she was. His beautiful, lovable Thea.

He cleared his throat.

'Well then. What about the carol concert. How did that go?'

'Oh, fine, all over for another year.'

Thea sipped her drink, catching her breath as the fiery liquid slipped down her throat.

'Dominic, I'm sorry to come straight to the point but you have to tell me how we stand. We were getting so close and then – nothing. Was the fault on my part? Did I say something I shouldn't have? You didn't even answer my text congratulating you on the outcome of the inquiry.'

'I know and I'm sorry.' He sighed. 'What with one thing and another it's been quite a time lately.

'You always say that,' Thea said dismissively. She frowned, as if something had just occurred to her. 'Where's Trina?'

'I've left her back at the hotel in Wexford. Remember Sue O'Hare, the proprietor's wife? She's looking after her for me.'

If anything, Thea's face went a shade whiter.

'You mean, you're going back to Ireland? You're not stopping here? But I thought once the case was finished you'd be free to take up your life again.'

'And so I am. Thea....' He leaned closer, taking her hands. 'This isn't going to be easy. Look, I've been offered my old job in Ireland. It's a thriving practice with no less than five horse specialists and I stand to occupy a senior position.

'It's my sort of work, Thea. I'd be a fool to turn it down. There's the matter of working out my notice here, but I've been speaking to Freddie Barnes. He thinks he knows of a vet to fill my place, in which case he's willing to waive the contract. That'll leave my way clear.'

'I see. And ... us?'

'Thea, this is why I wanted to see you. I love you, you know that. You're like no one else I've ever met, and for that reason I have to let you go.'

'I don't understand,' Thea said flatly.

He reached over and took her hands.

'Thea, I can't help thinking I'm no good for people. Wherever I go, whatever I do, things go wrong around me.' He grinned ruefully. 'I have an uncanny knack for it. I can't risk dragging you into all that.'

'All what?' Thea bristled. 'I can't make any sense of what you're saying. Are we talking about destiny? If so, then it's my belief that we make our own.'

'I'm telling you, it happens. Look at the Ferlann Ridge débâcle. Look what happened at the practice here. My mother would have called it the black dog of fate snapping at my heels.'

'Dominic, you were simply a victim of circumstances. It can happen to anyone. It was all just a knock-on effect. All this talk of fatalism ... it's just not true and you'll never convince me otherwise.'

Dominic's hands had tightened unknowingly over hers and now she disengaged them, rubbing back the circulation.

'So what other excuse have you for going back to Ireland without me?'

'You'd be lonely. It's all so different over there from what you're used to. It wouldn't be fair on you.'

She drew in a disbelieving breath.

'That's a good one! I'm not a child, Dominic. I'm a grown woman. I'm perfectly capable of making friends and settling down. We'd be together. Hasn't it occurred to you *that* might be all I want?'

'And give up all this?' In an almost angry gesture he embraced the crowded floor and bright faces around them. 'These are your friends, people you've known all your life. Not far away is the home where you grew up and the folks who love you. You hold down a respected position at the school. You have your own life here, Thea – the show ponies, the history group—'

'Don't they have all those things in Ireland?' she interrupted. 'Of course they do! Dominic, listen, just listen....' Thea's voice wobbled on the brink of tears. 'Don't give up on us until you've thought this through. OK, things were tough for a while – but you've come through it. You're still bruised by what happened through no fault of your own. Give it time to heal. Six months, a year. Whatever it takes. But please don't say it's over.'

Dominic gazed at her, hating himself for the desperate look in her eyes, his mind struggling to accept what she was saying. He was achingly tempted to swallow his doubts, take her into his arms there and then and ask her to risk all at his side. Just in time, he stopped himself.

'I'd be no good to you,' he repeated. 'Some men are cut out for going it alone and I must be one of them. It's a solitary road but there it is.'

Thea dragged her gaze from his and stared miserably into her barely touched drink.

'In that case, there's no more to be said,' she replied quietly.

*

It was late when Thea drove into the main yard at Woodhey. She hadn't been able to touch a morsel of her food and bitter unhappiness had swamped her all the way home. If it hadn't been for the weather, now working up to a sleety gale, she'd have taken her woes to the ponies.

She saw, with sinking heart, that the lights were still on in the sitting-room, indicating her mother was still up and waiting for her return. Facing Mae, having to put on a brave front to avoid worrying her, seemed a near impossible task.

Steeling herself, Thea went indoors, calling brightly as she crossed the kitchen floor.

'Hello…. Anybody there? I'm home.'

'Darling, hello,' Mae responded from the far side of the house. She came into the passageway, looking flushed from the heat of the fire and much improved after her recent spell of ill health.

'I was beginning to think you'd got lost. Do you want some cocoa? I was just about to make some.'

'Not really, Mum, thanks. I'm absolutely done in. Think I'll go straight to bed.'

She made to leave but her mother was quick, catching hold of her arm.

'Thea, darling, what is it? You look dreadful.'

'Oh … oh Mum!'

Sympathy on top of what had happened was too much. All Thea's control fled and the tears that had been held back now flowed unremittingly.

'I've just seen Dominic,' she said on a gulping sob. 'Mum, he says we're through and we'd b–barely started. But I know I love him and—'

'Hush, now.' Mae threw a cautious glance up the stairs where Chas was hopefully asleep and deaf to the world. She put a comforting arm around her daughter.

'Come in by the fire and tell me about it. And I don't want any nonsense about not wanting to worry me. Worry is all part and parcel of being a mum.'

Sitting together on the sofa before a replenished fire, Thea told

Mae what had happened. After the first bout of weeping had subsided, a strange calm settled over her. Thea barely recognized the dull tones of her own voice as she relayed the events of the past weeks, much of which had not been hers to broadcast and which she had kept closely to herself.

'You already knew why Dominic left Ireland to take up that vacancy with the practice here,' she began. 'It's true there was a big doping case and Dominic was implicated, but the evidence was flawed. It seems he took the blame to protect Aisling Cleary – well, they were engaged at the time. She wasn't guilty, though. The true culprit was a man called Murty Miles.'

'The jockey? Didn't he win the Dublin National three times in succession?'

'That's right. Murty was seriously ill and wanted to put his house in order. He managed to contact Dominic through Aisling and, well, to cut a long story short, Dominic's name has now been cleared by the Irish Jockey Club.'

'But … darling, that's wonderful!' Mae cried.

'Isn't it just.' A bitterness crept into Thea's voice. 'Oh, don't get me wrong, I'm delighted for Dominic. Mum, I *really* love him. This is different from how I felt about Geoff. It's … it's all-consuming. I can't imagine life without him. I know that sounds clichéd and melodramatic but it's how I feel. And he says he feel the same about me.'

Mae looked justifiably bewildered.

'So what's the problem? If Dominic's been exonerated, his career can now blaze ahead. And it will. He's a brilliant vet, everyone says that. And if this other girl no longer features in his life but you do, why can't the two of you give it a chance?'

Thea dabbed her eyes.

'Dominic doesn't see it that way. He's got this thing about being fated for things to go wrong. He says he's dogged by ill luck and he doesn't want to drag me into it. It's rubbish.'

Mae heaved a sigh.

'Oh, dear,' she said slowly. 'He's taken this hard, hasn't he? Maybe in time—'

'I said that, but he's so stubborn, Mum. What's more, he's been offered his old job back in Ireland and he's going to take it.'

'But couldn't you go with him?'

'He gave me a load of nonsense about it all being too difficult over there and how I'd be leaving all my family here and so on.'

'His confidence has really taken a beating, hasn't it? He seems so self-assured.... What's he doing over here all of a sudden? Working out his notice?'

'Not yet. Freddie Barnes wanted him to operate on a horse, a specialist procedure that Dominic's perfected. An animal from the Perrit yard.'

'Well, let's keep our fingers crossed that it's a success, love, which I'm sure it will be. What a feather in Dominic's cap! Good news for the practice too. They've lost quite a bit of trade lately, and all through that vicious gossip. I hope Bob Perrit is thoroughly ashamed of himself!'

She sounded quite fierce and Thea smiled wanly.

'Mum, what am I to do? I can't give Dominic up, I just can't!'

Mae reached out and touched her daughter tenderly.

'Darling Thea, if it were me I think I'd follow him.'

'You mean, give up my job and everything and move to Ireland?'

'I know it sounds drastic and there's a huge risk involved but … oh dear! Men can be so stubborn! They get these notions and often it takes drastic measures to make them see sense.' She paused. 'Tell me. Would you have done this for Geoff? Given up everything?'

Thea shook her head.

'No … no, I don't think so.'

'But you'd do it for Dominic?'

'Oh, yes,' said Thea fervently.

'Well, over the Christmas break, why not give it some thought, then?' Mae patted her daughter's hand decisively. 'Now for that cocoa. Fancy some nice hot, buttered toast? Believe me, darling, things won't seem as bad in the morning.'

*

After the gruelling day Thea half expected a night disturbed by dreams. It didn't happen. Next morning, she woke to the knowledge that she had slept the dreamless slumber of sheer mental and physical exhaustion – and she was thankful.

It was six o'clock and in spite of the very late night, she felt rested. To judge by the halogen lights of the yard streaming through the crack in the curtains, Chas was already up and about.

Leaving the bed, Thea pulled on her working clothes and went downstairs and out to attend to the first task of the day, the ponies.

'Hello, ponies,' she called as she trudged across the field in the early morning dark. During the night the wind had changed direction, bringing a biting frost that sent her feet slithering over frozen mole hills and clumps of rimy grass.

A chorus of whinnies answered her from the shelter of the stable. Letting the ponies out, she threw them some hay and set about making good the floor in the light of the overhead lamps.

She had finished clearing out and was shaking down some fresh straw, when something glinting over in the corner caught her eye.

It was her keepsake!

Pouncing on it, turning over the tiny pebble of glistening white crystal, Thea felt a strange lift of hope. Gladly she hugged the pebble to her, before stowing it carefully away in her trouser pocket. Now she had it back, would her luck change?

'Something's got to go right, Dancer,' she murmured to the little mare who had come back inside to investigate her pockets for titbits.

Thea rubbed the pony's furry ears and warmed her chilled hands under the thick mane. Then, aware of time passing, she checked the water trough and hurried home for a shower and breakfast.

All that day at school and in the long, boisterous hours of the children's party afterwards, the thought of the tiny semi-precious stone found by Dominic on the wind-swept Irish beach comforted and soothed her.

She had missed his endearing and energizing presence more than she had believed possible. Now, some vital ingredient seemed to have been restored to her. Driving home again in the black December evening, she found herself wondering about John Royle of long ago.

His circumstances hadn't looked good either. Had his fortune changed? Would she ever find out?

She didn't have long to wait.

After supper she opted for an early night. The characters in that long-ago play appeared the moment sleep claimed her.

'Where ... where am I?' Polly murmured, forcing open sweat-slicked eyes. Her head throbbed, her throat felt raw and her whole body ached. She was aware of a rustling of starched petticoats and the healing scent of lavender. In the candlelight, a figure bent over her.

'Hush, child. You had a fever but it's broken now. I'm Meg Shone. You once saved me from a watery end. Do you remember?'

'I ... yes ... you were trapped on the marshes. I remember ... what happened to me?'

There had been battering rain, a terrible weakness in her limbs, a confusing sensation of being both hot and cold and a deep unquenchable thirst. She had been drifting on the edge of darkness when strong hands lifted her and she knew no more.

The wise woman bathed Polly's face with cool water and offered a cup of strong-smelling beverage.

'Drink this. Slowly, mind. It tastes bitter but it will help.'

Polly drank, and presently she was able to sit up in the narrow truckle bed. She found she was in the small houseplace of Meg Shone's cottage on the heath at Thirstaston. Bunches of herbs hung from the smoke-blackened rafters and a bright fire crackled in the hearth.

'I came across you sheltering under a hedge,' Meg explained, straining some hot broth into a bowl. 'A few more hours and it would have been the end of you. Now then, child. Can you sup this broth?'

'I think so,' Polly said.

After she had taken the nourishing meal, Meg broke the sad news that Polly's mother had died.

'She's out of pain now, poor lady, and that is how you must look upon it. It's coming to my ears that your papa is taking it badly. Did you know he's lost his licence to trade? No, I thought not. He had a visit from the revenue men.' She gave a cackling laugh. 'That'll put an end to his tricks!'

Polly said nothing. Mama dead, Papa a broken man. What sort of homecoming was this?

'What of my brother?' she whispered.

'Edward? Oh, he's fine and dandy. Got himself betrothed to the clergyman's daughter and looking to the law as a career. Seems he's done with his wild ways and turned out a very personable young fellow. Your ma was proud of him.'

Her voice softened.

'Don't be sad, maid. These things happen and we must face them with courage. Set your mind on getting your strength back. Your papa will be overjoyed to see you.'

Polly had her doubts on that score. But when, several days later, she was strong enough to make the final leg of her journey to Parkgate and found her father slumped dejectedly in the deserted tap-room of the tavern, she was astonished at the smile that lit his clouded features at the sight of her.

'Polly, oh, my precious girl! It was your mama's dying wish that you'd come home and it's been granted!'

She ran to his side and that was all there was to it. Past differences were swept away by the shared sorrow of tragic loss, and a mutual gladness that ultimately, good feelings had been restored.

'They've taken my living away from me, Polly,' Wallace lamented. 'Devil take them! I can't trade any more. What am I to do? How will I earn a crust?'

'You mustn't fret, Papa. It could have been far worse. We'll think of something.'

But what, Polly was at a loss to imagine.

The door from the kitchens opened to admit Edward. Smartly attired in the sober brown of the lawyer, a cravat at his throat and his boots buffed to a fine shine, he was a marked improvement on the lackadaisical youth she had left behind. Polly's heart warmed towards the brother who, she was to learn, had saved their father and his shady dealings from a far worse predicament than this.

'There are ways to avoid the law from acting,' he told Polly over a meal she hastily made from leftovers in the kitchen. They were alone together, Wallace having taken himself upstairs to sleep off his excesses and hopefully waken in a more positive frame of mind.

'It's a case of knowing the system. Our papa had been playing with fire for some while and he was careless when in his cups. It was inevitable that the excise men would swoop.'

'But they didn't take him away.'

'No. I heard the men were on their way. We managed to empty the cellar in the nick of time. They couldn't pin anything on him, fortunately.'

'I see, but—' Polly threw a glance around the cluttered and greasy kitchen. The tap-room beyond was no better and neither, she hazarded a guess, were the bedchambers above.

'Edward, what are we to do?'

'Pray for a miracle? Papa can't trade any more, not as a publican nor a hostelry keeper. He's still at liberty to use the stable yard for the public stage-coaches and the riders bringing the mail. That will bring in a small revenue. It's something, I warrant.'

'Yes,' Polly replied on a sigh. It had been in her mind to turn the Harbour House into a hostel for travellers. Scrubbed from attic to cellar, the walls whitened and rafters swept of decades of dust and cobwebs, herself installed as housekeeper, it had seemed a way forward.

Now it appeared that this was barred to her.

They were still sitting there, pondering what to do, when hoofs rang out on the cobbled yard beyond. Through the grimy window they saw a rider, slim, darkly clad, familiar.

'Polly,' Edward cried. 'I vow our prayers may have been answered!'

Polly was already on her feet, running out of the door into John Royle's arms.

*

Thea swam slowly out of the realms of sleep. A strange gladness filled her heart, a certainty that for the lovers in her dream the problems were drawing to an end. Picking up the pebble from her bedside table, Thea clutched it tightly and willed the same for herself and Dominic.

It had been the most fantastic night out ever for Bryony. Geoff had taken her to the nightclub in Liverpool where they had danced until they dropped and feasted like kings on the grandly appointed dining floor above. Now, they were back at Roseacre.

There was no moon but the night was lit with stars and frost glistened on Helen's rose garden and the fields beyond.

'Warm enough?' Geoff drew Bryony into the encircling warmth of his arms. Beneath her long woollen coat, the skimpy black dress was not best suited to the temperatures of the winter night, but here in Geoff's embrace she felt she would never be cold again.

'I'm fine.' She smiled up at him. 'I've had a most marvellous time, Geoff. Thank you, thank you for a wonderful evening!'

He laughed gently at her.

'It's been my pleasure. You look beautiful tonight, Bryony. There wasn't another girl there to touch you.'

'Flatterer! Wait till I'm back in my jeans and wellies doing the milking. It'll be a different picture then.'

'You'll always look great to me,' Geoff said and, as if in agreement, a soft lowing from the winter cattle sheds carried over the air.

'Bryony, this might be an odd place to bring you in the middle of the night but—'

'It's the best place in the world,' she breathed. 'It's Roseacre.'

'Except the roses aren't out at the moment. Not to worry. They'll be in full bloom for the wedding.'

Bryony swallowed hard. Her heart was doing strange things in her ribcage.

'Wedding?'

'Ours, of course! Who else's?' Geoff was doing his best to make this a serious occasion but as always with Bryony, it ended in laughter. 'You're impossible and I love you to bits. Now, I've brought you out here to ask if you'll marry me and if you say no I shall pick you up and dump you in the—'

'You wouldn't dare! I won't. Oh, Geoff!'

Bryony's whoops of joy echoed around the silent garden and slumbering farmyard, bringing a chorus of affronted clucking from Helen's chicken-cotes.

'Of course I'll marry you. I'll marry you tomorrow. We don't have to wait till the roses are out. That'll be June! It's ages away!'

'No, it isn't. We're going to do this the right way. Tomorrow, we'll go into Chester and buy the ring.'

Bryony saw the sense in his words and nodded.

'So we're officially engaged? Wait till I tell Liz!'

And wait till Thea hears, she thought in the next breath. But then Geoff's lips came down on hers and all thought fled.

The following day, Saturday, they went early to town and chose the ring, a pretty platinum and diamond cluster.

Passers-by smiled at the happy young couple who seemed to have discovered the secret of perfect happiness, and when Geoff suggested they stop off at Woodhey on the way back to break the news to her parents, Bryony agreed readily.

They were driving up the bumpy track to the farm when the idea came to her. All at once she was determinedly calm.

She turned to Geoff.

'Geoff, d'you mind going in on your own and talking to Mum and Dad for a bit?'

'No, of course not. Why? It's not an attack of nerves?'

'Nothing like that. There's something I have to do.'

Emotion throbbed in her voice. Geoff reached out and squeezed her hand.

'Looks as if Chas is back from the fields. Great. Mae should have some food on the go.'

'You and your stomach!' Bryony laughed.

Having parked the car in the main yard, they went their different ways. Bryony headed for the corner of the old stone barn and the unmade cow-lane, making for the pony pasture where she knew Thea would be.

She found her sister hard at work in brushing the dried mud from caked manes and tails. At her footfall Thea glanced round, pushing wisps of hair from her face, squinting through the small dust storm she had created to see who it was. Immediately her face tightened.

'Oh, it's you. Hello.'

Ignoring the less than enthusiastic welcome, and keeping her left hand with its band of tell-tale diamonds hidden in her coat pocket, Bryony strode into the field shelter and began to make much of the ponies.

'Hi, Dancer. Goldie. Hello, Misty baby. Remember me?'

Taking her time, she went round each one tied to the long manger, stroking and petting, plucking up courage to speak.

She turned to her sister.

'Thea, there's something I want to say.'

Thea hesitated, then lifting a shoulder in a small gesture of compliance, she put aside the dandy brush and leaned back against the manger, waiting. Even in her shabby cords and old jumper, her hair escaping its long plait and a smudge of grime across her forehead, she appeared the picture of elegance, and Bryony experienced a remembered pang of envy.

Never in a million years would she develop Thea's sense of style.

She managed a smile.

'Thea, I want to apologize for the other day. I was an absolute idiot. It's really time I grew up.'

'No, it was my fault. I was in a state over something, and I took it out on you. It was unforgivable. Sorry, Bri.'

'That's OK. I truly didn't chase Geoff, you know, not when you and he were together. You're right, I had a teenage crush on him at one time but I never acted on it and neither did he.'

'I know that,' Thea nodded. 'He was flattered all the same. He used to say you were the cutest thing ever.'

'Did he?' Bryony swallowed hard. Heck, she thought, I'm not doing this very well.

'Thea, I honestly believed I could explain things but now I'm not so sure. I feel such a little kid all of a sudden.'

'It's called big-sister-little-sister syndrome. Mum still gets an attack of it when she meets up with the aunts. It's perfectly natural.'

'Is it?'

'Apparently. So whatever's bugging you, cough it up, otherwise we'll both freeze to death standing here!'

Slowly Bryony withdrew her hand from her pocket and displayed the ring. Gazing at it for a few seconds, Thea then gave a small smile.

'Geoff?'

'Yes. Thea, I....'

'It's all right. I don't mind, truly. I accept what you've said and I wish you both well.'

With a little cry Bryony sprang forward and embraced her sister. When they broke apart she was surprised to see tears on Thea's cheeks.

'Don't mind me,' she said, brushing the teardrops away with the back of her hand. 'You've caught me in an emotional mood, that's all. Bri, I really am glad for you. Is Geoff up at the house?'

'Yes, we called to tell you all but I wanted to see you first.'

'Thank you,' Thea said simply. 'You'd better go along in. They'll be wondering where you are.'

'Right. Are you coming?'

'In a moment. Just the ponies' feeds to do then I'll come in.'

Weak with relief that all had gone well, Bryony left, retracing her steps to the house. Here, Geoff had already broken the happy news.

'Sweetheart, I'm so happy for you both,' Mae cried, admiring the ring and hugging her daughter. She raised a brow suggestively in the direction of the fields and said in lowered tones.

'Am I to take it that things are all right with...?'

'Perfectly,' Bryony whispered, and was hugged again.

Chas, who had broken off a farming conversation with Geoff, came forward, jovial and beaming.

'I don't know, Bryony lass. If I'd had an inkling you were this taken up with dairying I'd have bitten the bullet and restocked myself. If I were to do that, would you consider giving Geoff up and come and work for me instead?'

'Not a chance, Dad.' Bryony sent her father a grin. 'But good try!'

Chas, his broad, countryman's face working with emotion, held his daughter close. Bryony, the last of the brood, the golden-haired child who had captured his heart from the beginning, now about to be married.

'You'll make a grand bride,' he said gruffly. 'Won't I be proud, walking up the aisle with my girl on my arm?'

'It seems to me we'd better start cutting back on cake and pastries,' Mae put in robustly, 'otherwise you'll never get into your suit on the day!'

Everyone laughed, stopping abruptly when the kitchen door opened to admit Thea.

'Hi,' she cried, deliberately cheerful. 'Congratulations and good luck, both of you.'

'Thanks!' Geoff grinned. 'Am I going to need it, d'you think?'

'Probably!' She rubbed her hands, eyes bright. 'My it's cold out there. Makes you hungry. Is lunch nearly ready?'

'Coming up.' Mae moved to the stove where a large pan of soup simmered fragrantly.

All in all, it was more like old times. There were still bridges to be built, but time would see to that.

'Why don't we celebrate, have a bit of a jolly?' Mae said suddenly.

'A Christmas do, d'you mean?' her husband queried.

'Dear me, no. That's far too soon for the preparations. New Year might be best. It'll give me more time to get ready. We'll have a proper party, invite all our friends. And Helen, of course, and as many family members from both sides as can make it at such short notice. What do you think?'

Bryony caught Geoff's gaze for confirmation. He nodded.

'Mum, you're on,' she said with delight.

It was New Year's Eve and spirits were high as Richard, Tracey and members of the jazz band left the Irish boat at Liverpool. They had agreed on a short break before embarking on the tour arranged by their agent. Exciting times were ahead, but for now the focus was on seeing their respective families again and seeing out the old year together.

Except for Richard, who was suddenly experiencing an uneasy qualm at the prospect.

'Cheers, Rich, Tracey,' shouted drummer Jack Roscoe and his best mate Danny Shine who played bass guitar. Both lived in the same street in Rock Ferry and were making the last leg of the journey together.

'Cheers, you guys. See you soon.' Richard waved the other band members off.

Laden with luggage and instruments, they vanished into the crowd. Richard and Tracey stood alone on the quayside, surrounded by parcels and baggage. Richard took Tracey's hand, on which sparkled a plain gold band as well as the simple diamond solitaire they had bought in Dublin.

'No regrets?' Richard said.

'None whatsoever. What about you?'

'Don't be daft.'

Richard dropped a kiss on the tip of Tracey's nose. She was a girl in a million and his love for her was absolute. Throughout the tour she'd been his rock, encouraging and supporting. Giving her utmost at every gig, night after demanding night, no matter how exhausted she might have been feeling.

Always a smile, always good to look at, always with a song that just about brought the house down around them. His Tracey.

'Let's go and find the hire car, eh? Here, give me the heavies. You take the lighter stuff. Ready?'

'After you, boss!' Tracey laughed.

Richard was quiet as he drove the hired car away from the city, leaving the motorway for the quieter roads of his boyhood. When he had last travelled this way, relations with his family had been less than good. Now, turning up like this – unexpected, unannounced – could turn out a mixed blessing.

What sort of reception would they get?

'You've gone quiet all of a sudden, everything OK?' Tracey's voice broke into his thoughts. 'No prizes for guessing why. You're anticipating trouble with Chas, aren't you?'

'I don't know what to expect, to be honest.' Richard slowed down as a highways lorry loomed up in the darkness ahead. 'Oh, they're gritting the roads, we must be in for a spell of bad weather. I hope it doesn't mean snow. We wouldn't want us to be marooned at Woodhey if things turn awkward.'

'Oh, Richard.' Tracey touched his arm lightly. 'I'm sure it'll be fine. Would you rather we went on to my mum's instead? We could always come back another time.'

'No, let's get it over with. I'm not concerned about Mum, she'll be fine. And Thea of course. Not sure how things are with Bryony, but no doubt she'll be doing her own thing anyway tonight, so I don't expect she'll be around.'

'What about us? How d'you think they'll react to our going ahead and getting married without them being there? While we were in Ireland it seemed the right thing to do. It was a great wedding, wasn't it? The boys made it such fun. And then when we walked into that bash they'd cooked up behind our backs it really made the day!

'Now, though, I'm having a tiny bit of guilt. How will your mum feel? You're her firstborn, and you know how she loves an occasion.'

'It's OK,' Richard said, chugging impatiently along behind the slow-moving lorry. 'It's crossed my mind too. I must say your mum's been great about the whole thing, didn't bat an eyelid when we rang and told her.'

'Oh, Mum's like that. She'll wait till we turn up and then see if we want a celebration. It's different for her. She's on her own and she's very tied up with her job. It would have been hard for her to get away at such short notice. All the same, it would have been great if she'd been there. I suppose....'

'Go on.'

'Well, I was thinking. Perhaps we could have one of those ceremonies where couples repeat their vows.'

'A blessing? No reason why not.' A clear stretch appeared on the road. Richard seized his chance and overtook, glad to be free of the slow crawl of the big vehicle at last.

'Let's get this over with first,' he said, 'then we can decide what to do.'

A blaze of lights met them as they approached Woodhey. The main yard was full of haphazardly parked cars. Music floated on the sharp night air.

'Looks like there's a bash on,' Richard groaned. Away from the stifling environs of home he had felt in command of his life. Now, confronted with his old home, previous grudges and misgivings came hurtling back. One glower from his father and that would be the end!

'Oh, well,' he said to Tracey, having found a slot to leave the car amongst the random clutter of vehicles. 'Let's go for it.'

The back door was unlocked. Lacing his fingers in Tracey's, he led her through the fragrant warmth of the big kitchen, noting the table and work surfaces laden with food and drink, the blast of jazz from the music system growing louder as they approached the spacious front lounge.

It was his own band playing, Richard noted with surprise. That had to be a good sign!

The door to the room was open, displaying a backdrop of glittering festive greenery and leaping log fire, and the first face he saw amongst the jigging crowd was his mother's. Spotting the couple, Mae's expression registered shock, then delight, and then seemed to crumple.

'Richard!' she said in a breathy whisper.

Geoff was here, dancing with Bryony who smiled up at him as if the world was theirs alone. Thea was handing round refreshments and had her back to the door but Chas, sipping a drink, caught sight of his son and the girl and all but choked.

He made a muttered comment to Mae, who put a restraining hand on his arm. Chas freed himself and came striding up. Richard was aware of Tracey's nervous intake of breath, of the dancing couples stopping one by one, of astonished faces and the music throbbing on regardless.

'Well, I don't know,' Chas said broadly. 'Look what the wind's blown in!'

'Hi, Dad,' Richard replied, offering his hand.

Chapter Twelve

Chas gazed at his son, his robust country face working with emotion. Around them the room was falling to stillness but for the dance music on the player which pounded on. Thea moved to switch it off, and suddenly the busy crackle of the huge log fire in the grate and the slow tick of the grandfather clock seemed very loud in the silence.

All eyes were on their host. Everyone knew what a difficult time Chas had gone through since Richard had abandoned the farm to follow his own path in life. Most could see both sides of the coin, but knowing Chas – and those present knew him very well indeed – expectations as to which side the penny would fall didn't rate the younger Partington.

Richard was aware of holding his breath.

'Hello, Richard,' his father said gruffly. 'What a surprise. New wife, as well. Hello, Tracey, lass. You're looking prettier than ever. It's good to see you both.'

And grasping his son's hand, Chas shook it soundly.

An audible sigh of relief rippled throughout the company. Chas, his eyes suspiciously moist, took his new daughter-in-law into his arms and kissed her cheek.

The room exploded once more into life. Mae was hugging Richard, laughing and crying at the same time. Bryony and Geoff – holding hands, Richard saw with surprise – came up to take their turn at welcoming the prodigal home.

Thea switched the music back on and the dancing started up again.

'Recognize it?' Tracey asked Richard.

'How could I not?' He grinned, hardly able to contain his gladness and relief at the turn events had taken. 'It's us!'

'Well, who else?'

That was Bryony, an older, slimmer and decidedly more pleasant-faced Bryony than the one he had left. Spotting the diamond on her finger, Richard's grin broadened.

'What's this? Don't tell me Geoff has let himself in for it! And I thought him a man of taste!'

'Oh – you!' Bryony beamed at her brother. 'The ring was Geoff's idea. Cool, eh?''

'Very, Geoff, this is just great. I hope you'll both be as happy as we are, right, Tracey?'

'Absolutely.'

The hugging and kissing continued a little longer. When the hubbub had died down and Richard had ushered Tracey to sample the delights of the refreshment table, it struck him that Thea's welcome had been restrained. His eyes roved the room, seeking her out, but she didn't seem to be amongst the laughing throng.

'Look after this a minute,' he said, handing a laden plate to Tracey. 'I want a word with Thea. Won't be long.'

Picking up his glass of wine, he headed off through the wide hallway where more food was laid out on trestles and through to the kitchen. A keen gust of air from the lobby directed him to the yard, where his sister stood gazing out into the frosty, star-filled night, a soft woollen evening shawl clutched about her shoulders.

'Thea? Are you OK?'

She turned sharply. Richard saw the glisten of tears on her cheeks.

'Oh, it's you, Richard. Yes, of course I am.'

He gave a disbelieving grunt.

'Look, sis, I'm sure I don't have to remind you what my credit rating is for observation, but even I can tell that things aren't what they should be. It's Dominic, isn't it?'

'Well....' She pushed a lock of hair back from her forehead. 'Richard, do you mind if we don't talk about this right now?'

'Yes, I'd mind lots. Tonight's been a massive breakthrough and—' He broke off, surprise and joy rushing through him afresh. 'I never expected Dad to come up trumps. Do you know, he's even asked what our future plans were for the band.'

'Well, with half the world looking on, what else do you expect? I know what you mean, though, and I'm really glad for you, Richard. And for Tracey, of course.'

'Thanks, sis. You've been great all the way along. I don't know what we'd have done without your support ... but this isn't what I wanted to talk about. Listen, Thea, I saw quite a bit of Dominic in Ireland. From what he said I understood you two had rather a good thing going. Early days after the Crash, I know—'

'Crash?'

'You and Geoff. It's what Tracey called it. She never did think you were right for each other. No spark, and all that.'

'Richard, please....'

'Give over. Putting on the schoolma'am hat won't work with me. This is a night in a million. I want everyone milking it to the full, including my big sister. So what's Dominic done to make you so down-in-the mouth? If he's chucked you over for that scheming ex-fiancée—'

'He hasn't, so stop jumping to conclusions. These are things you know nothing about.'

'So? Last thing I heard Dom was coming back here to operate on a horse. I told him the Parkgate practice couldn't do without him and I was right. So where is he?'

'I wouldn't know. His house is on the market, so I suppose he's in the throes of packing up. Please Richard. Dominic and I are going our separate ways, so let's leave it at that. How's Tracey's mum taking your news?'

'Oh, she doesn't know yet! But she takes things as she finds them. She's got this zen approach to life. Tracey's got it, too. Lucky girl!'

'Well, I must drop her a line. Is she still living at the same address?'

'Little rented place at Willaston, yes. We're going there

tomorrow.' Richard consulted his watch. 'Soon be time to see out the old year. Coming?'

'Right.' She shivered. ' Oh, the wind's changing. We could be in for more snow.'

Hugging her shawl more tightly around her, Thea gave her brother an over-bright smile and accompanied him back to the festivities.

Driving home from school, Thea made an impulse decision to call in at the Harbour House and check it out. It had been ages since she'd been there. What with one thing and another, the time had flown – or so she told herself. Being busy was as good an excuse as any for putting off visiting the place that had once held so much promise, and was now a white elephant of massive proportions.

What was to be done with it?

The snow had gone and the house stood out bleakly on the headland; a spacious dwelling, staunch, white-walled, intended for the thrills and spills of family life. For children and dogs, fishing tackle in the lobby and good cooking smells in the kitchen. Instead, there was emptiness.

Leaving her car on the paved forecourt that still bore remnants of building work – a pile of unused bricks, an old door flung against the wall, a heap of sand – Thea fumbled for her keys and went inside to the waiting silence of the old house.

Somewhere upstairs a mouse scuttled for cover, bringing a frown. Not quite empty, then, but giving more reason than ever for finding a solution to the problem.

Thea walked through the stone-flagged hall into the lounge, her footsteps echoing on the planked floor. In the original stone fire-place that Geoff had discovered when they were renovating, the apple logs she had put there back in the summer of last year still awaited a match.

Thea went on to the kitchen and sat down in the window seat that overlooked the estuary. This was where she had experienced the first of those strange waking dreams that spoke so graphically of the past, the dreams that caused her so much consternation.

In her coat pocket, her mobile jangled with a shrillness that grated on her nerves. She pulled it out.

'Hello?'

'Thea, it's me. Bryony. Is it OK to talk?'

'Yes, fine. I'm at the Harbour House, actually. Just giving it the once-over, you know.' She kept her voice deliberately light. 'I've been into school.'

'Oh? I thought the new term started on Monday.'

'It does. This was a preparation morning. Anyway, it's chilly in here. What was it you wanted?'

'Well, it's about the wedding. Thea, I know this is awkward for you. I keep putting this off.'

'Out with it, then. Is it bridesmaids and so on?'

'Yes. I'm having Liz for one. The other should be you, but—'

'Oh, I think we can safely bypass that little detail. Why not rustle up another of your mates?'

'Are you sure?'

'Absolutely. A seat with the family will do me fine. Mum and I agreed to do the shops together one weekend. That'll avoid the possibility of our turning up in things that clash. Nothing looks worse on the photographs than shouting tones of fuchsia pink.'

'Mum, in pink?'

'Only joking. She's actually thinking along the lines of ice blue. Rather striking, I thought.'

'Sounds lovely.'

'Quite. Problem solved?'

'Y ... yes,' Bryony said hesitantly. 'Thea, you really don't mind?'

'Not at all. This is going to be a beautiful wedding, so just go ahead and enjoy it. Mum's in seventh heaven. The binge of all binges to prepare for! Parkgate will never have known the like. She and Helen spend hours on the phone every night, swapping catering notes.'

'I wish Mum would leave the food arrangements to us. I don't want her wearing herself out and getting ill again.'

'She won't. This is a dream come true for Mum. Don't spoil it for her, Bri.'

'I won't – daren't!' She trilled a laugh, worries forgotten. 'Right, then, see you soon.'

It seemed quieter than ever after her sister had rung off. Sitting there in what had at one time been the rough and ready environs of a quayside tavern, Thea tried to visualize what life had been like then. According to her dreams, the kitchens had opened directly on to a coaching yard.

Stables could be glimpsed through the open doorway. Travellers stood in chattering groups on a straw and dung littered yard. The blast of a horn and the clamour and rattle of iron-shod hoofs and carriage wheels heralded the arrival of the public coach from Chester.

Thea shut her eyes tight to try to blot out the images that were taking over, but the act had the opposite effect. Dropping from wakefulness to sleep, the pictures came as they always did; vivid, powerful, real.

The roar of the wind and the oily slap of the tide against the quay cut through the air, and yet the small group at the grease-spotted wooden table seemed not to hear the noise, so flattened were they by the circumstances they had found here.

'You've a suggestion to make? A solution to … to all this?' Polly directed a despairing gesture at the ramshackle scullery and deserted tap-room beyond.

'John, tell us, do!'

For a moment John Royle hesitated, as if he could not find the words.

'Out with it, man,' Edward said with forced cheerfulness. 'Any ideas would be welcome, no matter how unlikely they might appear.'

'My idea would require your combined approval and efforts … and a great deal of trust.'

The gleam of ambition appeared in John's steady grey eyes.

'You know how for some time now I've been seeking premises to start up a school for boys? It's what I've wanted for long enough, but so far my every attempt to acquire one has failed. Until now.'

Polly and her brother stared, realization dawning.

'You mean … you're thinking of turning the Harbour House into a school?' Polly clapped her hands together in delight. 'Oh, John! What a perfectly splendid idea!'

Edward was impressed.

'It couldn't be more opportune. All would benefit. With your good self at the helm and Polly to see to the boys' comfort and good health.… But what of Father?'

'Wallace Dakin knows this place better than anyone,' John said. 'Someone will be needed to see to the outside chores and stoke the fires and so on. Wallace might well agree to the role of caretaker. What better way to make him feel needed and useful once more? And safe from the long arm of the law!'

Polly nodded in total understanding.

'You are right, John. A school with all of us running it. I'm in agreement.'

'As am I,' Edward said firmly.

'The sooner we make the necessary arrangements, the better.' John addressed Polly's brother. 'Edward, this is your area. Could you draw up the legalities? They'll need to be foolproof, mark you. We don't want the revenue people finding a loophole.'

'Indeed not. Yes, I'm sure it can be done. We keep the property in the family name and draw up a rental agreement for your good self. That way you will be held responsible for what goes on within these four walls. No black mark against your name, I would assume. The proceedings can go ahead with a clear conscience.'

'I shall be for ever in your debt.' John looked as if he had been given the world. 'I won't let you down, you have my word on it.'

Polly's hazel eyes dreamed. Her mind went back to a few moments earlier when John had turned up in the tavern yard and she had once more experienced the joy of his embrace. Had it been merely a gesture, or did he still love her? She hoped so.

She knew she would need to summon patience. First and foremost came the securing of her home … and John was a man with an idea. Knowing him of old, the school and the well-being of his pupils would take precedence.

Polly went to seek out paper and quill to pen a list of requirements for her new position of housemother to a lively bevy of
schoolboys.

Over the next few weeks, work went ahead. At the firm of
lawyers in Neston the updated set of deeds was duly convened,
signed and witnessed. Wallace, wrenched from his stupor by the
sheer weight of enthusiasm around him, took up hammer and
paintbrush and began working on the house.

At Fernlea, Jessica Platt put in her support, raising money for
investment in the new venture. With the proceeds John acquired
books, desks, beds and linen. Hanging up his fisherman's oilskins
for good, he had the tailor fashion a suit of clothes for his chosen
profession.

John Royle, to all intents and purposes, had realized his dream.

Polly, however, hid a sad heart. In the hope he would recognize
her motives for what they were, she had put all her energies into
John's scheme. She accepted that she owed him a great deal – her
home secured, her papa a changed man, herself able to hold up her
head amongst her peers.

But oh, how she longed for John to whisper the words she
wanted to hear.

Remembering the lad with sea-tousled hair and the love in his
eyes for her, Polly's spirits sank. Somewhere along the way that
love must have dwindled and died, for John had become a distant
figure, whilst her feelings for him had strengthened – uselessly, it
would appear.

'Polly?'

She looked up from the cauldron of beef broth she was
preparing for the boys' midday meal. Her father stood there,
staunch and workmanlike in his leather breeches and stout boots,
his freshly-laundered shirt open at the neck. She knew the boys
thought much of him and she chose to turn a blind eye to the
sweetmeats and other treats that sometimes found a way to the
dormitory for midnight relish.

'Why, Polly, lass. That was a great sigh from the prettiest maid in
all Parkgate. Is ought amiss?'

Polly shook her head.

'No, papa, not as such. I was merely thinking.'

'Of wedding bells and pretty gowns, no doubt. Susanna made a bonnie bride, did she not? Edward made a good choice there. Who'd have thought it, Polly? Wallace Dakin's tearaway lad wed to the parson's daughter!'

'And very happy they are, too. May they have a long life together.'

'Amen to that. Your mama would have been proud – God rest her soul.' Briefly his face clouded, then he brightened. 'Have you heard the latest news, Polly?'

'No, though I'm sure I'm about to. Papa, I vow you are becoming quite a gossip!'

'Not I!' Wallace gave his daughter a smile of deep affection. Neat and trim in her blue dress and white apron, she looked a picture.

''Tis your aunt, Mistress Uppity Jessica of Fernlea! It would seem that she and George Rawlinson are about to tie the knot. Poor man, he has my sympathies. She'll lead him a merry dance!'

Despite herself Polly pealed with laughter.

'Papa, you are incorrigible. It's a perfect union and well you know it. Think what a handsome couple they'll make. I for one am pleased for them and so should you be.'

'Aye, well, happen I am, girl. She was a good sister to your mama. Where are you going?'

Polly had set aside the iron pot of meat and vegetables and was reaching for her bonnet and shawl.

'I thought to walk as far as the churchyard for a breath of air. I've picked some flowers for Mama's grave. You know how she loved her roses.'

'Put some on from me and make it red ones, lass. She was a beauty in her youth, was my Marion. She'd have put any flower in the shade.'

Polly delivered a kiss on his bewhiskered cheek and left, walking smartly along the road and entering the lych gate of the little church where her mother lay.

That was where John found her. She was bent over the white

headstone, arranging flowers at its foot, and did not hear his soft tread over the grass.

'Polly? Do I intrude?'

'Oh, it's you, John. No, of course not. What is it? Am I required for anything?'

'No more than always, and certainly not urgently.' John's face was solemn. 'Polly, may I ask you something?'

'Go ahead.'

She was mystified. What was he about to tell her? Was he ... heaven forbid, was he thinking of getting wed? Two women in a kitchen....

'Polly. It's been in my mind to wait a twelvemonth before saying this, but I find myself unable to hold out any longer.'

'Why, John, what is it?' Polly's knees had gone weak.

'I can't go on like this! Having you there beside me, seeing you every day ... I thought ... dear me, I'm not putting this very well, am I? I'm as tongue-tied as one of the lads caught stealing apples!'

'You thought?' Polly encouraged.

'Last year when I went to Chester seeking you out, it struck me what a good position you'd held there. Your master wanted you back – in truth, the entire household wanted it. And I thought, who was I to stand in your way? You may have wanted the chance to return. Even now, it could still be possible. A secure position with a well-to-do family. It isn't to be sniffed at, Polly.'

She shook her head, her face brimming with emotion.

'John, I'd give up a thousand such opportunities to remain here at your side. Always.'

'Truly?' You will be my wife?'

'I should be honoured. I love you, John. I always have.'

He took her in his arms.

'My own dearest love. I have a confession to make. It was your papa sent me here. "Tell her what's in your heart, you young idiot," he said. "I know my Polly. You don't want to lose her, do you?" After those words I couldn't get here fast enough!'

John's lips came down on hers. And then, leaving that quiet

place to the rippling breeze and the scent of roses, the couple walked back home together.

A door slammed from somewhere at the front of the house, jerking Thea awake.

'Thea? Are you in here?'

'Yes, Dad. I'm in the kitchen.'

Chas came stomping into the room in his heavyweight rubber boots, leaving a trail of dried mud in his wake.

'I saw your car outside. Been having a look round?'

'Yes, I was just thinking—' Thea broke off, disorientated.

'About the house and what's to be done with it?' Her father sighed heavily. 'Blessed if I know!'

'Me, neither. It's such a lovely house. I'd hate it to go out of the family.'

'I daresay that's inevitable at some point. Funny old place. I wouldn't mind betting it's got a few tales to tell.'

'You could be right.' Thea shot him a wry look. 'It's the history group meeting tonight. One of the members is bringing in some early parish registers. I'll see if there's any mention of this house. It'll be interesting.'

'It won't find us a tenant, though, will it? Not to worry. Something's sure to turn up,' Chas said comfortably. 'Are you coming? Those ponies are tearing round the field shouting their heads off. They must know you're here. You look frozen, lass. A bit of mucking out will no doubt warm you up!'

That evening at the meeting, confronted with pages and pages of closely scripted copperplate, Thea's task seemed impossible. She tried a second volume and had more luck. About a quarter of the way through she found recorded the marriage of Edward Dakin, lawyer, to Susanna Marsdon, spinster of the parish. It was dated 3 August, 1835.

In the spring of the following year John Royle had wed his Polly.

In another leather-bound book Thea came across the baptism of Polly and John's only daughter. How the name Royle had become Partington was also made clear. The daughter had married a certain Charles Partington of Woodhey Farm, Parkgate, thus joining the two properties.

Thea stared, hardly able to believe what she saw, a monumental relief rippling through her. She wasn't going out of her mind. The people she had dreamed of really had existed!

She wanted, badly, to ring Dominic and tell him of her discovery. He'd be interested.

Later, back home again, Mae had some news.

'Tracey rang shortly after you'd left. She couldn't speak for long. They were at a gig – oh, the background noise! I could hardly hear what she said.'

'Was it something important?' Thea asked.

'Worrying, I'd say. She wants me to look in on her mother. Apparently Jenny Kent's been given notice to quit. Her landlord has plans for the cottage and wants her out. The very idea!'

'But surely he can't do that? Jenny's been there for years. As a sitting tenant she'll have rights.'

'That depends,' Chas put in behind the evening paper. He put it aside, rubbing his chin thoughtfully with his fist. 'Rentals can have small print that's easily overlooked – especially by those desperate for a roof over their heads. Jenny Kent was left with a small child – Tracey – to bring up, wasn't she?'

Thea nodded.

'That's right. Tracey never speaks of her father. He upped and left … I think.' She stopped, awareness blazing in her face. 'That's it!' she gasped. 'The Harbour House! It can go to Richard and Tracey.'

Chas shook his head.

'I don't think so. What'll they want with a house? If what Richard says is right they'll be spending the next few years on tour,' he said.

'But not all the time.' Thea gestured excitedly with her hands, words tumbling from her lips.

'Mum, Dad, don't you see? It'd be ideal for them. It's big, great for entertaining. They could even make a recording studio there if they wanted. It's isolated, no neighbours to be disturbed. Best of all, Jenny could live there and look after the house for them while they're away!'

'Of course!' Mae said wonderingly. 'It's all so obvious I can't think why we never came up with it before. Darling, you're brilliant!'

'I know!' Thea grinned at her mother. 'There's room for Jenny to make a flat if she prefers it. The old stables would do a great conversion.'

'Stables?' Chas frowned. 'You mean the garages and outbuildings?'

'Well, yes,' Thea said, thinking back, her smile broadening. What a story she'd have to tell her grandchildren one day. Always supposing she ever had any!

She drew out her mobile.

'I'd better text Tracey. I'll tell her to stop worrying, we've hit on a perfect solution, and suggest she rings back the moment she's free.'

Bryony wanted to hug herself. Her wedding dress had been delivered that morning and now hung in all its splendour in her old bedroom at Woodhey.

'It's gorgeous!' Liz pronounced soberly.

Doing the rounds of bridal boutiques and department stores with her mother, Bryony had discarded the modern look and gone for tradition. The gown was pure Victoriana, high-necked, long sleeves, frilled and flourished, a whisper of ivory silk and lace.

The one break with tradition was the reception, which was to be held at the groom's house instead of the bride's, Roseacre having the space to house the marquee next to Helen's celebrated rose garden.

'I'm so pleased with my dress, too.' Liz grinned. 'But when you insisted on the old-fashioned frock, I wanted to back out. I mean, ringlets, flounces and gold satin? *Me*?'

'Amber satin,' Bryony corrected merrily. 'The colour's perfect for you, especially now your hair's grown back to its natural shade.'

'Boring brown.' Liz made a little face, but her eyes were smiling. 'Wish it would grow longer. It's taken ages to get just to jaw length. D'you think Michelle will be able to do something with it on the day?'

Michelle, an old school friend, worked in a salon in town and was delighted to be second bridesmaid.

'Sure to,' Bryony said. 'She's got magic in her fingers, trust me – and anyway, you've time yet. Still six weeks to go. You'll look terrific, both being so dark.'

'Well, it'll make a contrast to the blonde bride! What colour's your mother wearing?'

'Ice blue. Thea's chosen a sort of silver-grey. A trouser suit with a long jacket, terribly elegant.'

'Thea's got class. That sort of look never dates.'

'I know. Just think, she'll still look a million dollars when the rest of us are grey and wrinkled!'

'Best make the most of things, then.' Liz grinned. 'You'll stun Geoff in that dress. He'll be knocked speechless!'

'He'd better not be. I want those marriage vows ringing out for all to hear.'

Sweeping up the dress, Bryony held it to her, suddenly serious.

When Liz left, Bryony hung up the dress under its layers of protective wrapping, headed for the sitting-room and sat down at her mother's polished kneehole desk. On the top of the desk was a stack of neatly written invitations that were stamped and ready for posting.

Checking off the names against the list she and Geoff had painstakingly compiled, Bryony picked up the pen and completed those that remained.

Her sister's face swam before her mind's eye. Tranquil, arresting, the eyes somewhat withdrawn of late, the chin upheld in typical Thea pose. She had been terrific over the events leading up to all this. What could Bryony do in return.

On impulse, she drew forward a final invitation card and wrote Dominic Shane's name on it. She had to scan her pocket book for the address. It came to light at last scrawled on the inside back cover – a coastal town in the Republic of Ireland. Having addressed the envelope, she realized it would have to go through the post office instead of the post-box.

It looked like rain and Bryony put the envelope aside, wondering whether to bother after all.

'Going to the post-box,' she called to her mother in the kitchen. 'Won't be long.'

'Right. Take your coat. It's April showers.'

Bryony had gone halfway down the farm track when her steps faltered. It was a pearl of a day, not raining yet, the air fresh and sweet. A walk would do her good.

Retracing her steps to the house, she snatched up the abandoned small, white envelope and set off again, cutting across the fields. She was smiling as she entered the village.

'How on earth,' Thea murmured to herself in the mirror, 'do I get through today?'

It was a perfect June morning, the birds singing, the sky gloriously blue and gold. As on the day before, the old farmhouse teemed with guests. Voices and laughter issued from the next bedroom, where the bride and bridesmaids were preparing for the big event.

The flowers had arrived. The horse-drawn carriage Bryony had insisted upon was waiting in the yard that had been hosed and swept to a pristine cleanliness by Chas. In the distance, the grey-green sweep of saltmarsh met an estuary sparkling in sunlight.

> *Oh Mary, go and call the cattle home*
> *And call the cattle home,*
> *And call the cattle home*
> *Across the sands of Dee.*
> *The western wind was wild and dank with foam*
> *And all alone went she.*

Throughout the night the poem so beloved by Dominic had prowled her dreams. A few days before she had heard from him.

Nothing much. A postcard featuring an Irish racing print on one side and a hasty scrawl on the other, enquiring after the ponies and wishing her well.

She had received other such missives from time to time, an email or a text, and had geared herself to look upon them as tokens of friendship rather than anything more serious.

The words of the verse were with her still; dark, full of imagery, poignant.

'Thea! The cars are here,' her mother's voice trilled from the hall.

'Coming.'

Arranging the broad-brimmed wedding hat over her hair that was dressed in an elegant coil on the nape of her neck for the occasion, Thea took a few sustaining breaths, lifted her chin resolutely and, collecting her handbag from the bed, left the room.

As she did so, the first pealing of church bells drifted across the fields.

Inside the church, all was hushed. There was a mingled smell of flowers, perfume and old stone. Thea, her silk-clad back ramrod straight, sat with her family on a front pew. To her right were her brother and his wife. Next to them was her mother, her handbag occupying the space shortly to be taken by Chas.

Mum and Dad, Richard and Tracey, aunts and uncles and all the rest. Couples everywhere the eye fell, here to celebrate the joining of yet another union. Only she, Thea, sat alone. She glanced down at the space on her left that would remain just that throughout the ceremony. It seemed to mock her.

Beyond, the north aisle was shadowed, although in the available pews an assembly of villagers had congregated in smiling numbers to watch the proceedings.

On the other side of the main aisle, Geoff's fairish head and the darker one of his best man could be seen.

Please, please let me get through this, Thea beseeched silently.

The organ started playing and Bryony was there, looking so ethereal and lovely that breath was collectively held as she drifted down the aisle on her father's arm. Chas cut a dignified and rather distant figure in his uncharacteristic wedding finery, and was almost bursting with pride as he beheld his youngest child.

As Bryony gained the altar where her groom waited and the vicar intoned the opening phrases, Thea realized her hands were clenched. She was making a concentrated effort to relax, when all at once the church door creaked open to admit a latecomer, closing again with a small, distinct click.

Aware of movement behind her, a tip-toed step approaching along the worn red and blue carpeted north aisle, Thea turned her head to investigate … and her eyes widened in surprise.

Dominic slipped into the empty space beside her. Tall, good-looking, smart in charcoal grey, the riotous dark hair hastily tamed with a brush, Dominic's intensely blue eyes were not on the bride, but on Thea. He reached out, took her hand and, lacing her fingers tellingly in his, sent her a hesitant smile.

Thea's heart pounded. Such a lot could be read in that smile. Remorse, contrition, a degree of hope and above all, love.

It was as if a fog had lifted. He had come for her. Now, they could move on.

Everything was going to be all right, after all.